KILL ME IF YOU CAN

A MIKE HAMMER NOVEL

MORE MIKE HAMMER
FROM TITAN BOOKS

KILL ME
IF YOU CAN

A MIKE HAMMER NOVEL

MICKEY SPILLANE

and

MAX ALLAN COLLINS

TITANBOOKS

Kill Me If You Can: A Mike Hammer Novel
Print edition ISBN: 9781789097641
E-book edition ISBN: 9781789097665

Published by Titan Books
A division of Titan Publishing Group Ltd
144 Southwark St, London SE1 0UP

First edition: August 2022

1 3 5 7 9 10 8 6 4 2

A CIP catalogue record for this title is available from the British Library.

Printed and bound by CPI Group (UK) Ltd, Croydon, CR0 4YY.

FOR KIM DEITCH—

a great storyteller
who appreciates Spillane

CO-AUTHOR'S NOTE

Kill Me If You Can takes place in the mid-1950s between the events of *Kiss Me, Deadly* (1952) and those of *The Girl Hunters* (1962).

The novel marks the 75th anniversary of Mike Hammer's first appearance in *I, The Jury* (1947). An afterword charts the detective's (and Mickey Spillane's) rise to fame, and discusses the extensive materials in the writer's files from which this book was developed.

Five short stories—two featuring Mike Hammer—are included here as bonus features, each introduced as to their histories and places in the Hammer-verse.

Max Allan Collins
August 2021

CHAPTER ONE

I had nothing to keep me company but my .45 and an itch to use it.

The intel was solid. I felt sure of that. But it was also sketchy as hell—they would hit this weekend, and that was all I knew. This very weekend the same robbery crew that hit the Civac reception last month would be dropping by unannounced.

They *thought* unannounced…

But the tip was solid. It came from Packy Paragon himself, the only mob guy in Manhattan worth trusting, ex-mob now but still tied in so tight he could hear a don pass wind. And he knew how bad I wanted the armed robbery crew who made the Civac score. They'd gotten more than just gems.

What they'd taken was far more valuable than any diamond, and they would die one by one until somebody spilled what he knew, and then he would spill, too, but it wouldn't be information.

This was my third day in the brownstone mansion on Central Park West, just me and tens of thousands in antique furnishings, hundreds of thousands in artwork by museum-famous names, and a refrigerator stocked to the brim. But it was Sunday night now and I was running low on Blue Ribbon. The client could keep his caviar.

I'd spent weeks tracking the robbery crew, shaking the trees and the monkeys that fell out of them, paying for info, squeezing it out of some, and getting nowhere beyond the general news that an unknown outfit—apparently unaffiliated with any of the half dozen New York City crime families—was scooping up precious stones like kids on the beach shoveling sand for a castle.

Nasty damn kids.

They invaded homes, any time of day or night, usually when the owners were away but not always, assaulting anybody who got in their way. They crashed fancy do's and don't you just know they'd go around to the intimidated guests with open bags to stow jewelry and wallets in. Shouting, slapping, waving guns like Old West stagecoach robbers.

Then Packy, who I'd asked to sniff around for me, showed up at my office, 808 at the Hackard Building. He had something for me, but wasn't about to use a phone—the feds were still tapping his, even though he'd gone straight, and who could say what cop or crook might be listening in on private eye Mike Hammer's line?

Looking typically sharp in a tailored sharkskin suit, his steel-gray hair brushed back with no grease, Packy was a tall, slender George Raft-style slick about fifty who'd been the best of a bad bunch. We'd saved each other's lives a couple of times and become unlikely friends.

"Don't ask me where I got this, Mike," Packy said in his radio announcer's voice, ignoring the client's chair, leaning in with a hand on the desk. He'd filled me in on everything he knew, which wasn't a little.

"Wouldn't dream of it," I said.

"But this seems to be a crew unconnected to any of the six families. Some new kingpin is putting together teams for jewel heists of society types and visiting celebs. Appears to be doing the same for institutional robberies, too—banks, jewelry stores, payroll hits. These are guys who go in heavy and come out flush."

"And this same crew made the Civac score?"

He straightened. "Can't swear to it. But that's the word."

I nodded. "Thanks, Pack."

"No trouble, Mike." Finally he pulled up the chair. Leaned in like a worried priest. "Listen, you don't mind my sayin'… you need to look out for yourself better. I heard they scraped you off the floor at the Hop Scotch the other night."

I shrugged a shoulder. "Ever since the Civac mess, I gotta drink my way into a good night's sleep."

He wiggled a forefinger at me. "Well, you better start doin' that at home. Keep snorin' into the sawdust at this slopchute or that one, and somebody who doesn't like you may catch up with you. Might take advantage of your current state of mind."

"They might not like it if I woke up, though."

"Right. *If* you woke up." His handsome head tipped back. "You, uh, gonna make it to my grand opening?"

"That this weekend or next?"

"Friday next. Victoria's on the bill."

I grinned at him, surprised I could still do that. "Who else *would* be, on opening night?"

Packy was married to Victoria Valance—they'd been hitched a year but she was holding onto her maiden name, already established in show business with a minor hit record and a few national TV appearances. She was a curvy torch singer who sang like Julie London and looked just as good.

Maybe better.

"I bought that club for her," Packy said, "so she'd have a home worthy of her talent. No more working the club circuit."

Any guy with a wife like that would want to keep her close to home.

"I got a ringside table for you," he said.

"Wouldn't miss it," I told him.

He got up and made his way to the door onto the empty outer office. Paused and looked back at me. "Mike, you really need to get a hold of yourself. Clean up your act. Would a shave and a bath kill you? And at least buy some Sen-Sen for Christ's sake. Word to the wise guy."

"Thanks, kid."

"Don't mention it." He gave me a little salute and was gone.

What came next had been no trickier than putting the pin back in a grenade when you had the shakes. I looked up a number and dialed it. I talked my way past a receptionist and then a mellow, confident voice came on the line. "Walter Greenway speaking."

"Mr. Greenway? Mike Hammer."

"I know. That's why I took your call."

"Well, we haven't met, Mr. Greenway...."

"No. But I've read about you in the *Daily News* and seen you make the eleven o'clock news. I figure a colorful individual as well-known in Manhattan as Michael Hammer may be able to afford a handsome investment or two."

"I can't even afford an ugly one. But something's come up that concerns you, sir, and I should share it. And I may be able to help."

* * *

Walter Greenway's Wall Street office was the size of a chapel, but mammon was worshiped in this walnut-lined masculine chamber. And he eyed me from behind a mahogany pulpit of a desk worthy of the Pope but didn't seem about to bestow a blessing. His gray vested suit was Brooks Brothers or better, his navy silk tie cost what my suit did; his frame loomed big with some heft but little fat, head oblong, eyes dark and sharp, features regular but grooved, hair white and perfectly in place, though the white eyebrows were out of control.

In early summer the fireplace off to my left went unlit, a gilt-framed oil painting over it, the subject of which was sitting opposite me. Skyscrapers were peering at us through windows at right, as if we had their rapt interest.

"I'm surprised, Mr. Hammer," he said, his voice as warm as the fire and just as deadly, "that you might think someone in my position would not already *employ* sufficient security."

"Normally I might agree with you. You have the usual door-shakers, the night watchmen making the rounds of your well-off neighborhood. They check the front and back and side doors three times through the night, and by day, too, if you and your wife are both away."

Greenway's nod took about as long as my words had.

I went on: "And you have the doors and first-floor windows hooked up to a real loud alarm, and wired to a central monitoring station by the same company you use for the door-shakers."

"By 'first-floor windows,'" Greenway said, "you imply the three floors above are somehow vulnerable."

"I don't know how they're getting in," I admitted.

That frown probably made his people pee a little. "But you've undertaken surveillance of our home, and have determined—"

"I haven't," I said, cutting in rudely, "done any surveillance at all."

The big head went back. "Excuse me? You've just outlined our security measures in some detail. Where did you get that information?"

"I didn't have to get it anywhere. Those are the best options available to you, unless you have live-in security, which almost no one does with a private residence in Manhattan."

Suddenly the eyes were as wild as the eyebrows. "Then what is the point of this, Mr. Hammer?"

"The point is, I have reliable information that this weekend… you *are* away this weekend? Hamptons, as usual?"

Greenway thought about that, before nodding. But he did nod, and not so slowly this time.

I said, "My informant says you'll be hit sometime this weekend."

He sucked in air, huffed it out. "Thank you for this information, Mr. Hammer. I'll share it with the police. If they think there's anything to it—"

I raised a palm. "You'd get some cooperation from them, sure. You could even mention my name and that would lend some credibility. But I thought you might like to prevent this from happening again."

"It hasn't happened for the first time!"

"Then tell the police. Their prowl car will go by a few extra times and maybe… *maybe*… stop the robbery in its tracks. And you'll file it away and in a few months you'll be ripe for the plucking. Again."

"I find this vaguely insulting."

"Really I'm behaving myself."

He sat forward, just a little. "Are you? I would say you need a shave. Have you been sleeping in those clothes? I'm disappointed by the way you present yourself, Mr. Hammer."

"You're not wrong, sir. I'm drinking too much and I'm disgusted with myself. You've read about the Civac robbery and its tragic aftermath?"

Another nod, neither slow nor fast.

"Then you must know," I said, "that my agency was in charge of the security at the Civac affair."

"I do indeed. Which colors my lack of enthusiasm for hiring you for a similar purpose."

Now I leaned forward. "Mr. Greenway, I will stop these thieves and make an example of them. No one will ever again dream of attempting the burglary of your home. And no scrimy bastard will dare try pulling a heist where the Hammer Agency is providing security."

He drew in a deep breath and let it out slowly, thoughtfully. "As I said, Mr. Hammer, I've read of your...exploits. In the tabloid press, where perhaps they may well be exaggerated..."

"They are not exaggerated."

"You would kill an intruder?"

"I would kill an armed robber."

A part of him obviously liked the sound of that. He might never admit it in public, but I could read him. And he read me, all right. Frowning, he said, "I could never sanction a reckless disregard of—"

"I'll do my best not to shoot up your antiques and artwork. Aren't you going to ask me my price?"

Eyes wide, mouth too, he said, "Uh… what retainer would be required?"

"It'll be a flat fee. One dollar, to make it legal. I work through an attorney and I'll have him send the paperwork over. And I'll handle his fee."

"This sounds personal."

I got on my feet. "It usually is with me. That's why everybody's heard of me, but I don't have an office like this."

If my client could have seen me after I'd camped out in his digs for the better part of three days, he might have changed his mind taking me on, even at a buck. I hadn't shaved or showered since I got here. I'd slept in this old brown suit the night before I came on duty, though here my bed had been the couch in the study with my .45 in my hand and in my lap. And I didn't sleep deep. A man in a living nightmare doesn't risk actual dreaming.

My belly was operating on beer and cold meat—good stuff from the best deli, and useful protein. They had fresh fruit on hand, oranges and apples and pears. I had some cheese, too, like the human rat I was becoming, scurrying around this house, checking out all the rooms. Not because I thought somebody had sneaked in but to familiarize myself. How many were on this crew I had no clue. Where in this house full of valuable items they might go, I couldn't be positive.

The safe was likely. More than. Packy had known about the safe in the study, which was a smaller version of the walnut chamber on Wall Street but with wall-to-wall bookcases on three sides, leather-bound volumes and pricey first editions. The safe was behind a row of deluxe Dickens volumes, a horizontal baby designed to tuck away nicely.

In that safe, I was told, were all the precious-gem-set jewelry Mrs. Greenway possessed. Some bearer bonds running to a hundred grand kept the rocks company, and some legal documents that wouldn't mean bupkus to burglars.

The study itself was a metal-padded, soundproofed room—a so-called Faraday cage—dating to when the brownstone had been owned by the Republic of Yugoslavia a decade ago, where officials of the Soviet puppet state and visiting dignitaries (and spies) could converse or make calls without the risk of being wiretapped or otherwise surveilled.

Packy said it sounded like an inside job, that someone on the household staff had shared the layout of the joint as well as info about antique jewelry in the master bedroom and the location of key paintings of value and precious art pieces, sculpture, vases and such. This I hadn't told Greenway. Some cards you play close to the vest.

Mr. Greenway's cozy little sandstone-fronted pad sported thirteen-foot ceilings and consisted of five bedrooms, six bathrooms, hardwood floors, an elevator, nine working fireplaces, a central staircase, a living room/dining room with baby grand and satin drapes and crystal chandelier, with a terrace off the kitchen onto a garden. The four floors had an atrium under a stained-glass skylight with cherubs dancing or maybe flying. Picasso, Miró, and Matisse paintings watched me expensively from the walls and all those antiques had a French look, like this building built around the turn of the century was mistaking itself for Versailles.

I wasn't just a fish out of water, I was a fish on the moon. But I looked past all that to focus on the overall layout. Top to bottom: basement had guest quarters with living room, kitchen, bathroom, bedroom, and storage area; first floor a spacious living room and kitchen; second—family room, guest bedroom, two bathrooms; third—a master bedroom and a master bathroom bigger than my two-room office suite; and fourth—two guest bedrooms, two bathrooms, and the study.

With the jewels and bearer bonds in that safe, the study provided the logical focal point. When I wasn't down in the kitchen feeding myself, or using one of the half-dozen bathrooms, I decided to wait for my guests in there—the comfy cream-in-your-coffee leather couch along one of the walls of books making a good place to camp out. When the help returned from the Hamptons with Mr. and Mrs. Greenway, their duties would include emptying the study's matching leather wastebasket for apple cores and empty Blue Ribbon cans.

No TV or radio in the study, but I couldn't have risked watching or listening anyway. So I lay back with my .45 handy and read a leather-bound copy of *The Prisoner of Zenda*—a good yarn—and was damn near the end when I heard the rustling on the roof.

I wouldn't have heard it in that sound-proofed chamber, only I'd left the door standing open for that very reason. I put the book back on the shelf, grabbed my gun and slipped out into the hall that circled the stairwell under the stained-glass skylight. Moonlight made the cherubs glow but some devilish shadows were joining them now.

Directly across from the study was a bathroom and I ducked in there. I watched in the dark, with the door open, until from above came the *screeeeeee* of cutting glass. I closed the door but left enough to watch the skylight where a cherub disappeared and night took his place. A head appeared in the opening—eyes in a face obscured by a balaclava, peering down for a look-see—and I shut the door some more.

Gradually, the cherubs lifted out, via suction cups probably—the leaded-glass panels heavy enough to be a chore—and then half a dozen cherubs had flown and some wooden framework got kicked out, the pieces falling down the stairwell like brittle rain. The hole in the skylight was plenty to accommodate the crashers at my one-man party. A black nylon rope dropped through and hung there, the end coiling snakelike on the floor near the stairwell.

The aperture was filled by first one and then another and another slender man in tight long-sleeve stocking-mask-to-boot garb, sidearms holstered at their hips; they came down like water gliding along a flower's stem, each man a globule. Two had fairly large canvas pouches slung over their shoulders, another a smaller variation. They dropped to the floor near the stairwell, one at a time, five in all, the first four scrambling out of the next one's way, every man getting a gun into his black-gloved right hand as soon as he could.

I could have shot them, one by one, coming down—and don't think I didn't consider it. But I needed one alive to ask some questions. I closed the bathroom door until it was shut, save for an edge I could spy through. Three intruders rattled down the stairs. With no one home, I wondered what the rush was. On the other hand, these brownstones were slammed together side by side, and any commotion heard or seen could attract unwanted attention.

My hunch was they didn't intend to go out the way they'd come in—more likely an amount of time had been set aside and a car would pull up and they'd go out the front door, loaded down with goodies. To hell with the stupid alarm—they'd be gone before any watchman or cop could react.

Only they weren't going anywhere. They didn't know it, but they weren't.

The two who'd entered the study left the door open. I went over there and stood to one side, back to the wall, .45 snout up, and eavesdropped. Tossed books were hitting the floor. I gathered they'd be cracking the safe, not blowing it. And that horizontal number behind the leather-bound books wouldn't take much to crack.

Time crawled, seconds adding up to minutes. Then:

"*Got it!*"

They laughed and congratulated themselves in profane jubilation, dumping gems and jewelry into the smaller pouch in a tinkling shower like the tiny pieces of ice the precious cut stones were named for.

"*Look* at this *stuff,*" the same voice said. "These are *bearer bonds!* Good as cash money. Better."

Stacks of paper thumped into the pouch, the gems making a percussive rattle. "Let's get the hell out," the other one said.

That was my cue.

I stepped in, pushed the door of the soundproofed chamber shut behind me, and before I had the chance to introduce myself, the man in black nearest me raised his gun, a silenced automatic, and I had to plug the panicky idiot.

Being dead made him lose his balance; he tumbled backward even as a ribbon of red celebrated his demise above him. The safecracker had his hands full of the pouch. I gestured with the .45 barrel to the couch where I'd been reading *Prisoner of Zenda.*

"Take a seat," I said.

The slender figure in black was frozen, looking at his fallen comrade, who stared out stocking-mask eye holes at the ceiling.

"Take… a… *seat*," I repeated.

The safecracker swallowed. Nodded. Backed over to the couch and, when he felt it hit the back of his legs, sat clumsily. The canvas pouch was in his lap.

"Whose crew is this?" I asked.

He was shaking, teeth chattering as if from the chills. "I don't know. I'm not one of them."

"You had me fooled."

"No! I'm just jobbing this. They needed that box open and I was here to open it. And I did."

He gestured with the bag, then with a lurch to his feet flung the thing and its contents at me and I was showered with gems and gold-and-silver jewelry and flying bearer bonds, but if he thought that would faze me, he was wrong, because the .45 thundered in the small space, the sound-proofing only making the roar more extreme, and the slug caught him in the throat and sat him back down. Then he was sitting there gurgling—his hands, his wriggling fingers trying to rise to staunch the blood oozing from his throat but unable to quite pull it off.

I swore to myself, brushing gems off like oversize dandruff. I stuffed the .45 back under my arm and plucked the silenced automatic, a .22 Browning, from the disinterested fingers of the dead guy staring up in filmed-over blankness. I figured making less noise dealing with the other three wouldn't be a bad idea, if they'd separated. When I slipped back into the hall, under the skylight where night was seeping through, the safe cracker had stopped gurgling.

The master bedroom, whose frou-frou pink-and-white decor reflected only the lady of the house, was home to a box of valuable costume jewelry—cheap stuff by the standards of the Greenways, but vintage material that could run into the hundreds and even thousands. I took the back stairs, the central stairwell making too much of a target out of me, and burst into the big room, staying low. One figure in black had been posted here, and he was at a fancy white mirrored dresser dumping out a fancy pink jewelry box into another modest-sized canvas shoulder pouch.

But when he swung my way, he had his own silenced .22 ready and I had no choice. My silenced rod coughed twice and he did a jerky dance and flung himself back, knocking over perfume bottles and knick-knacks and providing another festive stream of red to splash the mirror in a room dominated otherwise by pink.

That left two and I needed one alive.

I used the back stairs again and it brought me out by the baby grand. One of the black-clad burglars was helping himself to a Matisse over the fireplace and another was in the formal dining room area over at the right, grabbing a Picasso, the female subject of which gazed at me with one weird eye. He took off running toward the kitchen and, goddamnit, I tried for his legs and missed and had to take him down with a head shot; his momentum twisted him around and he gaped at me with only one eye left, a hideous gnarled scarlet exit wound taking the other one's place, making his ghastly stare worse than the Picasso's.

And then there was one.

His hands were filled with the framed Matisse, a landscape that looked childish to me.

He said, "You… I *know* you…."

I didn't know him. All I had to go on was eyes in a black mask, after all.

I said, "What happened to the woman on the Civac job?"

"…What?"

No, I didn't recognize him, but those eyes recognized me all right, those eyes filled with hysteria and terror, bugged eyes blinking under sweat-dripping lashes….

I was trembling. "The woman on the Civac job. Not the fat dame. Not the beast. The beauty."

"You're Mike Hammer. *Jesus!* You're Mike Hammer…."

He hurled the painting at me and I reflexively fired the .22 and he fell away, and over the mantle of the marble fireplace the wall displayed a brand-new abstract original.

In red.

"Shit," I said.

CHAPTER TWO

The Blue Ribbon restaurant on West 44th Street between Sixth and Seventh Avenues was a dark-wood-paneled paean to old Bavaria and German cuisine, beer hall music piped faintly in. Its bar was superbly stocked, with a narrow aisle between stools and tables, the latter along a wall of endless autographed celebrity photos—with a sketch by Caruso being the prize. My regular spot was in a niche where the famous faces included mine, which hung crookedly at the moment. I didn't bother straightening it.

Velda would have.

The place was our favorite, Velda's and mine. Most people called Velda my secretary, but she was more than that, much more—a full partner, the other licensed PI in *Michael Hammer Investigations*. But, over the years, what we had between us grew into another kind of partnership, signified by the ring I'd given her, a half-karat number a Diamond District client had paid me with.

She and I had sat together at this table more times than memory could calculate.

Big tux-sporting George, the Greek manager of the German place, paused to settle a disapproving gaze on me. "You've hardly touched your knockwurst, Mike."

"Takin' my time."

"That's your third Prior's Double Dark, Mike."

"Cuttin' me off, George?"

"Not yet. Not yet."

I forked a bite of knockwurst to placate him. I even chewed and swallowed it, and he nodded and went away.

A familiar voice said, "You look like hell."

I saluted Captain Pat Chambers of Homicide with my pilsner of Prior's. "Let me guess. They yanked my ticket."

He loomed over me for a moment, the picture of quiet disgust, a big dark-blond guy with gray eyes, the kind of pleasant face in a crowd that came in handy for a cop. His suit looked slept in, but compared to mine it just arrived from the cleaners. Finally he tossed his hat on the table and pulled out the chair Velda had so often used and sat and said, "Your private investigator's license has indeed been suspended, pending the results of the hearing into the shooting at the Greenway residence."

"It's been suspended before, but never *indeed* been suspended. I'm coming up in the world."

"I don't think so. Your permit to carry a gun is revoked, too. I'd say you finally crossed the line."

"How'd I manage that?"

He waved a hand. "Five dead on a home invasion? You working 'security?' Your client says you got a tip. Want to talk about it?"

"I didn't get a tip. I had a hunch Greenway was a sitting duck for the crew going around relieving rich broads of expensive baubles they never needed in the first place."

"So you're an ambulance chaser now."

"Usually the ambulance leaves *after* I get there."

George brought Pat his own Prior's and the two nodded at each other and for a moment they seemed to share a "what are we gonna do about this guy" look.

"By this 'crew going around,'" Pat said to me, "you mean the plunder squad that made the Civac hit."

I shrugged.

"You weren't working security at Greenway's," Pat said through his teeth. "You were playing your same old 'getting even' game. The Mike Hammer blue plate special—Revenge with a side of Murder."

I frowned at him. "I didn't murder anybody. They were armed robbers. They had guns they were getting ready to use."

"Like you were ready with *your* gun to use."

I leaned way forward. "Listen, buddy, I didn't want them dead. I wanted them alive and *talking*."

He made a sound deep within him that was half cough, half laugh. "You just miscalculated, 'buddy.' You thought you'd put three or four of them down and the remaining couple of survivors would be so scared they'd shit themselves and start running off at the mouth like bawling kids caught with their hands in the cookie jar."

My response was a mumble I barely heard myself. "I, uh... *tried* to... question them...."

Now he leaned across the table. "For years I been telling you this kill-happy spree of yours would catch up with you. That it would make you pay. Well, now it has, but *you* aren't paying. *Velda* paid. But *you* sure as hell didn't."

"I'll find her, Pat."

He shook his head. "You just don't get it, do you? You put her life on the line so you could pick up an extra paycheck. You already had something on the docket for the night of the Civac party—that suspicious death one of your precious insurance clients wanted you to make a murder out of. So you sent that girl in and she—"

"Velda was no 'girl!' Jesus, Pat, you know that. She was an experienced ex-policewoman with a Vice Squad background. She couldn't carry a PI ticket in this state otherwise."

He was shaking his head, his upper lip curling into a bitter smile. "A hundred people at that party, and half a million in rocks on just the lady of the house, never mind the damn guests, and you send in *one* operative? I call it negligence."

I slapped the air dismissively. "What the hell is it to you, Pat?"

He got rid of half his beer. Set the glass down with a slosh and a thud. "What's it to me? She was *my* friend, too."

"Quit talking about her in the past tense, Pat. I'll find her."

He jerked a thumb at his chest. "If anybody finds her, it'll be us poor underpaid public servants. And she'll be in the same shape as Mrs. Civac. I told you that at the morgue. But okay. From now on, I'll humor you. Present tense. She's my friend, too."

"She's my girl, Pat."

"Oh, *now* she's a girl."

"That's right. Get your own."

He took that like a punch. Then he got to his feet, stuffed on his hat, and said, "You better shower and shave before that hearing, Mike. And put on a clean pressed suit while you're at it. Maybe skip the orange juice at breakfast—you know, the half-vodka pick-me-up?"

"Thanks a bunch for the advice."

"You need it. Because you know what, chum? You stink."

I gave him two short words, and then he shook his head and was gone.

A few minutes later, George dropped off a pilsner of dark beer. "Last one, Mike."

I nodded. Sipped. Thought back.

The call came in six weeks before.

The voice on the phone had a distinct German accent. He introduced himself as Rudolph Civac, who had recently moved from Chicago with his wife Marta to an estate in Westchester County.

"We are throwing a little get-together to introduce ourselves to New York," Civac said, as if human beings could introduce themselves to a city or maybe an entire state.

"I'm a two-person agency, Mr. Civac. But I can put together a whole security team, if you like."

"That will not be necessary, Mr. Hammer." He spoke in a rather slow, unhurried manner. "We have a security service already. They won't be on the scene but will be on the alert. Still, I would feel better if Marta had a personal bodyguard nearby at all times."

"Why is that, sir?"

"Marta's first husband, her late husband, made a habit of giving her an annual anniversary gift of a precious gem, which would then be set in gold or silver, rings in particular. Half a million dollars' worth, over time. And..." The voice chuckled deep. "... she does like to show them off."

"Well, that could make her a prime target. There's been a rash of jewel robberies at private functions of late. Perhaps you've read about them."

"Oh yes. Which has spurred my concern, and my action. Of course, Marta has fine paste copies she could wear that would do perfectly well, but... you know women."

Most of the women I knew had more sense, but I said, "I do. What's the date of your event?"

He gave it to me and I checked my calendar.

"Mr. Civac, I have a conflict that evening. But my partner, Velda Sterling, is available. She's a pro all the way—fully licensed as an investigator and to carry a gun. I might have recommended her in any case, because over time I've had two heists pulled under my nose when they happened in a ladies' room."

A slight tightness came into the voice. "I would feel better if you handled this personally."

"Not possible, sir. But Miss Sterling can take on anything that might come up. I can drive out to your estate that night when my other business is finished. Where are you in Westchester?"

"Bedford Corners. Ours is a small estate. Eleven acres."

He didn't seem to be joking. Nor did he flinch when I gave him a quote at triple my usual rate. I told him I'd call back to confirm the job after I'd spoken to Miss Sterling.

Velda was in the outer office putting away a manila folder in a four-drawer filing cabinet. She was in a simple white blouse, a black pencil skirt, nylons and ballet flats, and made a Hollywood glamor-girl wardrobe out of them. Tall, damn near tall as me, her midnight hair a style-defying pageboy cut brushing her shoulders, she glanced at me in a smile that the lushness of her lips made special no matter how many times she sent it my way.

"You look like the cat," she said, "who ate the canary."

"We actually have a paying client, sugar."

But her smile disappeared when I told her she now had plans for a certain upcoming Saturday night. She came over to me in that slow, casual way that was as lithe as a leopard and as graceful as a runway model.

Almost nose to nose, she said confrontationally, "Don't you think you might have checked with me first?"

I touched that nose of hers lightly. "That's what I'm doing now."

Her smile returned when she heard what the client was willing to cough up for the privilege of her company.

"Grab your notebook," I told her.

Soon she was sitting across from me in my office, those long, lovely yet muscular legs crossed, her pen poised to write in the hand that sparkled with that half-a-karat ring.

"You'd agree this seems like a routine job," I said.

"I do."

"You sound like a bride."

"Promises, promises. But half a million in rocks is never routine. And with these jewelry heists lately…"

I nodded. "Can you handle it?"

"Don't insult me."

"Sorry, honey. But on that same Saturday night, I'm getting access to the penthouse apartment where that suspicious death took place, and the insurance people will be on hand, which means we can't do this one together."

When she shrugged, nice things happened in the white blouse; it was like a couple of kittens having a friendly fight. "I can handle it."

"I know you can, doll. But I'll drive out there when I'm done anyway. Make nice with our wealthy clients."

She cocked her head, frowned just a little. "I'm not familiar with Civac or his wife."

"And I'm not either. Understand, I haven't accepted yet. We need to check Civac's background, routine job or not. Call Irv Kupcinet in Chicago at the *Sun Times*, and I'll call Hy Gardner at the *Herald Tribune*. Between the two of 'em, we'll get the lowdown."

She nodded, closed her notebook and scurried off. I took time out to watch her, thinking what a lucky damn man I was, then started dialing.

In half an hour, she was back in the chair again, legs crossed the opposite way, steno pad open and we compared notes.

"Irv says hi," she began with a perfunctory nod. "Civac, a German emigre, was the European distributor for Singleton Manufacturing. Industrial machine parts. Singleton's wife, Marta, a Chicago girl, is very big in Windy City society, a real Gold Coast diva."

I gave a whistle. "Singleton Manufacturing. That's sizeable dough."

"Maybe you should have *quadrupled* the rate," Velda said. "When Singleton died of a heart attack—no suspicious circumstances— Marta inherited everything. No kids, it seems. A year later, a little over a year ago, she and Civac married. Apparently, Marta put good people in charge of her late hubby's business. Now she and Rudy have taken an early retirement to Westchester County and Marta has her eye on being a social influence in our little corner of the world."

"That tallies with everything Hy told me," I said. "His wife Marilyn says Marta is kind of a joke in society circles, but that doesn't mean she won't have a good crowd at her coming out party. He doesn't have anything much on Civac. Nothing suspicious, but Civac doesn't turn up in the newspaper files till ten years ago, when he went to work for Singleton. An unsubstantiated rumor is that he fled Germany to avoid a concentration camp. So. What do we think?"

"We think," Velda said with a big beautiful smile, "I am going to restore the health of our bank account after spending an evening with Mrs. Rudolph Civac, helping her audition to high society by hanging half a million bucks in gems on herself like a Christmas tree."

We both had a good laugh at that.

At eleven p.m. on the Saturday night in question, just as I was wrapping up work on the possible homicide, Velda called the prearranged number.

"Smooth as silk, boss," Velda said. "Nothing unusual. Guests are oozing with reputations and money. No suspicious or unknown characters have crashed the party, and we already cleared the household staff. We said it would be routine, and it is routine."

"What's your read on the host and hostess?"

"Marta's a ditz but nice enough. They're holding dinner awaiting the arrival of Mr. Civac, who got delayed in the city."

"Well, rich people like to eat late."

"Yeah, they're not five o'clock supper types like you, but midnight is overdoing it. He's expected momentarily. You can skip coming out, if you like."

"No. I think with the kind of loot they've invested in us, the famous Mike Hammer can put in an appearance."

She laughed. "Certainly. The famous Mike Hammer can introduce himself to society."

"Should I stop for my tux?"

"Like you own one. I better get back to it. Love you, you big lug."

"Love you, doll."

When I got to the estate on Succabone Road at just before one-thirty a.m., red and blue lights were stroking the night like a chef whipping up the night into a garish meal. A young cop stopped me at the gate and I told him who I was, showed him my ID, and was sent on ahead.

A thirtyish deputy sheriff named Garcia met me on the porch of the remodeled turn-of-the-century farmhouse. A swimming pool glimmered over to the right. All the lights in the big house were on.

I told him who I was and started to push past him, and he held me back. I held myself back till I heard him out.

"There's been an abduction," Deputy Garcia said.

"I want to talk to my operative—Miss Sterling."

"She's among the abducted."

Now I did push past him, and I don't remember much after that. Just the blur of shoving through cops and knocking a couple down, till I'd seen every room in the house, and there were a lot of those. A big living room had all the guests herded in and they were milling and disgruntled as sheriff's deputies and state police questioned them.

A detective with the state police grabbed me and calmed me down. I was ready for that, because Velda was nowhere in this place and I had to know my next move.

He was about forty and fleshy with a mustache and patient eyes. Introduced himself as Branford. "I know who you are, Mr. Hammer. If I didn't, you'd be in handcuffs right now. You assaulted three law enforcement officers this evening. Would you like to go to Sing Sing and have a reunion with everyone you sent there? Or would you prefer to calm down?"

We were back on the porch now.

"I'm listening," I said.

"They were holding dinner for the arrival of the host, Rudolph Civac."

"My client."

"Your client. He finally arrived at eleven-fifteen, greeted his guests, apologized for the delay, then went upstairs with his wife to freshen up. He'd apparently come from a long business meeting. Your operative, Miss Sterling, accompanied the couple. Half an hour later, a maid checked to see if something was wrong. The upstairs was empty."

"And she called the police?"

"No. Apparently the Civacs had been arguing on and off over the past several days, and the maid thought that unpleasantness may have carried over into Mr. Civac not arriving until late. She assumed they'd gone out the private exit at the rear of the estate, on the other side of the house from the kitchen and the living room. She took it upon herself to have dinner served, telling the guests the Civacs had been called away on a family emergency and sent their apologies and regrets. She's a longtime employee who came with them from Chicago."

"I want to talk to her. Right now."

The detective thought about that, then reluctantly nodded, and within a minute—with Branford listening in—I was talking to her, a skeletal woman in her fifties in the usual black livery trimmed-white; she was on the edge of tears. I did my best to press her, when what I wanted to do was take her by the shoulders and shake what she knew out of her.

"They've been fighting a lot lately," the woman said, nervous, snuffling, "and that's what I thought this was about. Then, while dinner was being served, I got to thinking—why was Miss Sterling gone? Why if they were arguing would a bodyguard accompany them? And why if they were fighting would they leave together? Then I checked the rear exit and it was forced."

I had a look and it had been pried open from the outside, providing entry and exit.

Finally, I was asked to leave.

"We've got a five-bedroom, five-bathroom estate," Detective Branford said, "with another half dozen rooms and a basement, all a crime scene now. And we don't need your help. We'll want to talk to you when…"

When I'd composed myself.

I nodded and left.

I drove back to the city. I drove fast but didn't get picked up, which was good, because I'd have probably punched another cop. Or two. And been in jail. Or dead.

My first stop was at Velda's apartment. I had a key. Maybe she'd made her way back here. I'd built a scenario where the Civacs had indeed argued and split up in two cars and Velda stayed with her ditzy charge and when Mrs. Civac was safely deposited in a suite at the Ritz or somewhere, Velda went home. She'd tried to call but I wasn't around. I was off in Westchester County chasing a wild goose.

So she'd be home. She'd be waiting. I'd be upset but relieved, and we'd both laugh and laugh, and for years we'd tell the story of this crazy night.

But she wasn't home.

I had been asleep in bed, managing maybe two hours, when the call came from Pat.

"Mike," he said. "Can you meet me at the morgue?"

Maybe the worst question I was ever asked.

I said, "It's not Vel...?"

"Get over here."

A city hearse was unloading a passenger in a wicker coffin through the black steel doors at the rear of the morgue when I pulled up in the early morning shadow of the beehive of office buildings surrounding it. I was shaking as I walked down the white-tiled tunnel to where Pat Chambers was waiting at a door marked CORONER.

He curled a finger at me, like a father summoning a kid who'd been using crayons on the playroom walls.

They hadn't filed her away yet. She was on a metal carrier when the assistant coroner flipped the sheet back to the woman's waist. She was maybe sixty, fat and her make-up trying too hard, her henna hair permed professionally, her dress the finest evening wear that ever got soaked in filthy river water. She had a bullet hole in her forehead and her open eyes were still surprised about it.

"Marta Civac," Pat said.

I grabbed him by the lapels. "You *bastard!* You could've told me it wasn't Velda!"

He brushed my hands away. Hard. "No, it isn't Velda. But it could've been. And it may be any day now, if she and Rudy Civac haven't been washed out to sea. Have a look."

The fingers of both her hands were gone. Cut off at the knuckle.

"She was a hefty gal, the former Marta Singleton," Pat said. "She must've had a hundred grand or two stuffed on her thick pudgy fingers. To get those rings, they had to sever the fingers. Gardening shears, you think?"

"Lousy bastard…"

We walked out together. I fumbled a Lucky into my face and Pat lit it up for me.

"They were abducted to steal those jewels," I said, "and do it away from all those people, those witnesses. Even any male guest who might have waded in and tried to play hero."

"Why did they take Velda?"

"She was just there."

"If she was as capable as you say, why didn't she make a try for them?"

I stopped where my heap was parked. "Pat, that's standard operating procedure for an operative in a situation like this. Better to give up the valuables than get yourself killed. Jewel thieves aren't usually killers. Not unless you corner them."

"You figure Velda would've played along… encouraged the clients to cooperate, figuring once the thieves had the gems they'd let the hostages go and take off?"

"Yeah. But then those rings wouldn't come off."

"And the only question," Pat said, "is whether they shot Marta in the head and then cut off her fingers…"

"Or vice versa," I said.

CHAPTER THREE

Scarlet lettering cut across an ebony slab—

THE PARAGON

—over a red-black flame design canopy and a red carpet leading rather grandly into the well-appointed hole-in-the-wall that was Packy Paragon's new club at 70 East 55th. As you went through double glass doors, you were welcomed by a standing marquee with the same picture of Victoria Valance in a low-cut evening dress (pic cropped just under the generous bosom) that graced the cover of her bestselling album, *I Carry a Torch* on Rendezvous Records. A similarly busty babe, if not as classically beautiful, took your hat and coat in exchange for a smile and a ticket. Just over where the maitre d' greeted you at his podium was draped a GRAND OPENING banner.

The place had a cozy feel, a row of red leather booths slightly elevated at right, a stage with a piano at left, divided by two rows of small round tables for four—white cloths, red chairs. The ceiling, with its modest stage lighting, was rather low and paneled in orange-ish wood, as were the walls, and a fieldstone fireplace was along the far wall with a faux electric fire going. The shallow stage had a curtained backdrop continuing the flame motif.

Classy in its way, this was a far cry from the chrome-and-glass nightclub casinos Packy used to operate in every borough, and from here to Albany. The only false note was a big young handsome broad-shouldered guy in a sharp suit wandering the room, smiling and nodding if anyone made eye contact. Despite his relative youth, he had a hardness to his face and a thoroughness to how he was checking out the crowd. That impressed me, and not entirely in a good way. A bouncer, most likely. But even though that suit was well cut, I could tell he had a rod under his left arm.

Of course, so did I.

The opening night crowd was impressive enough. Over here were Rex Harrison and Kay Kendall. Over there were Ernie Kovacs and Edie Adams. Dan Dailey and Robert Q. Lewis had a couple of showgirl types with them. And I had a ringside table all to myself.

For a guy whose last Broadway appearance was at an automat, I had a lot of eyes on me. My columnist pal Hy Gardner had warned me the word was out I'd cracked up. That I was drinking myself to death. That bums were embarrassed to ask me for a handout because they didn't want to be seen in such company. Hy advised me to get hold of myself, if I insisted on going out in public.

"I know what that doll means to you," Hy said over lunch at P.J. Moriarty's, where only the sufferance of John, a bartender I considered a friend, allowed a slob like me a spot at that long, legendary mahogany bar.

"Pat thinks Velda's dead," I said, looking into foam. "He's written her off."

The eyes in Hy's hound-dog, seen-it-all face peered over the top of his dark-rimmed glasses at me. "Pat may be right. But if she's alive, you want to find her. And if she isn't, you still want to find who took her. Don't you, Mike?"

"I killed those bastards already," I said and drank some beer.

He put a hand on my shoulder. "You got the flunkies. Don't you want who sent them?"

"You know I do."

"Then snap out of it, man. Rejoin the human race."

So tonight, at the Paragon grand opening, I was bathed and shaved and wearing my best suit. I hadn't had a drink since lunch, either. Of course, the first thing I did was wave over a waitress in a short red skirt and white apron and order a highball.

It came and I took my time with it—a good three minutes. Then a waiter brought me food I hadn't ordered—a thick, rare cut of tender prime rib served on the bone, a baked potato with sour cream and chives, and French-cut string beans. I just stared at the plate like I hadn't seen food before in my life.

Packy sat down. He was in a tux tonight, looking more like a tall George Raft than ever. He looked amused but sympathetic. "You *have* eaten in the last month and a half, haven't you, Mike?"

"Sandwich here and there," I admitted. "When I got faint. Soup. Breakfast once or twice."

A waiter put the same meal in front of Packy and the host started eating at a reasonable pace, as if otherwise I might get sick here at ringside and ruin his famous clientele's night. Joke was on him—I didn't have anything in my stomach but that highball.

He asked, "How did that hearing go?"

"Having the District Attorney himself testify against me," I said, "I'm told was a first, for the state licensing commission. My PI ticket has been suspended for a year." I opened my suitcoat and gave him a glimpse of the .45 in the sling. "Good thing I can reapply for my gun carry license in two years."

His eyeroll was subtle. "Well, you're a young man."

I shrugged. Tentatively cut a piece of rare roast beef off the hunk of dead animal and studied it like a clue. "If nobody kills me first."

Packy ate for a while, then said, "I wish I could tell you I had any luck."

He meant finding out who the kingpin behind the armed robbery crew was.

"I took a chance just sharing the tip about Greenway," he said very quietly.

Was he all right? He seemed a little nervous. But then it was opening night.

He was saying, "And I honestly think none of my low friends in high places… and I have a few… know who that is, either. As I told you, the big man appears to have several crews. You shot his home-invasion-party-crashing squad to hell and gone. But he'll find new recruits."

"No shortage of criminals in the greater metropolitan area," I said. I took the bite. Swallowed.

"No shortage," Packy agreed. "Never has been, never will. A separate crew is doing jewelry stores and another handles payroll robberies. But there's also a group doing institutional knockovers. That Brink's truck a week ago? That was them."

"A new take on taking."

Packy nodded as he swallowed a bite of baked potato. "In the past, the six families have underwritten independent operators in that field of activity. This is a whole new organizational approach."

The bite seemed to be staying down; I tried another. Swallowed and said, "Will any of the families step in? It's cutting into their action."

He shook his head. "I doubt it. They're concentrating on their various brands of servicing the public's forbidden desires. How do you make people not want the easy money of hitting a number or making a small fortune on the turn of a card? How do you convince anybody not to pursue their darker sexual desires? How do you discourage someone from hiring the death of someone else who displeases them? Human nature hasn't changed since the dawn of time, Mike. You know that."

"You're a philosopher, Packy. And yet you went straight."

He touched his lips with a linen napkin, then said, "I have enough money. Why take chances? And I have a beautiful, talented wife. I'm investing in her future, and mine."

Bite number three. "Anybody ever tell you you're a lucky son of a bitch?"

He grinned. A hood hadn't been this handsome since Legs Diamond. Ex-hood, now. "You have, Mike, a couple of dozen times. Listen, uh… you look good. Damn near healthy. You should stay that way. Maybe even leave your unlicensed gun at home." He shrugged. "I mean, Mike… it's not like you can't kill somebody with your hands."

He had a point.

"I want to find somebody and kill him, Packy. That makes me suspect somebody's out there wanting to kill *me* first. I'll risk a Sullivan Act beef."

"Okay," he said and shrugged again.

His manner was cool, cordial as ever, but I couldn't help but feel something had him a little on edge. Or was I so caught up in my own paranoia it was bleeding into how I read other people?

Soon I had managed to put away about a third of my plate. I pushed it aside and waved a waitress down for another highball and slurped that to oblivion while Packy finished his meal. He was brought a cocktail without asking, a Manhattan. He already had the staff trained well.

When he was done, a waitress materialized and took our plates away. He used the linen napkin again and said, "Mike, I appreciate you coming tonight. I know Victoria will be thrilled to see you. You and Velda are two of her favorite people."

I appreciated that, unlike Pat, he was sticking to the present tense.

"We're on our second copy of Victoria's LP," I said. "Wore the first one out."

Packy beamed at that, then gestured to the stage. "She'll join you after her set. This is going to be her home—she'll play here all but a few weeks a year. A handful of dates in Vegas and Hollywood are necessary in her business. But we're going to record her next album right here. *Victoria Valance—Live at Paragon's!*"

I had to smile. "You got it made, Pack."

"There's, uh, a matter… Mike, I need you to trust my judgment on something."

Was he finally getting around to whatever was bothering him? *If* something was bothering him…

"Oh? Well, sure."

"The young buck who's been keeping an eye on things around here tonight…" Packy gestured to the handsome character who was discreetly milling. "…he's my new bodyguard."

"Why does somebody who's gone straight need a bodyguard?"

"Because most of my life I was crooked as a dog's hind leg. I have old enemies who even now wouldn't mind seeing me freshly dead."

"Tell me about it," I said. "He looks familiar, your new right hand. But I don't think I know him."

Packy nodded toward the guy, who nodded back with a smile. The bodyguard had black hair and a deep tan. He had the look of a cocky punk on *Gunsmoke* who gave Matt Dillon trouble and got killed before the last commercial.

"That's Sonny Gray from L.A.," Packy said.

The back of my neck talked to me. "You're kidding. The word on him is *not* good, Pack. They say he's a trigger-happy psycho."

A big smile blossomed on the '30s movie-star face. "Well, they say the same thing about you, Mike, but I don't hold it against you."

Again, he had a point.

"Look," he said, leaning close, "Sonny's reputation is deserved to a degree, but that psycho, trigger-happy stuff is just the bunk. He lets people buy it because having that reputation can be an advantage in his line of work."

"Killing people, you mean."

"Mike…"

I raised my hands, palms out. "If he's okay with you, Pack, he's okay by me. I heard he was a rising star out there. He got to about number three on the West Coast Cosa Nostra hit parade."

"He did. Then he found himself in the middle of a power play after Jack Dragna died and he did what I did—went straight—before he wound up choking to death on bullets. He's strictly working security now, exclusively for me. I pay him well." Now Packy raised his hands, palms out. "Mike, if you have *any* trouble with him, and I do *not* think you will, you have my blessing to handle it any way you please."

I nodded slowly. "I'll take you at your word, Pack."

"Thank you, Mike." He half-stood and with a wave summoned the bodyguard, who made a beeline. Tall Sonny had a carved look, despite his youth, like a cigar store Indian or an Easter Island statue.

But he also had a big, Hollywood smile and he extended his hand as Packy said, "Sonny, this is—"

"I know who this is," Sonny said pleasantly. His grip was strong as we shook but stayed just to one side of showing off. "It's Mike Hammer himself. You're kind of a legend where I come from, Mr. Hammer."

"Call me 'Mike,'" I said. "I would think my name would be mud in certain L.A. circles."

"Sit, sit," Packy said to the bodyguard, who sat between us, grinning at me like a kid meeting Mickey Mantle.

"They tell stories about you, Mike. Like that one time you bumped off a couple of hoods and left them under a 'Dead End' sign."

"That was never proved. Like it was never proved you draped a movie director over the 'O' in the Hollywood sign."

Sonny shrugged a shoulder and his grin turned shy. "He'd been banging a starlet who was tight with my capo. They say."

I gave him a grin in return. "People say a lot of things, don't they? Listen, you take care of my buddy here. He saved my bacon more than once."

"You bet, Mr. Hammer."

"Mike," I reminded him.

Sonny said he'd better get back to work, and got up and did so, after smiles and nods to us both.

"Mike," Packy said, "that night they snatched Velda and the Civacs—a hundred people were there, and a gaggle of household staff."

I nodded.

"And *nobody* saw *anything*?" he asked.

"It's a big house. There was a back way out. The cops interviewed everybody. Packy, I'm the one laid out under a 'Dead End' sign this time. I've hit a wall. I don't want to put you in a bad spot, but if you can shake anything loose, I would owe you big time."

"See what I can do, buddy." Packy stood and said, "Now, you'll have to excuse me, Mike. I'm my own M.C. at this venue. I'll be bringing Victoria on in a few minutes."

"Go ahead, you big ham," I said.

"Hey, I don't cost me anything," he said with a laugh, then made his way to the stage, pausing to greet and shake hands with his mostly celebrity patrons.

When the lights came down, applause came up—and my tuxedo-sporting friend strode to the microphone to welcome the opening night attendees.

"Ladies and gentlemen," Packy said, "it's my honor, and pleasure, to introduce the lady of the house.... Rendezvous Records recording artist, Miss Victoria Valance!"

Applause and more than a few whistles greeted her as she glided slowly onto the stage, in no hurry, looking like that marquee picture at the entrance had decided to come to life. She wore the same silver sparkly clinging gown that looked like all it would take was a tug to bare that high, full bosom in a way the law would not allow. The silver of the second skin stood out sharply against the red-and-black fiery backdrop.

Her golden hair fell to her bare shoulders in waves the ocean might have envied, her forehead high and broad with a hint of widow's peak, her eyes wide-set and big and a rich unlikely green, her nose well-carved, almost Roman, her lips full and defiantly sullen, the moist red of her lipstick touched with orange, a fiery willful challenge.

She didn't even nod to the audience or make them wait for her hit version of Billie Holiday's "My Old Flame," just going right into it, accompanied only by Bud Gregg on the piano. She nodded and granted them smiles at the clapping that opening created, and then went through a set of classic torch songs reimagined in her breathy but perfectly pitched way: "The Man I Love," "Lover Man," "Don't Smoke in Bed" (I was having a Lucky at the time), "Since I Fell For You," and more.

"I got it bad and that ain't good," she sang in her encore, and winked at me midway. Velda would have got a kick out of that. I think.

A scattering of audience applause greeted her when, half an hour after she left the stage, Victoria returned to join me at my table. She was in a simple gray and black suit now, and she had pony-tailed her hair back and her mouth, her entire face, was make-up free. She was no longer glamorous, just gorgeous.

She sat next to me and took my right hand in both of hers and said, "Mike, I am so sorry. I can't imagine what you've been going through."

"She's not dead," I said. "I'll find her."

"If anyone can," she said, and nodded and smiled bravely.

Packy came over, gave his wife a quick kiss, told her how great she was, and said to me, "Babysit my baby, would you, Mike? I have to mingle with our famous guests. If I neglect just one of them, I'll get crucified in Earl Wilson's column."

The songbird gave me my hand back, patting it first, then a waitress came over with a glass of white wine for her and another highball for me.

Victoria leaned forward, her brow creased. "Are you doing all right, Mike?"

"Flying high, kitten."

She cocked her head. "You *look* good. But, uh… your eyes give you away."

"Really."

"You ought to try blinking once in a while. Kind of breaks up the monotony."

I laughed. "Suppose it does."

Now she smirked, mocking me just a little. "And I can give you some make-up for those dark circles under your eyes. Not sleeping much?"

"I find sleep's a habit you can shake, with the right motivation."

She nodded archly. "So I hear." Then her voice became soft and serious. "You want to tell me all about it? The papers have been pretty vague."

"You mean the abduction, or the Greenway fun and games?"

The big green eyes tightened to slits. "The abduction. The Greenway robbery you interrupted, that was covered in the press pretty accurately, wasn't it?"

She didn't seem to know the role her husband had played and I wasn't about to change that.

So I said the papers were right about Greenway, and filled her in on the Civac job and how it went wrong.

When I was done, she said, "You shouldn't blame yourself for anything in this. Velda could take of herself. And I think you're right—she may still be among the living. I grant you, I... can't come up with exactly *how*, but I know how strong she was. *Is*. And you'll find whoever's behind those robberies. I just know you will."

"Thanks, kid." I lit up a Lucky. I studied her. That crease in her forehead was still present. "Something's on your mind. What?"

I could sense it. I could almost smell it. *Fear*. Something big was worrying her.

"I'm fine," she said. "Never better. Having a club like this to call home, and having a chance get off the damn road... it's a dream come true. But Packy... I don't know."

I frowned. "Everything okay between you two?"

She smiled a little and waved that off. "Sure. We get along swell. It's not that. It's..."

"Spill it, Vickie."

That stopped her. The smile returned, bigger. "You're the only person in the world who calls me 'Vickie.' Only person I *let* call me 'Vickie.'"

"Thanks for the honor. Now what the hell's bothering you, lady?"

She shook her head, sighed. "I really don't know, Mike. It's not me. It's Packy. Something's worrying him."

Despite what I'd noticed myself, I tried to shrug it off for her benefit. "Honey, he seemed fine."

She shook her head. "He puts up a good front, but I can tell."

Had one of his former partners among the six families got wise to him giving me that tip about the Greenway job?

"This new bodyguard," I said. "Sonny Gray. What's your read on him?"

She shrugged, shook her head like she was getting rid of a fly. "He seems all right. He seems fine."

"When did Packy hire him on?"

My line of inquiry seemed to confuse her. "Few months ago," she said. "As the club was coming together."

That predated my asking Packy to do some digging.

I stopped a waitress for another highball.

Victoria gave me a stern look. "You're hitting those a little hard, aren't you, Mike? Is that how you're dealing with this thing? Prescribing yourself alcohol with every meal? And between meals? And at bedtime?"

"There is no bedtime," I said, "without it."

She almost looked like she might start crying. "I hate to see you hurting like this. What can I do to help, Mike?"

I let out some Lucky smoke. "Not a damn thing."

51

She arched a single eyebrow. "Not a damn thing that… wouldn't betray a couple of people we love?"

"You and that yen you got for tough guys," I said, grunting a laugh. "It's what attracted you to Packy in the first place."

We were at that place now—that place where if either one of us said another word we were going to get ourselves in big trouble.

So I skipped the last highball and gave her shoulder a squeeze as I got up and left, then made it to over where Packy was saying goodnight to Sidney Chaplin. The place was near closing and the crowd was thinning.

"Mike, thanks for coming," Packy said. "I know it was tough for you to, uh…"

"Pull myself together? Make myself presentable? Naw. Easy as falling down three flights of stairs, backwards. Look, uh, Pack… if something was bothering you… the kind of something that I could handle for you… you'd tell me, right?"

He grinned. "Mike, I don't know what the hell you're talking about."

But his eyes were lying.

CHAPTER FOUR

You spend over a week beating the bushes, looking for a vague somebody who is smart enough, tied-in enough, to assemble armed robbery crews for a wide range of ripe-for-the-picking targets. If this new kingpin really isn't somebody inside one of the half dozen Mafia families controlling greater New York, he still has to be known to the dons, and has to be *somebody*—somebody credible enough, fearsome enough, to carve out a profitable corner of criminal turf for himself.

Even if he kicks back a piece—pays his taxes, as the mob boys say—only those at the very top of the six families are likely to know who he is. So the foot soldiers are of no use, and they wouldn't talk to you anyway without you killing a few of them first. And then you'd have a real problem on your hands.

You don't rule that out, but have enough sense left to know you are in no kind of shape, mentally or physically, to make that kind of move. And your usual sources prove no help, either—cops, stoolies, prosties, newshounds. So you start turning over rocks in parts of town where Mike Hammer is just a name they know from the papers, a reputation they are happy never to have rubbed up against.

In the beginning you are damn near yourself, advice from everybody from Pat Chambers to Hy Gardner to Mr. and Mrs. Packy Paragon getting your attention enough to put you in a clean suit and tie. Mornings you even shower and run a razor over your mug, avoiding the ugly red-eyed face in the mirror as much as possible. Of course, mornings usually mean noon since the night before is always a late one.

You systematically try joints where you aren't known personally, starting with the West Side and then Midtown, working up conversations with bartenders, using your name and a few bucks to try to loosen tongues. Tongues stay tight, though, or maybe they don't have anything to share except free pretzels.

You can't go into a bar and just plop onto a stool and start trying to pry information out of barkeeps. You have to be more subtle than that. You can't go in flashing dough out of the gate, you need to be the next walk-in customer, low-key, friendly, just another joe making conversation. You edge your way up to offering folding money to those who seem like maybe they know something, or anyway who can at least direct you to somebody down the bar who does.

And you don't want to order a coffee or a Coke—something about that seems wrong. So you have a beer. And then after dark, a beer doesn't seem right, seems cheap or maybe doesn't make enough of an impression, so you move to bourbon and branch. Yeah. Classier that way.

Of course by about four days in, somewhere in Midtown, you've become a whiskered sleepwalker in a ruined suit and didn't you just shower yesterday? Why make a habit out of it? And at first it doesn't occur to you you're doing all your looking in gin mills, and when it finally does, what the hell, where else were you supposed to look for the kind of dirt you're after?

But did you really think you'd learn anything in Harlem about a big-time armed robbery ring hitting Brink's trucks and high society parties and posh jewelry stores? Mostly they just look at you and unfriendly eyes come out of the gloom to make you feel unwelcome. At the Hi Ho Club, Big Sam comes out from behind the bar with a billy to stop a couple of guys from rolling you and calls you a cab and sends you home. You saved his life once from protection racketeers, but now, he tells you, your white ass is even.

The next afternoon, late afternoon, you start in the low Forties and hit one spot after another. Short stops, just long enough for some questions and a beer, then some questions and a highball. You don't linger anywhere because this isn't about having a good time. This is about... what is it about?

Velda.

You sit there at the bar and cry. It's Pullen's Bar in the Thirties. You've done a lot of walking, so much walking you staggered your way in. Harvey Pullen is his own bartender and he delivers a rye and soda water. The place is pretty busy, not that you've noticed. A jukebox is going. Pat Boone is singing "Ain't That a Shame." A couple in their twenties are dancing to it, swaying rhythmically, plastered together like unfortunate Siamese twins. Girl's a little drunk. The guy is happy about that.

"Mike," Harvey says.

A big man with a walrus mustache and a cueball skull, Pullen shakes you.

"I'm not sleeping!"

"Well, damnit, wake up anyway." Pullen leans in. He smells like Old Spice. "There's two guys watching you."

"So? Free country."

"You know 'em both."

"I don't give a shit." You wipe tears away with the back of a hand and have a gulp of the rye and soda water, like it's medicine you're taking. Maybe it is.

"*They* give a shit."

You don't look. "Who?"

"Terry Bailey and Buster Crenshaw. You beat Bailey to a pulp last year when he slapped Rosie."

You try to focus on this information; focusing on Pullen's puss is too much effort. "He's her... he's her pimp, right?"

"He was. She was only about sixteen. You called her parents and put her on a bus to Akron. Gave her a hundred bucks and never even got laid for your trouble."

"Who's the other guy? Buster who's-it?"

"He's a pal of Terry's. Well, a customer. Rosie was his favorite."

You look over your shoulder. Two men are staring at you without love from a little table among a lot of little tables, mostly empty. Terry and Buster have a young woman with them. The two men are in their thirties or maybe early forties. One is in a black suit with pinstripes out of *Guys and Dolls* and a tie so loud it screams. The other is in denims and a short-sleeved red-and-blue pullover; he has biceps like a couple of footballs and a tattoo of an anchor on one. You are enough of a detective even in this condition to figure he's a stevedore.

"I don't want a fight in here tonight," Pullen says. It's half advice, half warning.

"When do you?"

"I don't want a fight in here ever, Mike, and you have been in more than one."

"There a limit?"

"Yeah, and you've reached yours. For fights. For rye. Drink up. Go home."

You drink up.

The couple are slow dancing in one spot to "Moments to Remember" by the Four Somethings. The guy has one hand on her ass and his face in her neck. She either likes it or is dancing in her sleep.

You go out into the night. You can smell the river. Fresh with a pinch of rancid. You fumble for the deck of Luckies in your suitcoat pocket. There's a couple of Luckies left, and they are crinkled things, almost as ruined as your suit. But you get one going. You have a Zippo and are glad you do. You are not sure you could manage striking a match.

The sidewalk is sparsely populated and cars going by are a slow blur. You wonder if there's a chance in hell a cab will come by in this neighborhood and then the hands, a whole lot of goddamn hands, grab you and yank you into the alley and toss you up against some garbage cans that make a metallic clatter and spill their innards in what will be a feast for some lucky cats.

You are not a lucky cat.

The two men, the pimp and the stevedore, are hovering over you as if they intend to help you to your feet, but that's not it at all. They are swinging their fists into you, your torso, your face, and there's a part of you that just wants to take it, that sees this as the punishment you deserve for getting that sweet woman killed, for sending her out on a job you should've handled yourself or at least shared, and you barely feel the blows—but the thought of it, the thought of her dead because of you makes you scream, not in pain, just scream, and it's such a banshee thing it throws your attackers off for a second.

And in that second, you take out your .45 and there on your back you slap the pimp across the face, tearing open a future scar, and his teeth break like cheap china and he's backing away, windmilling, barely maintaining balance, spitting little yellow shards he used to chew with—and the stevedore, the big bad stevedore, starts to run toward the mouth of the alley, and somehow you are on your feet and you holster your gun and you take off after him, no staggering now, and you throw a championship tackle into him and bring him down. He's almost to the sidewalk and you drag him back into the alley by his ankles, pulling him on his belly like a big fish you're hauling on deck. Then you crawl up onto his back and sit on him and you take him by his ears and you pull back and then smash his face into the brick alleyway, and he yelps, and again, and he whimpers, and again, and he gets quiet.

You go back to where the pimp is leaning against the wall and he's crying, poor baby, and you hit him in the torso where he hit you and in his face where he hit you and then you grab his hair and slam him into the side of the wall. Very faintly you can hear "Rock Around the Clock" on the jukebox playing inside.

The pimp slides down the wall and sits there, leaning against it, his nice pinstripe suit more ruined than yours. He is not unconscious. You kneel by him and take the .45 out and you press the nose to his left temple and his eyes get so big it's comical.

"Next time I kill you," you say.

"No… no next time… no… no next time."

"Good."

The other one is on his back. He's breathing. You are neither relieved about that nor concerned. You kneel by him. He has left some of his face behind on the bricks and what's left of his nose is blotted out by blood and torn flesh, not really a nose at all anymore.

"Next time I won't be so nice," you say.

"No… no next time."

You laugh. "That's just what your buddy said."

You get up and you go back in the bar. You are enough of a mess, more of a mess than you already were, to get Harvey Pullen's attention.

"Somebody knocked over your garbage cans," you say, pointing vaguely.

Harvey leaves his waitress in charge and rushes out.

When he comes back, he looks white as a sheet. As a ghost. As a blister.

"Mike… what happened out there?"

"Ask them."

"Ask who? There's nobody out there, but there's blood puddles and… and I don't know what? Teeth? Skin? Christ!"

You make a noise that is sort of a laugh. "They walked away, huh? How bad can it be then?"

"What am I gonna do with you, Mike?"

"You're gonna get me another rye. Skip the water."

Your barstool is waiting.

You fill it, and rest your head on the counter a little. You go to sleep, and in the dream Velda is shaking her head, saying, "Mike, Mike, what am I going to do with you?"

But it's not Velda's voice, it's Pat's.

I came awake slow, with no idea where I was. But even in my bleary state, it didn't take long to realize I was home. This was Apartment 9-D all right. The only light on in my little living room was a standing lamp over in the far corner, the shade making a yellow glow. I was stretched out on the couch and the smell of booze hovered like smoke. Somebody was in the recliner, which was usually aimed at the TV, but had been turned toward me, and somebody was in it.

Pat.

And he was saying it again, to himself: "What the hell am I going to do with you? What the hell am I going to do *about* you?"

Those were rhetorical questions, so I skipped any answer and got myself into a sitting position, which made me nauseous and a little dizzy, but I didn't let on. I wasn't about to give my best friend, if that's what he still was, the satisfaction.

This time I asked the question and it sure as hell wasn't rhetorical: "What are *you* doing here?"

The captain of Homicide was in a brown suit and it was rumpled enough to say this had already been a very long day. His hat was shoved back on his head like he was giving his forehead room to breathe, a few tendrils of blond hair falling over the creases above his eyebrows. "Don't you want to ask what *you* are doing here?"

I thought about shrugging and decided against it. "I live here."

He shrugged—easy for him. "I suppose you're used to it by now, waking up, not knowing how you got home. You still have a few people who give a shit about you. Harvey Pullen, for instance. Of course, he might have called me just because he wanted somebody to get rid of the drunken bum cluttering up his otherwise respectable establishment."

I gave him those same two words I'd been reserving for him lately. I hunkered over and put my hands on my face and tried to stop shivering. And why was I? It wasn't cold or anything.

"I don't think you're going to," he said.

"Going to... going to what?"

"Puke. You already did that at Pullen's, in the men's can, before I dragged you into the back seat of my car and lugged you home."

"You're not big enough to carry me."

"You helped. I got you by the waist and your legs and feet pretended they belonged to a functional human long enough for us to get up here. Key was in your pocket."

My mouth tasted like death. "Okay, you did your comradely duty. Now scram. Get the hell out and leave me to my own devices."

"To your misery, you mean." His laugh would have been perfect coming from somebody torturing a guy. "Mike, you are one pathetic sack of sad shit. You need to get over this, already. Snap out of it."

I gave him the two words again, then added, "Leave me alone, Pat. Will ya?"

He got out of the chair and loomed over me. Looked down on me both figuratively and literally. "Oh, I intend to. This is the one ride home you get from me. I'm not bailing your ass out anymore, Mike. Not from jail, not from whatever slopchute you might pass out in. I am willing to help you book a permanent berth in the drunk tank and that's it. Clear?"

"As mud, buddy."

He started to go out, quick, then with his hand on the knob he stopped. His head was hanging. I heard him let out a bushel or two of air and then he walked over and sat beside me on the couch. Not close. But beside me.

"Face it," he said. His voice was soft now and drained of anything antagonistic. "She's gone."

"I'll find her."

His laugh was a ragged, awful thing. "Not *that* kind of 'gone,' Mike. *Dead* and gone. It's been seven weeks, for Christ's sake. They killed Marta Civac. Why would they leave Rudolph and Velda alive?"

"The Civac money," I said. "There may be a ransom."

His sigh went on a while. "Yeah. Right. Any year now. Mike, I don't like it any better than you do. But if Velda were alive, she'd have got in touch by now. Somehow. You don't kill one hostage and let the others go. You don't dump one abductee in the river with her fingers lopped off and make the other two comfortable. Face it. She's gone. You killed the robbery crew and cut off the only avenue to finding out what happened. You can blame yourself for that."

I did. For that and more. Velda had been a vice cop before I knew her and she'd gotten through some tough scrapes with me at her side. Twice her little .32 had spit flame and lead and taken big men down for the long fall. But that didn't mean she could handle what had come at her at the Civac place, a squad of armed men ready to kill to get what they came for, and no Mike at her side to even the play.

"If she's breathing, Pat, I will find her. I don't care if she has amnesia or got sold to some rajah for his damn harem. But if she's dead, I will find the one who killed her. And they will die nice and slow, by inches, right up to where they are begging for that big black curtain to come down and put them out of their goddamn misery."

Shaking his head, he got up again and began to pace, his hands stuffed in his pockets. "That's your answer to everything, isn't it, you kill-crazy lunatic? Kill the only people who could have led you to their boss. Kill whoever took Velda. Kill anybody who gets in your way. Kill anybody who looks cross-eyed at you!" He stopped and glared at me. "What happened in that alley by Pullen's? He was a little tight-lipped about it. Hell, it looked like a murder scene where the body got hauled away and dumped by the perps! Maybe *you* dumped it."

"I left it on your doorstep," I said. "Maybe you can solve something on your own, if you trip over the evidence."

His smile was the worst I ever saw on him. It was as bad as something I might have cooked up. "There's only one dead body that's likely to get dumped during this little merry-go-round ride, Mike... and it's yours!"

I managed to fish one last Lucky out of the crumpled pack in my pocket. The Zippo did its job, and I said, "Nobody's killing me, Pat. I do the killing around here."

He was already shaking his head again. "Not in the shape you're in, buddy boy. Harvey says you took on a couple of guys who were half in the bag themselves. What happens when you piss off one of these hoods you've been sniffing around about? Or when word gets back to the Mafia crowd that you're on the warpath?"

I frowned. "You been tailing me, Pat?"

"You're not worth tailing. But I hear things."

"Yeah, you're really on top of it. Nothing gets past you."

He took a step closer, still looking down. "This is the last advice I'm going to give you."

"That's something, anyway."

"You want to find out who those plunder boys were working for? You want to go around town asking questions and maybe going on tour with your intimidation song and dance? Then sober the hell up! Rejoin the human race. But I don't think you can do that. I don't think you have the guts."

Through the fog in my brain, something clear emerged, something down under at odds with the surface of all these words he was flinging.

I laughed. "You want me to find the armed robbery kingpin for you, don't you, Pat? You want me to take the bastard down. And *kill* him, Pat? Not give him to you and the justice system to coddle?"

He reached inside his suitcoat and pulled a gun out of his waistband. Not just any gun.

My .45.

"I could put you in jail right now," he said, very softly. "In violation of the Sullivan Act and, coming so soon on the heels of your hearing, you can bet you will never get a permit to carry again. Not in this state, anyway. Maybe nowhere."

I put my wrists together as if begging for handcuffs. "Why don't you then? What's stopping you, Pat?"

"Get sober," he said, "get shaved, showered, dress yourself like a professional not a panhandler. Get your head on straight—or as straight as Mike Hammer's head is capable of getting—and maybe, just maybe, I'll give this baby back to you."

He hefted the .45.

Then he said, "Maybe I'll just look the other way about you packing without a permit. Could be I'll somehow just overlook that little detail."

I didn't say anything to that.

He stuck the .45 back in his waistband and was heading out again when the phone rang. He went to the phone-stand over by the kitchenette and said to me, "I gave my number here. Hope you don't mind, chum."

"*Mi casa es su casa*," I said, "you louse."

"Chambers," he said into the phone. "Yes... yes.... All right, yes, I can be there right away." Frowning now, he hung up and stood there thinking for a few moments, then turned to me.

"How quick can you make yourself presentable? Shave and a fresh suit would do it."

"Why?"

"I think you might want to tag along on this one."

"Why?" I said again.

What in the hell could have made Pat want to take me along anywhere?

He answered the unspoken question: "Your pal Packy Paragon just got himself murdered."

CHAPTER FIVE

Packy Paragon and his wife lived high, high up in one of the man-made cliffs of stone and steel that line Riverside Drive. The lobby welcomed us with thick russet carpet and marble corridors and suggested a timeless elegance. But apartment 5-C itself—once we were up the self-service elevator, and Pat had ushered me past the two uniformed officers at the door—was an ultramodern place, stark geometric lines against soft pastels with abstract paintings here and there, daring you to make something of them. Similarly, furniture with amoeba-shaped cushions defied you to try them out for comfort, but if you broke your ass trying, that was on you, brother.

At one end of the spindly-legged living room couch, Victoria—again in a ponytail and no make-up, in a white shirt with rolled-up sleeves and black capri pants hovering over black ballet slippers—was clutching a cloth hanky and staring blankly into her state of shock. A plainclothes guy from Pat's division was seated opposite her with his notebook out, patiently asking questions and getting nods and curt mumbles.

When she saw me, the songbird rose and bolted to me and threw herself into my arms. I patted her back and did the "There,

there" bit while she bawled into my shirt. Pat gave me an eye and nodded toward the couch. I nodded back.

I ushered Victoria over, gentled her down and slipped an arm around her shoulder and let her cry. The bawling turned into sobbing and then eased into sniffling as Pat stood halfway across the room talking to his underling, who had vacated the chair where he'd questioned the newly minted widow. I let her calm down and gave her occasional words of support. I was still half in the bag, but the homicide of a friend can sober a guy up in a hurry.

Then Pat took over the chair opposite Victoria, who clutched my hand, her other one still busy with the hanky.

"I'm Captain Chambers. I knew your husband fairly well, Mrs. Paragon. I asked Mike here to come along because I know he was a friend of both you and Mr. Paragon."

She nodded and kept nodding. "Good friends. Good friends."

"I got the basics from my associate," Pat said, "but I'm afraid I need to hear it from you."

She nodded once more, composed herself further, then said, "My husband had a headache and didn't accompany me to the club tonight. I perform there every night but Monday—we recently opened, perhaps you're aware of that."

"I am."

"My last set is over at around eleven o'clock. I have a full dressing room with shower. As you can see, I wash up, remove my make-up, get into comfortable clothes, and head home. Which I did. By cab."

"When was that?"

"Midnight. I have an arrangement with a cab company. I'm picked up at the same time every night. Packy usually comes with me. *Came* with me." She swallowed. Shook her head slightly. "I'm sorry, it's just so hard to grasp."

"You were home when?"

"Twelve-twenty-five. Maybe twelve-twenty. It's a quick ride this time of night. I used my key—the door wasn't open and didn't seem to have been forced or anything—and called out for Packy. The few times we haven't been together after an evening at the club, he waits up for me." She swallowed. "*Waited.* But not this time. Of course, he'd had a headache, so I went to our bedroom, thinking perhaps he'd gone to sleep... but no. The bed was made. No sign of him. Not in the den, either. I finally tried his study. And there he was."

She began to cry again.

Pat said, "Mrs. Paragon, just take it easy right here. I'm going to ask Mike to have a look at the study with me. Just calm yourself as best you can. This won't take much longer."

I squeezed her hand, exchanged sad smiles with her, and followed Pat as he went down a connecting hall to the study. The medium-size room, longer than it was wide, had cherry-wood paneling with another abstract painting taking up much of the right wall, a floor-to-ceiling bookcase at left, and between them, at the far end, a very modern walnut desk with a phone, a blotter, some pens, a black leather-cushioned leather chair—in which Packy Paragon in a maroon dressing gown leaned back, his head turned toward the bookshelves, a purplish black-rimmed hole in his left temple. His expression suggested disappointment to me, and why wouldn't it?

He seemed to be looking toward the wall of books next to him. Its shelves were taken up by mostly bestsellers and Reader's Digest

Condensed Books, but also some framed photos of Packy and celebrities and his wife and himself, plus a few knickknacks. Nearer where he sat was a dictionary, a thesaurus, an atlas, and some of the inside of Packy's head, which had dripped and clotted there.

What struck me, however—and even cut through my alcohol-induced fog—was an exposed wall safe on a middle bookshelf, which had been tucked behind volumes that were now stacked on the floor underneath. The safe door had been left in a swung-open position and I could make out a stack of papers but nothing else inside—basically, empty.

Or emptied.

The M.E., a bald man in wire-rim glasses with a round face that didn't go with a slender body, was off to one side, by an abstract painting that wasn't unlike the impromptu artwork the inside of Pack's skull had provided; he was making notes in a spiral pad with all the compassion of a bank examiner, a wicker casket waiting nearby. A photographer in a rumpled hat but no suitcoat was taking flash photos of the man at the desk and the red-green-white glop hanging on the bookcase like melted wax. A couple of lab boys in smocks were waiting patiently for their turn. The bulbs popped like little gunshots and the bursts of light hurt my delicate rye-ravaged eyes.

Without going over to him, Pat said to the M.E., "Any take on time of death?"

His voice was high-pitched and unmodulated. "Judging by rigor and body temp, several hours ago. I'd guess three or four. Better idea for you tomorrow."

It was a little after one a.m.

"That clears the wife," Pat said.

I nodded. "She'd have been on stage in front of maybe one hundred witnesses. She does three sets a night of about forty-five minutes each. Goes on at eight. Takes forty minutes or so between. Is off at eleven. Sneaks out during one of her breaks, maybe? But if getting here from the club is twenty or twenty-five minutes, one-way? Little tight. And what's her motive?"

"Since when does a wife need a motive?"

He had me there.

But I said, "Far as I know they were happy."

Pat nodded. "How do you read this, Mike?"

"Two people."

"How do you figure?"

"Pack was shot in the side of the head by somebody facing him while he was turned to one side, looking at whoever was getting in that safe. No powder burns, so the shooter may have been as far back as just inside the door."

"The wife would know the combination to the safe, probably."

My shrug was dismissive. "That's an easy jug to crack—an old Mosler I believe. Anyway, under the gun, Packy might have given up the combination."

"Jewels in that safe, you think?"

"Ask her, why don't you?"

Pat studied me. "You're taking this pretty calm, buddy."

"What do I care? He was a hood."

"An ex-hood."

"You can take a guy out of the mob but you can't take the mob out of the guy."

Pat's smile was suspiciously tiny. "Good to hear you say that. I don't need you running around with a wild hair up your tail, trying to get even for another friend."

"Make up your mind, Pat. Am I a pitiful drunk or a danger to society?"

He grunted a laugh. "I'll let you know."

We resumed our conversation with Victoria. She was sitting quietly with her hands in her lap. Only the pink-tinged whites of her eyes said anything was wrong at all.

"This isn't easy to ask, Mrs. Paragon," Pat said, leaning forward in the chair, "but when you found your husband, what did you see? When you first stepped in that study?"

"I saw *him*, of course. Sitting there…" She shivered; bit a knuckle. "As I told your… your associate, I didn't touch him. I didn't touch *anything*. It wasn't like… wasn't like I needed to check his pulse. That… that awful hole in his head told me everything I needed to know."

Pat kept his voice easy. "Did you notice anything else?"

"Like… like what, for instance?"

"You need to tell *me*, Mrs. Paragon."

She thought about it. Then she straightened. "Well, the safe was open, of course. Is that what you mean? The safe was open. This was a robbery, certainly. Gone tragically wrong."

"What did you keep in the safe?"

The green eyes flared. "I didn't keep *anything* in the safe but my jewels."

Pat and I exchanged sharp glances.

He said, "There are no jewels in the safe now."

"Well, there wouldn't be. Lately I've been keeping them in a jewel box in my dressing room, locked in a drawer of my make-up table, and wear certain pieces occasionally on stage."

"Are they valuable?"

"Oh no. Well, perhaps a few thousand. Costume jewelry that I sometimes wear performing. From the 1920s and '30s. Just… fun things." She almost choked on the word "fun."

"Was there *anything* valuable in the safe?"

"I don't know if you'd call them valuable, Captain Chambers, just the kind of legal papers and documents you might normally keep in a safe deposit box."

"Nothing else of worth?"

She glanced at me and the glance lingered long enough to indicate she wanted my advice. I wasn't sure what she was after, but I said, "You should tell him. Whatever it is."

She swallowed. Nodded.

"Packy kept one hundred thousand dollars in cash in that safe. A mix of twenties, fifties and hundreds."

Pat's eyebrows went up. "That's not an insignificant amount."

"Well…" Her eyebrows lifted too, and she glanced at me again, fleetingly this time. "…he called it his 'getaway money.'"

Pat smiled. "Ah," he said.

She leaned forward. "Don't misconstrue. My husband wasn't involved with… *those people* anymore. He had gone straight, completely straight, genuinely turned over an entirely new leaf. I was the instigator of that."

"Oh?"

She nodded several times. "I told him I wouldn't marry him unless he cut those ties."

"I see."

"Nonetheless… old habits die hard. He said, 'You never know when things might start closing in.' That money would get us somewhere—Mexico, maybe… really, I don't know where. Nor do I know what he meant by 'closing in.' As I said, he called it 'getaway money.'"

"Could he have been lying to you about changing his ways?"

Her shrug was barely there. "I suppose it's possible. But I don't think so. I really don't."

Pat sighed. "Nothing else in that safe?"

"No, unless Packy put something in there recently that I didn't know about. In any case, I didn't have the combination. It was *his* safe. Not mine. Not ours."

"Even though you kept your jewels in there."

She found a tiny smile. "Even though he *let* me keep my jewels in there."

"Do you have any idea how someone might have got in? In your apartment, this building?"

Her shake of the head made the ponytail bob. "No. But I would say the security here is, if not quite lax, not exactly stellar either. There's no doorman or night man of any kind. Someone has to buzz you in, but that's all. And sometimes people are careless about how they buzz folks in. There are fire escapes in back, and I would assume anyone who knows anything about burglary could find their way in."

Pat closed up his notebook. Gave her a tight smile. "All right, Mrs. Paragon. Thank you. Sorry to put you through this at such a difficult time. I'll be following up tomorrow or the next day, but for now I've put you through quite enough."

She leaned forward and gripped Pat's sleeve so quickly he almost jumped. "Captain Chambers—I don't want to stay here. In this place. Not now. Not *right* now, at least. Could you possibly put me up at a hotel for a few days? My husband handled the finances, and my personal funds are limited."

His head went back for a moment. "Well, it's not a bad idea for you to stay elsewhere tonight, Mrs. Paragon, at a hotel or with a friend.... Your apartment is a crime scene and the processing will go on for several hours. But the department is not budgeted, I'm afraid, to provide lodging in such circumstances."

I said, "I can put her up, Captain."

Now it was my sleeve she gripped. "Oh, would you, Mike? I'd be ever so grateful."

"Go pack an overnight bag."

She got to her feet and disappeared down the hall.

Pat gave me a look. "What do you have in mind, Mike? Or do I want to know?"

"Get your mind out of the gutter. She's an old friend."

"Not so old." He leaned back in the chair. "You don't make your jewel robbery kingpin as behind this, do you?"

"No. For a bunch of costume jewelry that wasn't even there? Don't be stupid, Pat."

"How about for a hundred grand that was? Maybe word about that tidy little bundle got around somehow. Your robbery czar isn't just jewel happy—he goes after cash, too, anything valuable that ain't nailed down."

"Maybe."

He studied me. Then he got to his feet. He waved me to mine. I complied. He glanced around, and seemed to be checking whether any of his men could see us. But the uniformed guys were still in the corridor outside the door, and everybody else was piled into that study. They hadn't even filled the wicker basket and brought it out yet.

He unbuttoned his coat and took my .45 from his waistband. He almost whispered: "Take it."

I did.

What was I going to do, argue with him?

"You be discreet, Mike."

"Discretion is my middle name."

"No, I'm pretty sure the 'D' is for dumb shit."

I grinned at him. He grinned back. Some of the friendship was hanging on.

She came out looking about sixteen in that white shirt and black pedal pushers, carting a pink overnight bag, her ponytail swinging. She said goodnight to Pat as she passed and I fell in after her, and Pat whispered, "You be good, Mike."

I took the couch.

My suit I hung in the front closet, since my bedroom was hers now. I put a boxer's robe on over my shorts and t-shirt. My socks were still on and I looked like a guy in a stag film. She came out in a pink silk dressing gown she'd brought along and looked like a girl in a Hollywood movie; the way the fabric clung to her curvaceous figure told me a little more than I wanted to know right now.

We'd caught a cab and her expression had started out grateful but before long turned troubled. Hardly a word was spoken on the ride, and now she looked even more bothered.

I arranged the extra pillow I'd borrowed from the bedroom. Mid-summer, with the window cracked to let in air and sirens and drunken war cries and car backfires that might be gunshots, no blanket was necessary. She had found a 7-Up in my fridge and had poured it into two glasses with ice and brought me one.

"No Seagram's tonight," she said, plopping down next to me. "Just Seven."

"Hey, fine by me, honey. I'm on the wagon."

She toasted me with her glass. "I don't think you can be on the wagon until the booze already in your system works its way out."

"You sure are hard on a guy."

"Yeah. But not on myself." The green eyes fixed themselves on me. They were so deep you could dive in and swim. They were so wide set you had to look at them one at a time.

"Not hard on yourself, huh? How so?"

She sipped 7-Up. "I wasn't entirely honest with your friend. Captain Chambers."

I waved that off. "Oh, don't worry about that."

"No?"

"I'm never entirely honest with cops. Really, I would say I'm rarely entirely honest with cops."

She laughed a little. It was a good sound. She had something she wanted to tell me, but I wasn't going to go looking for it. She lost her husband tonight. She could share whatever was nagging at her whenever she felt it was time.

Turned out it was time.

"Packy has this ledger."

I already didn't like the sound of that. Something was sneaking up my spine and I almost wished it was a real spider and not just a crawly sensation at what might be coming.

"Okay," I said. "Packy had a ledger."

The big eyes looked at me. "Did you already know?"

I shook my head. "But Packy was a crafty character and he would want an insurance policy. I take it that's the purpose the ledger served."

She nodded. Gazed into the 7-Up glass like she was looking for tea leaves to interpret. Then: "It was filled with more incriminating info than you would believe."

"Oh, I believe, all right."

She looked toward the open window, where my filmy curtains were making ghosts of themselves. "He had the goods on just about every crook, cop, and politician in this town. And I mean every damn borough—and you can throw Albany in for good measure." Her sigh took its time. "I didn't have the nerve to ask Captain Chambers whether…. Mike, was that ledger still in the safe?"

"No. Whoever killed him must've got it. Kitten…" I touched her shoulder gently. "…had he been blackmailing anyone? Holding what he had over them, maybe to fund your club?"

That thought alarmed her, the big green eyes getting bigger. "No. Oh no, he was a *lot* of things, Packy, but a blackmailer was certainly not one of them. And when he sold out his interest in his nightclubs—his, you know, casinos, the illegal holdings—he made more than enough money to buy the entire building our club is in. Enough to live out the rest of his life."

He just hadn't known how short a period of time he had to bankroll.

I said, "Do any of his former partners hold a grudge?"

She thought about that for a moment. "The only one I can think of is Mel Hazard. Know him?"

I knew him. Hazard was a squat toad of a Prohibition-era leftover who rumor had it was one of the real-life lowlifes Edward G. Robinson patterned Little Caesar after. He was a vicious, conniving shitheel who made a fortune peddling tires and horsemeat on the Black Market during the war. Yeah, I knew him.

"What grudge did Hazard have with Packy?"

"My husband sold several properties to Hazard, somewhat reluctantly. He had no love for the odious little beast. But Packy wanted to keep everybody happy in the six families, and Hazard has strong ties to the Bonettis, so…. Then a few months later, Hazard made an offer on another of Packy's properties, a good offer, but Packy went with another family's lesser offer."

"A slap in the face."

She gestured with an open hand. "Still, it's not the kind of thing you'd kill somebody over."

You might if you were a gutter rat hoodlum like Mel Hazard, I thought. But I didn't share that observation with her.

"Any idea why he refused Hazard?" I asked. "Packy apportioned his holdings among any number of disagreeable types."

She shook her head. "I'm not sure you're right about that, Mike."

"Oh?"

"Packy had lines he wouldn't cross. To some, how he viewed things would probably seem hypocritical. He made a lot of money off human weaknesses—gambling, specifically. But to him, that was a form of entertainment, and a personal choice. Call girls, that was never his line, but as far as Packy was concerned that was a financial transaction between consenting adults. But outright crime—contract killing, peddling schoolyard dope, armed robbery—he wanted nothing to do with."

I was sitting up. "Plenty of people Packy did business with crossed all sorts of lines. Was there a specific line that Hazard crossed lately that Packy couldn't condone?"

Her eyes widened again. "Mike! He said something…. I should have thought of this *before*!"

I took her arm, the fleshy part above the elbow. "Thought of what?"

"You're hurting me… please…"

I let go. "I'm sorry. I'm sorry. What should you have thought of, Vickie?"

She swallowed. And when she spoke, it was as softly as if she were afraid someone might overhear. "When he read about what happened at that society party, where Velda was abducted—and this was after that woman's body was found all mutilated—he said, 'That's *exactly* what I'm talking about!' And I said, 'What do you mean?' And he said, 'That's precisely why I was careful about who I sold my businesses to.' Could he have been talking about Mel Hazard?"

If it was Hazard, I'd have to work to wrap my hands around his fat throat. It would take some real effort to get through those rings of blubber and squeeze the goddamn life out of him till his eyes popped and his tongue lolled and lolled and finally turned black. But it would be worth the effort.

"Possibly," I said, throwing it away. "But I'm afraid I already know who's responsible for Packy's murder."

"You do, Mike? Who?"

"You're looking at him," I said.

I was shaking. Rage was in there, but some of it was just... just me shaking.

I said, "Pack isn't the first friend who's gotten himself killed trying to help me out. It's a long list of decent people who gave their lives in a bad cause—Mike Hammer. And it's why it's hard for me not to just crawl in a bottle and drown myself."

"No, Mike, no." She put her arms around me. Her kiss came sudden and warm and giving and not entirely sexual.

"You loved her," she said, drawing away just a little. "And I loved him. No... you *love* her and I *love* him. It... it hurts, doesn't it?"

I nodded.

"Come to bed," she said.

"No."

"No? Because it's wrong? I don't care. I want to be held, Mike. I want you to hold me."

"I'll hold you right here until you fall asleep and then I'll carry you in and put you in my bed, but nothing else is going to happen tonight. Hell." I laughed. "I couldn't do right by you anyway. Even if the booze in me doesn't shut off that option, I'm not about to make love to you and risk not remembering it in the morning. If that ever happens, sugar, we're both going to remember it. For a long, long time."

CHAPTER SIX

The headache wasn't bad—if your idea of a snappy tune is the "Anvil Chorus." I made it off the couch in slow motion and then picked up speed heading into the can where I bent over the porcelain altar and made an offering of dry heaves that only lasted five minutes.

I stumbled back out into my little living room and plopped into the recliner. My wristwatch said eleven and sun was streaming in the window, so presumably this was the morning after, or anyway what was left of it. The best thing I could say is the D.T.'s weren't kicking in. I'd been drinking heavily, on and off, for several weeks, but I was still in the early alcoholic stage. There was hope for me yet, I just didn't remember where I put it.

Getting upright again, I shuffled to the closed door of my bedroom, cracked it open, and Victoria was still sleeping soundly. I had no air conditioner in the place, so she'd slept on top of the covers, not even crawling under a sheet. The pink silk robe clung to her like a jealous lover.

But looking at one long lush leg extended from the slit of the garment, and one full breast whose tip was defiantly obvious beneath the fabric, I could only regard them clinically. Like a painting at the Met. Doing anything about it was blocked by guilt for even registering such feelings in tandem with a physical impossibility.

And Velda's framed picture, smiling at me from the nightstand, did not help.

I made coffee. Fried up some eggs. Let the bacon sizzle like it was pissed off at me. Stood over the pan daring it to make me puke again knowing the joke was on it since my stomach had been empty in the first place. If the pan wanted to get at me, it would have to wait till the chicken fruit and strips of dead pig had made their way down my gullet and then maybe I'd puke. Maybe.

When I sat on the edge of the bed, the springs sang a squeaky melody that opened her eyes to sleepy slits.

I said, "I got coffee. How do you take it?"

"Cream. Sugar."

"You can have milk and sugar."

"That'll do." She sat up and stretched. Fists high. "What time is it?"

I told her.

"Well," she said. "Aren't we a couple of bums? Is that bacon I smell?"

"It is."

She made a brief trip into the bathroom, then joined me at the little table for two I'd managed to squeeze into my kitchenette area. I had the coffee waiting, steam sending smoke signals off the two cups. She watched me with an amused smirk as I stirred in milk and sugar.

"I thought you tough guys took it straight," she said.

"I'm not much of one anymore."

We both managed to eat. Her eyes were still red and I was still shaky, but we made pretty good approximations of living human beings. No ponytail this morning; her hair was at her shoulders, brushed rather carelessly and the color of the hay any healthy guy would like to roll in with her.

Not much conversation accompanied the meal—all our effort was going to just taking it in and keeping it down. We did fine.

I cleared the table and dumped the dishes in the sink and returned with freshened cups of coffee. We sat and talked. She took the lead.

"Packy had no family to speak of," she said. "Some dead, others not speaking to him."

"The dead aren't speaking to him either."

"Well, maybe now they are." She sipped. "We talked about it once and he said if anything happened to him, he didn't want a funeral. He said he wanted to be cremated. Wanted his ashes sprinkled over Marilyn Monroe."

I laughed. "Good. That leaves Hedy Lamarr to me."

"I'm going to put Packy on my mantle where he can keep an eye on me. But even so, I have arrangements to make. I'll pick out a funeral home and put things in motion. And I'm going to ask Sonny Gray to take over running the club, at least on a temporary basis."

"Little young, isn't he?"

Above the wide-set green eyes, her eyebrows did a little shrug. "He's past thirty. And got a lot of experience on the West Coast. I know, I know, he's another reformed bad boy, but he and Packy were close. My husband was like a father to him. I'll close up for at least a week, while Sonny gets a handle on the business side of things, and then when I reopen I'll have someone fill in for me until I can… can face going back on stage myself."

"What happened to the show must go on?"

"Oh, it'll go on. Just not for a while. Too soon would be in bad taste, and… Mike, the Paragon was Packy's gift to me. No. That doesn't say it. It was more like his… shrine to me."

"I get that."

She shrugged, just starting to tear up. "Normally I am a trouper. A show biz gal who lives to be on stage, whose greatest love affair is between her audience and herself. But going on at the Paragon seems, right now, to be something I just can't make myself do. Singing songs of lost love? Not now. Not for a while."

I sipped coffee. It actually tasted good to me. "You should call Pat and see when—I'm sorry, honey—but when Packy's body can be released. It's evidence in a homicide at the moment."

She nodded. "I know. I understand. Thank you for… putting a roof over my head last night."

"You're welcome to stay on as long as you like, kitten. I'll stay put on the couch and throw in breakfasts."

Her grin was nice to see. "You'd make a decent short-order cook, Mike. But I'm going back to the Riverside Drive digs. Back to 5-C. It's my home. And the sooner I shake any residual uneasiness, the better—don't you think, Mike?"

"Sure. Why don't I drop by there this evening and we can maybe go out for a bite."

"That would be swell."

We both laughed a little—it sounded like teenagers making a date to meet at the malt shop.

Half an hour later, I was walking her and her little pink overnight bag to the elevator, where we paused for a moment, not knowing whether to hug or kiss or what, and wound up just smiling and nodding instead.

Back in my apartment, I opened the refrigerator door and stared at the Blue Ribbon bottles lined up like soldiers ready to salute and serve. A beer wouldn't hurt, right?

But I slammed the door shut and went off to take a long hot shower. I was going to get myself cleaned up and rejoin the human race, like Pat advised. I had places to go and people to see and maybe to slap around or even kill if I had to.

When I left the apartment just before four, I felt like me again. You remember the guy, don't you?

Mike Hammer?

From the garage down the block I collected my heap, which wasn't a heap at all really, but a bribe Carl Evello left outside my building a few years ago with a couple of accessories meant to blow me to Kingdom Come. I sent Carl there instead, and kept the maroon Ford to make up for the souped-up jalopy of mine they shoved me off a cliff in. I'd made it back but the heap hadn't. This replacement had twin pipes and finned aluminum heads flanking dual carbs. Who said the Mafia never gave me anything?

I left the wheels in a 52nd Street parking lot and headed down the block. The gin mills were the opposite of hopping and the niteries were mostly still asleep, but things would pick up soon with the after-work crowd, and when darkness came so would the night people. What, ten years ago, had been Swing Street had become Sleazy-Second Street, the jazz of Dizzy Gillespie and lilt of Billie Holiday exchanged for the guns of hoodlums and needles of drug dealers.

My destination was a study in false advertising, starting with the big painted white letters:

GLASS HOUSE

on a windowless wooden facade coated with a shiny black acrylic, where smaller white letters at cockeyed angles danced above a single door:

MUSICAL REVUE, DANCING, FLOOR SHOW, CABARET.

The interior was chrome trim and plastic everything else, including the split-upholstery of the zebra-striped booths, and the only glass in this phony joint was the bottles that fed the plastic tumblers. About twenty years ago, under a slightly different name, they catered to boys with boys and girls with girls, but then a certain mob guy bought it, left the '30s musical look of the joint to age in a way wine didn't, threw the gay crowd out into the cold cruel world, and curtained off two-thirds of the joint into a gambler's paradise and a sucker's Hell.

Only one bartender was behind the half-circle bar at left. Those cauliflower ears didn't go so good with his tuxedo shirt and he hadn't put his tie on yet. His forehead was strictly caveman and the dull brown hair was a fuzzy parcel where nothing would ever grow again. Small pouchy eyes locked onto me.

No customers yet, the hatcheck stand un-womaned, the lights up lighter than they ever should be in a joint like this with its cigarette-burn and nicotine-stain decorative scheme. Just empty tables with upside-down chairs piled with legs as unenthusiastically in the air as a back-seat pick-up. Also, a bandstand where a redheaded stripper in a sweater and denims and sneakers was trying out her moves with the help of a bored little four-piece combo (drums, guitar, bass, sax) playing "Night Train."

"Not open yet, bud," the bartender said, wiping down the counter with a rag worthy of its name.

"Not drinking," I said and slid onto a stool.

"This look like the *Christian Science Monitor* reading room to you?"

"Dunno. Never been in one." I put a five-spot on the bar. "Too early for a few easy answers?"

He looked at Abe Lincoln. Pushed the assassinated president back at me like he was adding to a poker pot. "Yeah. Way too early. Blow."

I didn't touch the fin. Kept my voice friendly, my manner easy. "You work here long?"

"No."

"New in town?"

"No."

"New job, this?"

"No." He filled his barrel chest with air. Let it out. Said, "I own the place."

"No kidding."

The combo was playing "Blues in the Night," a little early for late afternoon. The stripper was trying to remember how to look sultry.

The bartender leaned on his left arm. "You wanna see my license?"

"No. I believe you. Pity about Packy Paragon."

"What?"

"Packy Paragon. You're a club owner. You must've known Packy. Or heard of him, at least."

"Maybe. But you need to go now, bud. We're open in an hour or so. Come on back when I can sell you a drink and still not answer your goddamn questions."

"Now, be nice."

"Look. Friend. I don't know if you're just a wise guy, in which case you can get out by yourself. Or a tough guy, in which case I can toss your ass out for you. Your choice."

"Look. Friend." I opened my suitcoat just enough to let him see the leather of the sling that ran across my chest. No need to show him the .45 that went with it.

I said, "I'm guessing you have a silent partner, uh… what's your name again?"

"Joe."

"Good bartender name. All-American bartender name. Now, Joe, you don't have to tell me who your silent partner is. I already know. I just want you to tell me if he's in. And if not, when will he be?"

"I don't know who you're talking 'bout. I own the place. I told you, I can show you the license."

A voice behind me said, "Problem, Joe?"

I must have been slipping because I hadn't heard him come in. Of course, if he came from the casino, he'd have slipped through those curtains, not a door.

"Gentleman don't understand," Joe said, "we're not open just yet. Maybe you could see him out, Billy."

Behind me the newcomer came nearer, changing positions enough that I could see him in the mirror above the lined-up bottles. Billy was big, as big as me, but young, not out of his twenties; he had a blond pompadour and a pale oval face and sky-blue eyes and his teeth were just a little buck. He had a checked sports jacket on and pleated trousers. Despite his brawn, he was in the wrong business—he ought to be looking for a record contract.

"No help needed," I said pleasantly to his reflection. "Joe and I are just having a friendly chat."

Billy strutted up to the bar and took a stool three down from me. He leaned on both forearms and looked at me with an arrogant smile and said to the bartender, through puffy Elvis lips, "Did you want to talk to this gent, Joe?"

"I'm talked out," Joe said. "He needs to be somewhere else."

"You heard him," Billy said to me with a smile that would drive a teenage girl batty.

"Billy... maybe you could do me a favor," I said, still genial.

"Yeah? What's that, deadbeat?"

"Go get your boss. He's in the back, right? Go get him and tell him Mike Hammer wants to see him."

The kid was unimpressed. He didn't know Mike Hammer from Glenn Miller. But the bartender backed away so fast he bumped into the back counter and made the booze bottles rattle.

"Get your old ass out, Mac," the kid said with a sneering smile. He slipped off the stool and stood there like a gunfighter. His right hand edged into his jacket pocket.

Now here was a problem. First off, I really did just want to talk to their boss, no rough stuff in mind. Second thing, I had my .45 under my left arm all right, but if I used it, and put this little asshole at the top of my hit parade, my lack of a gun license could get the weapon grabbed and me jugged.

His pale white hand withdrew something, not a gun. Then the snick/click announced a switchblade, which he held up till it caught some light and winked at me. And he winked, too, his smile settling on one side of his almost pretty face.

"Hit the road, Jack," he said.

With my left hand I opened my suitcoat enough that he could see that leather strap and with my right hand I extracted my spare .45 caliber ammo magazine. I held the clip in my hand and my thumb sent a .45 cartridge rolling down the bar, where its metallic whir stopped right in front of Laughing Boy.

His smile was gone. The switchblade blade was still pointing up.

"Get rid of that," I said.

He pitched it across the room.

The combo had stopped playing. I could feel eyes on me. I put my eyes on the kid, whose face had turned into so much putty with some features stuck on.

I nodded toward the .45 cartridge.

"Eat it," I said.

He frowned. His eyes were bewildered.

"*Eat* it," I repeated.

He reached a trembling hand toward the slug. Picked it up, and slipped it into his mouth like a cough drop.

I grinned at him. "Be a good girl. Don't spit. Swallow."

He swallowed twice. First in contemplation of my demand, and second in carrying it out.

"Now go get your fuckin' boss. I'll wait. Tell him to come alone!"

He scurried off.

Behind me the little combo started playing "Hound Dog." I glanced at them and they were all smiling at me, including the redhead, who was laughing so hard her sweater was doing all her work for her.

Joe was right there now. "Can I, uh, get you something to drink, Mr. Hammer?"

"Yeah." I was lighting up a Lucky. "Seven-Up."

"Seven and seven?"

"Do I stutter? Seven-Up. I'll be in a booth."

I took one of the zebra-striped banquettes and made myself comfortable. That included getting out the .45 and putting it next to me on a split cushion. I drank my 7-Up. Smoked my Lucky.

When Mel Hazard made his appearance, slipping out from behind the curtain like an actor taking an encore, he was alone, as requested. But a hood or two would be right on the other side, keeping an eye on us through where the curtain halves met.

I almost laughed out loud at the sight of him. Not that there was anything funny about the squat, obese little character with his big jowly face and big ears and bug eyes and flat nose with its distended nostrils. It wasn't even what he was wearing exactly—a modified zoot suit that had been a tasteless joke a decade ago—just the color of it: a light green set off by a wide dark-green tie. And alligator loafers!

Was he *trying* to look like a toad?

No, I knew he was going for classic gangland sartorial elegance, the black tie and diamond stick-pin bit. I'd known another froggy-looking gangster once, but he at least tried to downplay his unfortunate appearance. Well, hell, maybe Mel had just decided to embrace his amphibian ancestry.

I almost expected him to hop into the booth like it was a lily pad, but Hazard had surprising grace for a man of his excess of girth and lack of stature. Then Joe materialized with a drink for his boss—a whiskey sour.

Hazard's voice, appropriately, was a raspy croak. "Why all the cops and robbers crapola, Hammer? Why not just send word back you wanted to see me like a civilized son of a bitch?"

"I tried, Mel. But it took a while for Joe to warm to me." I took some Lucky smoke in and let it out. "How's your rockabilly bodyguard doing?"

The frog face's wide mouth curled into half a sneer. Or maybe that was a smirk. Hard to tell. "What did you do to him, Hammer? He's back there crying his eyes out, after puking."

"Maybe you shouldn't recruit guys from a sock hop."

He chuckled. "You are a stitch, Hammer. Always have been. I suppose you're here about your pal Packy."

"No flies on you, Mel."

His liver-spotted mug worked up a scowl. "I had nothing to do with that kill. These rumors Packy and me had a falling out, they're pure bullshit."

"You two were tight, then?"

"Not tight." He plucked the maraschino cherry off its cocktail stick. Popped it in his puss and chewed. "The guy was a pain in the ass, tell you the truth. What's a moralist doing in this business, anyhow? But we put up with each other. Takes all kinds. When he started divesting himself of his interests, I was right there at the head of the line and he was fine with the color of my money."

Green like his suit.

"But he turned you down," I said, "the last time you tried to do business."

The big head sitting on the nearly non-existent neck bobbed up and down. "He did. Won't lie to you. He had a crazy idea I was the mastermind behind all these high-end robberies. Does that sound like me, Hammer? I am strictly a goods and services man. And an entertainment impresario. Not a damn thief, not a damn backer of heist artists who stick guns in people's faces that sometimes go off. That's where I draw the goddamn line."

But apparently not at bodyguards who waved around switchblades. Still, at least Hazard drew the line somewhere—or anyway said he did.

He was about halfway through the whiskey sour. "What's your stake in this, Hammer?"

"Packy was my friend."

That smirky sneer returned. "Yeah. Yeah, that's what they say about you, Hammer. You'd rather get even than get laid or paid. Well, fine. But does that mean you're your own client?"

Christ, now *he* was asking the questions!

"Well, I'm working with Packy's widow."

"The thrush, huh? That's a choice piece of ass, no offense."

"Watch it, Mel."

The bulging eyes went half-lidded. "So your interest is finding who took Packy out? And if it was a hit, you want who hired it?"

"Yeah. Size of it."

His chin came up. A neck was under there, after all—where else would he keep his Adam's apple? "What about that secretary of yours? That beautiful broad who got herself snatched by these lousy vicious thieves who I got nothing to do with? Is that a separate concern or a motivating factor?"

"Don't know just yet."

The chin came down but the bulgy eyes came up. "How would you like a client for a change?"

"Who might that be?"

"Yours truly, Hammer. They took Packy's ledger, didn't they?"

"What ledger?"

"*The* ledger, Hammer. The one somebody snatched from Packy's safe when they bumped him."

"How would you know about that, Mel?"

His laugh was as low and raspy as his voice. "What, you think the cops are sealed tight like a jelly jar? There's gonna be a hundred people after that ledger. Every one of the six families. Every bent cop in town. Every pol with the wrong kind of campaign contributions. I'm in there, too. You might've guessed."

"Which makes you a suspect."

"No! Which makes me a customer. You find that ledger, Hammer, and bring it to me, and I will pay you more money than you will see in a lifetime of missing persons, window peeking and insurance fraud. How would you like ten thousand in cash as a retainer? That's yours even if you can't deliver."

I gave him the kind of grin nobody liked to see from me. "All to tear a page or two about yourself out and burn 'em? Or maybe use it for insurance like Packy? Or blackmail every damn name in it?"

The wide shoulders shrugged. "Who doesn't like options?"

He'd come prepared. His plump hand reached carefully inside his green suitcoat and withdrew an envelope, and it was plump too. He lifted the flap and thumbed the hundreds inside like a card sharp doing his magic.

And when he handed it toward me, I took it. I would rather have slapped him with it, but a business relationship with Mel Hazard might come in handy in this thing. And if he was lying to me, having him close by might save me looking for him when it came time to give Mr. Toad a wild ride the likes of which he never dreamed.

"If ten G's ain't incentive enough," he said, "you might be interested to know one of the names in that ledger is a pal of yours. Certain Captain of Homicide?"

And he hopped out of the booth.

CHAPTER SEVEN

The restaurant seemed as though Mother Nature herself might have played interior decorator to make the sprawling Victorian building fit in better with Central Park, the color scheme a leafy green with touches of pink and other floral shades. Like most New York natives, I generally avoided Tavern on the Green, where the specialty of the house was tourists on the half-shell.

But Vickie insisted we go there—she'd never been. She also insisted it would be her treat, in return for my hospitality last night. Her late husband's attorney had arranged funds for her, so she was (in her words) "no longer a destitute dame in need of a handout."

We weren't the best-dressed couple in the place, not among these cocktail dresses and dinner jackets. But her low-cut navy-check pencil dress and my off-the-rack-at-Gimbels gray suit would just have to do. No pearls or high heels for her or folded white breast-pocket handkerchief for me. This suit was the only clean pressed one available and it hadn't been cut for my shoulder holster, unlike most of my wardrobe. I felt a little naked without the rod, but I didn't figure to have to shoot it out with anybody, starting with the doormen in silk hats and hunting coats.

I'd been sober long enough to face a real meal—Southern fried chicken with corn fritters—but Vickie only picked at her filet of lemon sole. We shared a strawberry tart but she didn't hold up her end. She brightened up a little after dinner when we danced to Milton Sanders' big band before having drinks on the terrace, surrounded by trees festooned with twinkling lights that echoed a star-flung summer sky. She was having a champagne cocktail and I was sticking with 7-Up.

Vickie looked great, her arms mostly bare, her shoulders entirely so, and her cleavage getting peeked at from guys left and right—and frowned at by the gals with them.

She said, "Could I be a more horrible person? My husband dead a day and I'm drinking champagne?"

"You really think Packy would mind?"

She laughed a little. "No. Not really. Not Packy. You know, Mike, I'm surprised you let me treat tonight."

"Figure me for more pride than that?"

"Something along those lines."

I saluted her with my glass of 7-Up. "Honey, I'm a private eye without a license. Considering my options, being a kept man doesn't sound half bad."

Another little laugh. "You *are* terrible, Mike Hammer."

"So I been told," I said.

We were seated under an elm tree the room had been built around.

"Not bad for a former sheep pen," I observed.

The big green eyes blinked. "What?"

I shrugged. "Twenty years or so ago, a couple hundred sheep used to huddle here by night, and graze that pasture next door by day. Then they got shipped to Prospect Park in Brooklyn. Now kids neck in the pasture, and people have been getting fed in this joint ever since. You're not from here, are you?"

"No," she admitted. "Lincoln, Nebraska."

"Ouch."

"Somebody has to be from there."

"Somebody who left, obviously."

She sipped her champagne cocktail; twinkling lights in the trees winked off the glass. "I'm just one of thousands of girls who graduated from cheerleading and school plays to chorus lines and burlesque shows in Chicago and Vegas. That's where I met Packy—Vegas. He had a little club downtown on Fremont Street."

"I remember."

Her smile was crooked. "I was working as a showgirl at the Sands and auditioned for him and he put me with a little combo."

"And the rest is history?"

She shrugged her bare shoulders, but wasn't looking at me when she said, "Packy had money in Rendezvous Records. The rock'n'roll fad hadn't really taken hold yet and we did well with a couple of singles. Packy had to grease some record-spinner palms to get me any airplay, but *Downbeat* magazine liked what they heard and that got me off the ground in a more legit way. From that came the album, which charted, and I started working the club circuit, getting some TV spots."

"I saw you on *Sullivan*."

"Me and the trained seals."

I chuckled. "Packy was your manager."

A nod. Still no eye contact. "I owe him everything. Owed."

"Were you two an item from the start?"

Now the green eyes fixed on me. Unblinking wide-set orbs that held mine like a magnet kissing metal. "There are things you need to know, Mike. About me. About Packy. About... me and Packy."

I shook my head. "No I don't."

But she went right ahead. "I didn't get from Lincoln to Omaha, and Omaha to Chicago, and Chicago to Vegas, without some rough stops along the way."

"Okay. Let's leave it at that."

"No, Mike. These names familiar? Emil Backus. Lamberto Pastore. Ugo Tomasino. Wade Merlin."

"Stop it, kid."

She leaned forward, daring me with her décolletage, and her smile wasn't her prettiest. "Why, were you expecting a longer list? Isn't that Rogue's Gallery enough?"

I shifted in my chair and frowned at her. "So show business is a glittery cesspool. What else is new? You paid your dues. So what? You want a list of who I slept with over the years? It's not just Sunday school teachers and more than one expected payment."

Her eyes looked moist now and she finally started blinking occasionally. "I'm not proud of how I got here. Even Packy.... Mike, he was the best of a bad lot. In a way, he was just another... well, gangster. But he had a heart. He came up out of nothing and never stabbed a single back on the way. And he had those lines he wouldn't cross. With me, he liked what he saw, but also liked what he *heard*—talent I had that had nothing to do with a willingness to stare at ceilings or get on my knees or—"

"Enough."

A red-nailed hand shot across the table and gripped my sleeve. "Mike, I need you to understand." Urgency tightened her voice. "There's been an electricity between us since the first time we met. You know it and I know it. Even when Packy and Velda were sitting right at a table with us. We never let the sparks turn into anything hotter—we had that much decency. Anyway, I saw what you and Velda had, while Packy and me... well."

"What about Packy and you?"

Sadness half-lidded the green eyes. "I did love him. Hell, I *still* love him. He was warm and giving and being with him... in *that* way... was nothing I ever came to dread. You need to grasp this. He was like a brother to me—no, a father."

"Incest is illegal, baby."

She drew her hand away. "I'm making you mad. I'm making you unhappy with me. I'm sorry. I shouldn't have got into any of this, but..."

"But what?"

Al Castellano's band was playing a rhumba. People were laughing.

"I'm someone now," she said. "*Somewhere* now. Packy built me a platform where I can perform and thrive. I'm not kidding myself. I know my neckline on the cover sold as many albums as my music—more, probably. But as long as my looks hold up, I'll have a career, and maybe beyond that. The point is, I don't have to return any favors on my back or my knees. I don't have to sleep with anybody I don't love, Mike. Never again."

"Must be a relief."

"See, you *are* mad. What I'm trying to say is, every man in my adult life has been temporary. A step up the ladder, another landing

I reached climbing the stairs. I thought Packy was the last rung, the last landing up those stairs. I loved him. Not the way I could.... I *did* love him, and had no designs on anyone else, on being with anybody else, understand? But I have a feeling you and I could be different."

"Do you?"

One slow nod. "I really do. Maybe not forever, but not just another stop on a trip to, where? The next booking? Success as a torch singer who isn't carrying the torch for anybody but herself?"

I didn't say anything.

"I've ruined it, haven't I?" she said, more a statement than a question, really. She had another awful smile on that lovely face now. "Yes, Packy had lines he wouldn't cross, but I think I just crossed one with you."

Tears started streaming now. Her mascara running. A few other diners were noticing. This lovely woman's date must be a real heel.

"No, kitten," I said, and now I took one of her hands in mine, gently. "You didn't have to go down memory lane with me, but you did. I knew about most of those bent-nose beaus of yours. I had a hunch you and Packy made a great team but never took it for a many splendored thing. But it means something, you leveling with me."

"Thank God," she said softly. "Thank God."

The night was warm with a cooling easy breeze as we strolled aimlessly. The restaurant was on the west side of the park near West 72nd. That left us eight-hundred-some acres to explore if we felt like it. We stopped on an ornate cast-iron bridge to lean at the rail over a pedestrian walkway.

"Did I mention," she said, her shoulder brushing mine, "that I'm not from here?"

"Think you might have."

"Well, it probably sounds corny to you, but speaking as a girl from Lincoln, Nebraska, I don't think there's anything in Manhattan more beautiful than Central Park at night."

"Oh, I can think of something."

Her amused expression seemed to dare me to kiss her.

Instead I just touched her hair and said, "A golden waterfall in the moonlight. Or does that sound corny to you?"

"Awful," she said. "Just awful."

And she kissed me, lightly at first, but blossoming into real warmth, her tongue darting in at the close with a promise of wild things to come.

We wound up in a quiet area of elm trees and took a bench. She gazed into the thickness of trees and shrubbery, her hand finding mine. My eyes were on her, that golden waterfall of her hair, the wide-set green of her eyes, the clinging fabric of the dress, the pale fullness of her bosom, the plump redness of her lips. Here, among undulating meadows and rock formations, flowering gardens and glassy lakes, wooded paths and dense foliage, we were at once a world away from Manhattan and in the very midst of it. I wanted to take her in my arms and let forever start right now, but I had walked too many times with Velda in this emerald refuge and the open wound had not begun to heal yet, and despite that wonderful kiss on that rustic bridge, I doubted it ever would.

The arm looped around my neck and jerked me back. I heard Vickie's scream, a jagged thing ripping through the quiet night, and I was pulled from behind and into bushes, the rustling shake of tiny leaves on skinny gnarled branches like tambourines around me, a mocking gypsy serenade with no melody, just percussion, the sharp joints of boughs almost like thorns as I was pulled out onto a more open patch where my assailant could better get at me. I glimpsed the blackjack silhouetted against the moon, its dark shape hovering over me, a knee keeping me pushed down on the grass on my back and my hand reflexively went for the .45 that was not under my arm. Then I was squirming and slapping at his torso and the blackjack wiggled and wavered, hanging above like a guillotine blade waiting for its moment to fall as my attacker tried to get the best angle on my skull. I clawed at him, he had a jacket on, and my fingers felt his shirt and then a leather strap and I risked a grin that might get shattered with a blackjack blow but it was too good, just too damn good—he had a gun where I didn't, a revolver of some kind worn where I usually would, and I gripped the gun butt and turned the thing sideways, still in its sheath, and the weapon fired. The dark shape atop me howled in shock and surprise and sudden pain and tumbled off, and as I got to my feet a gurgling was in my ears, like the last water going down a drain. It came from the shape on its back, a figure all in black, wiggling like an overturned bug, a balaclava keeping his features secret but his hands grabbing under his mask at his throat where the bullet had gone through and blood ran from between his fingers in dripping scarlet rivulets.

I took the revolver with me and there on the crushed rock path was Vickie, in a crumpled pile, and another figure in black was running away, fast, as if death was on his heels and he wasn't wrong.

Then came: "*Mike!*"

And I had to stop. I knelt next to her, the gun in my right hand, my other hand on her shoulder, bending to look at her, her head hanging, her hair no waterfall now, more a golden webbing the green eyes looked through in round wide fright.

I said, "Are you all right? *Are you all right?*"

"Yes… I… I think so…"

Up ahead the figure had disappeared.

Damn!

She began to get to her feet and I helped her, steadied her. "He said… said… if I behaved… he wouldn't kill me. He was dragging me off somewhere, Mike! I think he was kidnapping me!"

"Slimy son of a bitch. What changed his mind?"

"There was a gunshot."

"That was me. Guy who jumped me's gun, not mine."

A whistle blew, as shrill as the earlier scream, as a uniformed cop ran up to us and stopped; he had a revolver in his hand, too. He yelled at us, wanting to know what the hell was going on.

"I'm Mike Hammer," I said.

"Oh," he said, as if that explained it. He was in his forties, his face a white smear in the dark. "I know who you are. What happened here?"

I told him, gesturing to where a corpse was waiting.

He asked, "Any idea what this is about, Mr. Hammer?"

"Just get to a radio and get Pat Chambers over here. Have them call him at home if he's not at the station. I'm walking Mrs. Paragon back to the restaurant. Tell Pat to come over there."

He gave me a cockeyed look. "You're giving orders to the captain of Homicide?"

"I started doing that a long time ago."

The cop shook his head. "You really shouldn't leave the scene."

"We're the victims, pal."

And I slipped my arm around her waist and we headed back.

At the Tavern on the Green we both freshened up. Then the manager provided a private dining room not in use where he sat us down. He asked what he could bring us and I said coffee. We were on our second cup when Pat finally showed.

I didn't figure we'd be his first stop—he'd want a look at the scene, and at the dead guy. Homicide dicks are sticklers for detail.

He sat at the head of the table. We were side by side nearby, the three of us alone in a room that sat sixty. His gray-blue eyes focused on me with distrust as he tossed his hat on the table. His suit was as rumpled as an unmade bed. Caught him at home again, I'd bet.

"Mike," he said, "you left the scene of the shooting."

"Central Park was the scene of the shooting," I said. "This *is* Central Park, in case you're new around here or maybe lost your sense of direction."

"Who is he?"

"Who is who?"

"The guy you shot."

"How the hell should I know?"

I told him what happened.

"You're using the other guy's gun now," he said.

"When you don't have a license you have to make do."

Pat wasn't boiling, but he was starting to simmer. He swung his attention to Vickie.

"What can you tell me about this incident, Mrs. Paragon?"

She shrugged. Having waited for Pat for over half an hour, her composure was fine.

"It's just as Mike told it—we were sitting there on that bench, quietly talking, and suddenly Mike was pulled back into the bushes and a figure was just... just right there in front of me. Like the other one, he was in a black stocking-mask and black, uh... black *everything*, jacket, shirt, slacks, shoes, even gloves, like... driving gloves, I guess. So I got no actual sense of what he looked like. He was about Mike's build, a little shorter. But strong. Very strong. He grabbed me and really just... overwhelmed me."

"Could it have been a mugging?"

She shook her head. "No. He was after *me*. Said if I behaved he wouldn't... kill me."

Pat's eyes narrowed. "Sounds like things were leading up to a sexual assault. Was that your sense of it, Mrs. Paragon?"

"That's certainly possible. With all the underbrush, that certainly could be what he had in mind." She thought for a moment, then: "But I don't think so."

"Why is that?"

"Just not how it... felt. He was calm, businesslike. There was nothing... sexual in his words or manner. It felt like a kidnap attempt, if anything."

I said, "Pat, a two-person rapist team? Are you serious?"

He said, "That's more common than you'd think."

I opened a hand. "If sex is what they were after, why not wait for a woman alone, or a couple of girls walking? Not a healthy guy out with his date."

"Since when are you healthy," Pat muttered.

"Very funny. But you know as well as I do there are hookers working the park, particularly later in the evening. Yeah, yeah, you guys cracked down on that, but it still goes on. And if sex was the point, why not grab one of them? They're less likely to file a complaint."

"And more likely," he said, "to have a knife or small rod on them."

He wasn't wrong.

"Look," I said, "Victoria here has been through the mill tonight, and I've had more relaxing strolls through the park myself. How about releasing us? You know where to find me, and Mrs. Paragon is back at the Riverside apartment, if you need to talk to her again."

Pat thought about that, rose, said to Vickie, "If you'll excuse us a moment, ma'am? I'd like a word with my *friend* here."

He said "friend" in a way I hadn't heard before.

She nodded and started to rise, but Pat gestured for her to stay put. The room was large enough that he could walk me over to one corner and have enough privacy for a little chat.

"I know you like this dame," Pat said quietly, "but I wouldn't trust her with change for a dollar. Her husband, yeah, he was a nice guy, as mob guys go, but Mike—he was a mob guy. And I could give you chapter and verse on half a dozen other mob guys she was a high-class moll to from here to Omaha, Nebraska."

"Isn't it a shame," I said, "when a bad girl tries to take advantage of a clean-cut youth like me. I have should have paid attention to those movies they showed us in the service."

"Fine. Make a joke out of it. But you're asking for trouble right when you're at your most vulnerable. I know you're torn up about

Velda. You think *I'm* not? Screw your head on straight, Mike, before somebody shoots it off for you."

"You finished?"

"No. You think I don't know why you're cozying up to the widow? Packy was your pal, right? And what does Mike Hammer do when somebody rubs out one of his pals? Why, he goes all crusader on us."

"Is that what I do?"

His shook his head and his smile was a frustrated thing. "Come on, Mike. Isn't this getting a little old? Packy wasn't your war buddy like Jack Williams—he didn't give an arm to keep a Jap bayonet from searching for your heart. No, Packy Paragon was a mobster. The very kind of lowlife you have devoted your life to hating. So being a mobster finally caught up with him, if a little late. So what? Good riddance."

"Tell me about the ledger, Pat."

He frowned. "What ledger?"

"You want me to believe that you don't know about the ledger that was the really valuable item in Packy's safe? That made a hundred grand look like chickenfeed? The book that got him killed?"

Pat drew in air, let it out slow. "Yeah, I've heard about it. And I think it's a bunch of b.s. A bluff Packy ran to keep himself alive."

"Didn't that work out great for him."

He seemed genuinely amused. "Why, you think this mythical ledger's for real? Are you that gullible, Mike?"

"Pretty gullible. But if it *does* exist, my question is… are *you* in that book, Pat?"

He got red. It started at his neck and worked its way up. In the cartoons his head would've turned into a radish. "What are you saying, Mike?"

I drained everything but sincerity out of my voice. "Not that you're on the take. You are as straight a cop as I ever knew, and that's from the heart, old chum. But your uncle was city comptroller back when you became the youngest captain in the history of the New York Police Department."

He grabbed me by a lapel. "You know I got that job because of a mass murderer I put away!"

"I know, I know. If strings were pulled, you never knew. But blackmailers tend to have no scruples, and nuance seems to elude the public. You want to let go of my coat before it rips? I don't have that many decent suits that I can spare one."

"You bastard," he said.

"Now who's casting family aspersions?" I said, and I collected Vickie and we left.

CHAPTER EIGHT

With Victoria the obvious target of the Central Park attack, I figured neither my pad nor her Riverside digs were suitable to keep her off the firing line. What came to mind was Velda's apartment, which was just a couple of blocks from mine, and I had a key of course.

We went straight there from the Tavern on the Green. Vickie was about the same size as Velda, their tall, full-breasted, leggy beauty strikingly similar. Temporarily she could borrow clothes, till we could make a stop tomorrow at apartment 5-C for some of her own things.

I opened the door and hit a wall switch that turned on a couple of lamps. Then I led the way and for several long moments I thought I had entered the past—the recent past, but a time not long ago that was already seeming distant. Was I imagining I was smelling Velda's Chanel No. 5, or was that floral aroma the flowering potted plants spotted here and there in this simple but feminine apartment?

Vickie, stepping inside, said, "Very nice," and I shut the door behind her.

For someone who lived on Riverside Drive, her remark might have been sarcastic or patronizing, but it was neither. The small space was functional with a quiet, quirky elegance. We'd entered directly into the small living room—where, on a cobalt-blue throw rug, a light gray overstuffed couch with zebra pillows faced a white fireplace alongside a rose wall I'd helped paint. A low-slung glass coffee table had an oversize art history book and a *New Yorker* that was already well out of date. Over the mantle hung a red, white and black cubist painting she'd bought in Greenwich Village. To the left of the fireplace was a little stand with a rabbit-ears TV.

Over by the window onto the street—near a radio console with a warm wood cabinet nearby—was a darker gray comfy chair and an ottoman. The impression of her was still on the cushions.

Vickie was at my side suddenly, her hand on my sleeve. "Are you all right, Mike?"

"Yeah. Fine."

But I felt like a ghost haunting this cozily familiar world. A ghost who kept looking around for another spirit who wasn't there and yet was all around me.

The kitchenette, looking as clean and gleaming as something out of a model home, was beyond a dividing counter at left. Velda's bedroom was behind the kitchenette. A bathroom was off the hallway that cut between the kitchenette and a wall with a landscape Velda's mother had painted, badly, over a bookcase filled mostly with popular paperbacks and small framed photos. A portable stereo HiFi was on a stand with a lot of LPs stacked on the rack below. Somewhere among them was *Victoria Valance—I Carry a Torch.*

She frowned as she glanced around. "Is somebody else living here already?"

"No, these things are all hers. About a week after she.... I paid six months' rent on this place. In case... you know."

"I know." Vickie edged around in front of me. "Do you mind if I take a shower? Maybe get into a nightgown of hers or something?"

"Go ahead."

"I tore my dress in the park, and got a few scrapes. I'll see what the medicine cabinet has to offer, if you don't mind."

Somehow, from somewhere, I found a pathetic little smile. "Whatever you need."

But she paused. "Mike—could you stay here tonight? I'm pretty shaky. That couch looks like it would suffice for you. I don't mean to be a baby, but…"

"We'll see."

She nodded and I pointed her to the bathroom. She disappeared and I went over and sat on the couch, where Velda and I had been together so many times, watching a fire. But this was summer and the fireplace was cold. I looked at that stupid painting she bought in Greenwich Village that I'd told her was ugly and had grown to like.

The shower drummed pleasantly in the background as I rose and wandered into the kitchenette. I checked the refrigerator and the only things left in there were four bottles of Blue Ribbon. My laugh sounded like somebody hit me in the belly.

"You mocking me, kitten?" I asked Velda softly.

A key worked in the door.

For the second time tonight, I reached for a gun that wasn't there. Then I plucked a carving knife from the knife block on the counter and came around quickly, snugging to the wall at left of the door as it opened.

The knife was in my fist, ready to stab, raised high, when Velda's landlady stepped inside. I quickly tucked my hand with the knife behind me as the pleasant older woman stepped inside. Short, a little plump, in a daisy housedress, this woman was about as threatening as the small red watering can she held in one hand.

"Oh!" she said, startled. "Mr. Hammer. I didn't see you come in."

"Mrs. Murphy," I said with a nod.

She had blue eyes and a pleasant face that was still pretty despite expansion by time and sampling of her own baking. "I just remembered I'd forgotten to tend to Miss Sterling's flowers today."

"Go right ahead and tend. I should have let you know I was stopping by."

She went around freshening flowers, first at the windowsill and then the counter that separated the living room from the kitchenette and finally the table by the gray chair where Velda would sit and read. As she did, the landlady said, "I've kept the place clean and aired out, as you requested, Mr. Hammer. Got all the perishables out of the icebox. Most everything in the cupboards should be fine. I do hope you'll get word soon about Miss Sterling... one way or another."

"Yes," I said. I'd discreetly rested the carving knife on the dividing counter when her back was to me.

"She so brightened up the building," the landlady said, shaking her head sadly. "And I know you must miss her terribly."

I hadn't even noticed the shower had stopped. But just then Vickie emerged from the hallway, her head lowered as she dried her hair with a towel, her still somewhat damp body making her pink robe cling to her hourglass shape in ways I wouldn't have minded at all if company weren't watering the plants.

"That's a nice big bathroom," Vickie said, toweling, "for such a small apartment.... Oh!"

Mrs. Murphy caught herself watering the floor and also said, "Oh!"

"This is a friend of mine," I said to the landlady. "Victoria Valance. The singer? She needs a place to stay tonight and maybe longer. I should have called."

"No, no," Mrs. Murphy said, understandably flustered. "You're paying the rent, Mr. Hammer. None of my business."

Vickie, embarrassed, excused herself and disappeared back down the hall and shut herself in the bathroom.

"That's a very forward-looking attitude, Mrs. Murphy," I said, "but you misunderstand. Miss Valance, actually Mrs. Paragon is her married name, is a client. Her husband was murdered last night and I'm hiding her away here."

"Oh dear."

I took the woman by the arm and gentled her toward the door. "If anyone asks about Miss Valance, you don't know a thing. They might ask for her by her married name. I doubt any of that will come to pass, and I should have let you know before."

She nodded, said, "Uh, well, uh… thank you, Mr. Hammer."

And I shut the door behind her.

I waited perhaps thirty seconds, then called out, "Olly olly oxen free!"

Vickie came out with her head in a towel-wrap turban, her nakedness beneath the pink dressing gown a bit less apparent but for the impertinent tips of her breasts. She was laughing, so lovely sans any make-up at all.

"Well," she said, "that wasn't *too* embarrassing, was it?"

I laughed. "Not very, no. No worse than farting in church. Good and loud."

She started to laugh and so did I.

"You missed the part," I said, "when I almost stabbed the old girl with a carving knife."

That made her howl, but I just chuckled. After all, that had been a close call.

Then we were sitting on the couch and she was giggling, nestled against me. She smelled fresh, of Velda's Camay. A small narrow rose-shaded lamp on an end table on my side of the couch cast a soft glow. The Greenwich Village cubist painting glared at me.

"You'll be fine here," I said.

The laughter stopped. "No, Mike."

"No?"

"Please stay. Camp out here on the couch. I'll be a good girl. I promise."

"I don't know if I trust myself."

"Nothing's going to happen here." She glanced around us. "Not here."

I swallowed. "I'm glad you understand that."

She got up, disappeared for a few moments, before returning with a pillow from Velda's bedroom. "You won't need a blanket."

After handing me the pillow and giving me a modest little kiss on the cheek, she ran off like a little girl. Except little girls didn't have a shape like that.

But with the lights out, and me stripped to my shorts and t-shirt, the thoughts I was dealing with had nothing to do with a longing to join her in that bedroom. This was too much Velda's world. Her presence hung like a pleasant but watchful phantom, that faint floral aroma tickling my nostrils… the flowers the landlady watered? A lingering hint of Chanel?

That, and not the nearby presence of a woman so achingly beautiful it hurt to think of, was what nagged me, what made me toss and turn on that little couch for maybe an hour and then, when I finally felt the welcome blackness of sleep about to suck me in, came her voice.

"*Mike!*"

It straightened me up as if by spring action.

Was she in trouble?

I ran to the closed door of her bedroom.

The door spoke. Not a yell or shout this time, but a request.

"Mike. Come in here. Please."

I opened the door. The room was dark, but the light from the hall illuminated the lovely woman in that other lovely woman's double bed. That light had a sense of humor or irony or maybe it was just sadistic, because my picture with Velda one happy afternoon was grinning at me from a bedside-table frame.

"I lied," she said, very quietly.

That hallway light caught her green eyes and the waterfall of golden hair, but she had a sheet tucked up to under her chin, so at least the rest of her was leaving me alone.

"Lied?" I said numbly, leaning in the doorway.

"I've been waiting for you. I want you, Mike. I want you tonight. I want you right now."

"You don't understand…."

"Come be with me. You've been in this bed before, haven't you? It's ready to welcome you again."

I sat awkwardly on the floor. In the doorway. As if her words had pushed me down. "I *said* you didn't understand. I've never been in that bed, baby. I gave her my ring. I was going to marry her. But like a dope I kept her on such a pedestal that... I never had her."

Her expression had gone from demandingly yearning to outright startled, as those words took hold. Then that expression changed into sheer confidence, as her chin raised and her big eyes turned into glittering green slits.

She flipped the sheet away.

She lay on her side with a pillow propped behind her head, her beautiful features needing no help from cosmetics, the lushness of her mouth made moist by a flicking pink tongue, the impressive hemispheres of her breasts firm and high as if gravity had been banished, that high ribcage sweeping to a narrow waist, her stomach flat but with a fetching layer of baby fat giving her navel a dimpled home, hips angled toward me, bottom leg extended, top leg with knee raised and foot flat on the mattress to audaciously, unashamedly reveal a golden triangle bookended by the pale, creamy flesh of inner thigh, such a supple part of those legs that seemed to go on forever, feminine and yet muscular and flexing almost imperceptibly.

"Have her now, Mike," she whispered. "Have her *now....*"

I had her.

The next morning I went to a delicatessen down the block and brought back bagels with lox and cream cheese for breakfast. I told Vicki to lie low till I got back, but warned her it might be a while. Velda's cupboards and the refrigerator's freezer were stocked well enough to provide plenty of meal options till I got back.

She wanted to know where I was going, and I said, "Hunting without a license."

I started at the *Trib*, where behind the door with HY GARDNER in gold letters I sat across the desk from the syndicated columnist and heard something interesting.

"I talked to Jack Ross and Lou Feinstein both," he said, then paused to relight his cigar, "and neither one has picked up a single solitary rumble about that ledger being stolen."

Those were the *Trib*'s top two crime beat reporters.

"Oh," he went on, puffing to get it going, "they've heard the rumors, all right. That it was hands off Packy among the Mafia crowd because he had the goods on everybody and their mothers. But it obviously didn't stop somebody from sending Packy eternally packing."

I frowned at him. "What about somebody on the outside who's playing kingpin over these robbery crews?"

"Well, it may not be somebody from the outside." He looked over the dark-rimmed glasses at me like a lazy hound dog. "Those guys you made dead and littered around the Greenway townhouse? They had long histories as breaking-and-entering boys. But not with each other. Somebody seems to be organizing these crews, like a damn casting director, which suggests an inside knowledge of the New York crime scene."

Vitale's, a brick-fronted *ristorante* in Little Italy, looked like just another option for locals and tourists alike. The guidebooks said the food was fine, but the hours were limited—from two to four, they were closed. But if you had business with Don Alberto Bonetti, that was the perfect time to drop by. Of course, you didn't get that information from guidebooks.

Sometimes it comes in handy being a guy known for ignoring rules. When the old don looked up from his plate of linguine and clams and saw me strolling into the otherwise empty back dining room, he waved his two overgrown altar boy bodyguards to sit back down at their nearby table.

As I approached, I held my suitcoat open and displayed the lack of hardware or for that matter even a shoulder sling. The don's face was a soft oval thing with dark hard deadly eyes in it, like gunshot in a bite of duck. His hair was salt and pepper, heavy on the salt, and his attire was unassuming, a black suit and black string tie, like he'd ridden in on a burro from the Old West.

"Been expecting you, Michael," he said in a warm voice with a sinister edge. He was in a half booth, on the booth side; he gestured for me to sit opposite. "Something to eat?"

"No thank you."

"Some red wine?"

"I'm off the sauce. Even the vino."

His eyebrows frowned and his mouth smiled. "Mike Hammer on the wagon. I shudder to think. Does that make your mood better or worse?"

"I am on the edgy side." I sat forward in a non-threatening way, elbows on the red-and-white tablecloth, hands open and empty. "I'm here because I am hoping a few honest questions can get honest answers from you. In any case, whatever the answers, I will leave quietly, respecting this neutral ground. But I'd like to ask them."

"Pose your questions."

"Was Packy Paragon's killing a hit by any of the families? Or combination thereof?"

His head shook once, slowly. "Not that I am aware of."

"All of the families did business for years with Packy, when he was active in gambling until not long ago."

A slow nod.

"Apparently a ledger was taken from his safe."

The don said nothing.

"What do you know of that ledger?"

"Nothing directly. Its existence was a rumor."

"Used as a threat by Packy?"

"No. Merely a rumor."

"Do you believe he had such a ledger?"

"He may have."

"Has it been offered to you?"

"No."

"Has anyone old or new tried to use it against you?"

"No. But, Mr. Hammer, I might not be forthcoming about that. You are not a fool and I am not a fool."

"Understood. I have only one more question."

"Go ahead."

"Are you involved in any way with this series of high stakes armed robberies?"

"No."

The answer came so quick I blinked.

I broke my promise of just one more question and asked, "Do you know if any of the other families *are* involved?"

This came slower, but it came: "I don't believe so. This is someone from the outside. This kind of reckless behavior is bad for business. None of the dons would countenance that just when we are endeavoring to move into legitimate enterprise."

That was bullshit, to a degree, because gambling and prostitution and loan-sharking and protection and illegal narcotics and union plundering were still in play and probably always would be. But those activities would be cushioned by layers between the top and bottom, and political and police payoffs, though certainly some of what had once been front business was now turning into paying concerns.

"That was my gut instinct," I said, "but I had to ask. And I felt with you, Don Bonetti, I would get an honest answer."

"I will give you more than that. I will promise that if I hear anything that might help you in your pursuit of those who took your secretary—and who mutilated the wife of a wealthy individual, which is very bad public relations, as the term goes—you will hear personally from me."

"Thank you."

He paused to reflect. Then: "I appreciate how difficult it was for you, Mr. Hammer, to come to me like this. The courage it took for you to beard the lion in his den, so to speak…. I respect that."

I stood, slowly. "I respect you for allowing me my questions, Don Bonetti, and risking me sticking that fork in your neck."

His eyes widened and I gave him a smile and a nod, and went out.

I didn't have to travel far to get to the baroque old building on Centre Street. The exterior was a promise of grandeur that got immediately broken by a decrepit interior, and that included Pat's third-floor office, which was tucked to one side of a busy bullpen.

The door was closed, muffled conversation going on the other side. I knocked, then went right in—I was expected. I'd called ahead.

Roy Rollins, Pat's counterpart on the Robbery Division, was in a chair across from the captain of Homicide. His ankle resting on a knee as he leaned back, Rollins was in his mid-forties, a slender ferret-faced guy with a thin mustache and a suit that was a little too nice for a cop. I found him cocky and full of himself, but he didn't like me, either. Of course, cops generally don't like PIs, even though we're almost all ex-cops.

Pat's desk was typically tidy, as orderly as that scientific mind of his, but his loose navy tie split the distance with a tan suit that this early in the day hadn't got itself rumpled. It would. Say what you will about him, Pat always worked long, hard hours.

He and Rollins were hardly tight, but I'd leaned on what was left of the Hammer/Chambers friendship to get Pat to arrange this meeting.

"Have a seat, Mike," Pat said, gesturing to a chair. "Roy was nice enough to work you into his busy schedule."

There might have been some sarcasm buried in that, because I knew Pat considered Rollins a guy who dogged it.

"Appreciate it," I said. "I just wondered where you are, Captain Rollins, on the robbery side of the Civac investigation."

Rollins had a laugh that was too high-pitched for an adult, but then so was his voice in general. "Since you *killed* every one of the poor bastards at Greenway's, Hammer, somehow not much has turned up."

Ignoring that, I said, "I hit a snag in my inquiry."

Pat somehow kept himself from reminding me I had lost my investigator's license and just said, "Oh?"

I nodded. "Let me confirm right now that the tip I got about the Greenway home invasion came from Packy Paragon."

"The *late* Packy Paragon," Rollins said with a smirk.

I ignored that, too. "And, of course, Packy was tied in with every one of the six families. Back when he was the gambling czar around here."

"Which seems like yesterday," Pat said.

"It *was* yesterday," Rollins said.

"But," I said, "I have it on good authority that the crew I took down at Greenway's was *not* tied to any mob faction. So... where did Packy get the information?"

Rollins frowned in thought, then said, "Could Packy himself have been the mastermind behind these armed robbery crews?"

"Highly doubtful," I said. "Not his style, and why would he tip me off to the Greenway hit?"

Pat said, "To get rid of his accomplices in the Civac job, after it went so badly wrong."

"Maybe," I said. "Captain Rollins—can you confirm sophisticated armed robbery crews are targeting specific kinds of targets? Individual crews for home invasions, jewelry stores, banks, payrolls, armed cars?"

"That would seem to be the case," he said, then scowled. "That's not for public consumption, Hammer."

"Noted. But no matter how you slice it, Packy's killing is part of this thing. You both know about the ledger supposedly stolen from the Paragon safe?"

"We do," Rollins said. "But we can't confirm it. We can't even confirm the ledger's existence."

I turned to Pat. "You must have noticed, chum, that the pair who jumped Victoria and me at the park last night wore the same black garb as the robbery crews."

Rollins let out his pig-squeal laugh again. "The attackers wore black? *That's* a connection? You are *reaching*, Hammer."

Again, ignoring him seemed the better part of valor. Slapping cops can get you in dutch. "Pat, tell me—who did I kill last night?"

Pat just looked at me. "Why? Do you have a ledger you want to record it in?"

"Funny. Who?"

"Burl Lambert."

"And who is Burl Lambert? Make that, who *was* Burl Lambert?"

Rollins said quietly, "His package says he did a stay at Sing Sing for a bank job. Out a year or so."

"*That's* my connection," I said, getting to my feet, "you dumb-ass jerks."

And I got out of there.

CHAPTER NINE

I snugged my hat down and turned my trench coat collar up against the sudden gust of cold.

What started out a sunny morning had deteriorated into a chilly afternoon, the sky one big gray sodden rag waiting to wring itself out over the city. I'd made my rounds on foot so far, but hoofing it from Centre Street to East 55th would have taken at least an hour and I had no desire to get caught out in what the gray overcast seemed to have in store for me.

That endless gray ceiling and the sudden shift in temperature had me on edge, but that was more my fault than the weather's. Even after that violent assault last night in Central Park had me caught without my .45, I had nonetheless set out unarmed again today.

Yes, Pat had sneaked my iron back to me and implied he'd look the other way if I went gallivanting around packing; but I didn't want to risk getting the piece confiscated, particularly not when one of my planned calls was police headquarters. I figured when night fell and my hunting took on a different tenor, I'd head back to my apartment and strap on the shoulder sling with the

Colt. Trouble was, night had arrived hours early, those grumbling hellish heavens floating overhead like a fat filthy ghost.

So I caught a cab to the Paragon, which wouldn't have been open yet even if it hadn't been shuttered temporarily to honor its owner's death and give its new manager a chance to get his feet under him. I walked in under the fiery canopy through unlocked doors and in past the unattended hatcheck stand to be greeted at the entryway by the Victoria Valance standee. Just like before, only this time the songstress was turned to face the wall, her cardboard backing on display like a guy in a hospital gown with his ass hanging out.

After all, Vickie wouldn't be performing here for a while, again out of respect to the man the club had been named for. Of course, it was the man himself who'd done it in his own honor. And, frankly, I had a feeling Vickie would be back on stage as soon as she could get away with it. And she would definitely not be facing away.

The Paragon didn't take on the shabby look of most clubs when the lights were up and the fantasy of nightlife took on the reality of day. Packy's remodeling was still fresh, and anyway there was an inherent brightness to its red leather booths and chairs, and a lodge-like warmth to its open beams, orangish paneling and fieldstone fireplace—unusual touches for a nitery. The only tip-off was an olfactory cocktail of cleaning fluids, old beer, and cigarette smoke.

Way to the right, beyond the row of booths with their slightly elevated view of the stage, a bartender in street clothes on the tier above was taking an inventory of the impressive array of bottles along the mirrored back of the bar. A couple of good-looking girls, who I recognized as waitresses here, were in blouses and slacks with their hair pinned back as they cleaned the tabletops, which were absent their linen cloths. They looked more like young housewives than drink hawkers. On stage left, a slender, attractive short-haired black woman in a white blouse and black toreador pants was standing near the piano with Vickie's accompanist Bud Gregg massaging the keys.

She was singing, minus any amplification: "*I'd rather have the blues than what I've got…*"

Not bad. Velda would've liked her.

"I recommended her to Victoria," a husky male voice said just behind me.

I glanced at the big handsome black-haired guy, his teeth blindingly white against his West Coast tan; he wore an Aloha shirt, a green-and-orange-on-white tropical design, and pleated tapered trousers a black-speckled light gray. He looked like a guy in an *Esquire* fashion layout only with more hair tonic and less shame.

I said, "She's good."

Sonny Gray said, "Kitty White. I brought her out from L.A. I used to hear her at hip little clubs out there. I knew the boss would dig her."

"Packy, you mean?"

"No—Victoria. To sub for her till she's ready to get back in the ring. That's a Nat King Cole tune."

"*…the web has got me caught…*"

"Not familiar with it," I said.

"It was in some movie."

"Must've missed that one."

We listened a while, then I said, "When do you open back up?"

"This weekend, already. So much still to do! I been playing catch-up, big time."

I gestured to the empty room. "Can you find a moment to sit and chat, Sonny?"

His smile shared no teeth this time. "Sure, Mike. I'm glad to get the chance to talk to you…. Let's take a booth. My little office is pretty cramped for a pow-wow."

I fell in with him as he went up the short flight of carpeted stairs. "I hear you're the manager now, Sonny. Don't you have Packy's old office?"

"I'm *in* Packy's old office, a cubbyhole backstage. He did business out of their apartment, mostly." Again, the white grin flashed in the tanned face. "But you should see Victoria's dressing room! Shower, a couch, couple comfy chairs, vanity mirror with lights like Broadway—hell, I've *lived* in smaller apartments."

"Good to be the star attraction."

"And married to the club owner didn't hurt. Can I get you a drink, Mike?"

"I could stand a 7-Up."

Another grin. "Hey, we can do better than that. It's cocktail hour, isn't it? And if it isn't, it's gotta be cocktail hour *somewhere*."

"No thanks."

"Since when is Mike Hammer a teetotaler?"

"Since Mike Hammer started waking up in his own vomit."

"Oh. Well. That'd do it."

My image as a legendary tough guy had taken a hit with Sonny.

The new manager deposited me in one of the red-leather booths and headed back to the bar and put his order in with a flat-nosed character who looked like he doubled as a bouncer. Sonny waited back there while I listened to the singer. Unamplified, just rehearsing, she was still easy to hear. She'd moved on from the Nat King Cole number to a lovely "Sky Lark." I wished Velda had been there to hear it.

I heard Sonny behind me telling the bartender, "No calls, Jack, till I've talked to Mr. Hammer."

Then my host delivered me a glass of 7-Up on ice and brought along for himself what looked to be a Scotch and soda. I hadn't thought about having a drink at all today but I had to work to keep my eyes off his glass, like a guy on a date trying not to look at any other women.

His manner was low-key, friendly. "I'm glad to have a chance to talk to you, Mike. I've spoken with Victoria on the phone several times since the, uh, tragedy... and she seems to me to be doing okay. What's your take on it?"

I sipped the 7-Up, hold the Seagram's. It was like having a bite of hamburger bun without the burger. "I'd say she's handling it well."

I had to play it a little cagey, not being sure what Vickie had shared with him.

His chin lowered and his eyes fixed on me. They were Rock Hudson light brown and he was damn near that good-looking, too. But Hudson didn't have tiny scars here and there on his handsome mug in memory of countless brawls. And was that a knife scar on Sonny's forehead?

"Mike, I know you been looking after Victoria. Looking out for her. I even know you've got her squirreled away... just not where. Or why."

Since he hadn't posed that as a question, I didn't answer it.

Instead, I said, "We finally went out for a little air last night. Took in Tavern on the Green. Maybe she mentioned that."

He shook his head again; I ducked back, not wanting to get hit with Vitalis drops. "Mike, I had the impression you had her stowed away someplace. Sequestered like a jury."

So he didn't know about us getting jumped in Central Park. Good information to have, but it limited what I could say.

"Might be she's in trouble," I said.

That rocked him back. "Why *would* she be? Wasn't Packy just a, you know, casualty in that robbery?"

"That may be what we were meant to think. And not see it as a hit on Packy."

He was really shaking his head now, and I swear I saw droplets fly. "No, Mike, that makes no sense. Victoria told me the thieves got a hundred grand out of that safe. That *has* to be the reason they were there."

I got out my deck of Luckies, shook one loose. "Does it? Good way to make it read wrong and pick up a tidy sum in the bargain."

"But… why would *Victoria* be a target?"

I fired up the smoke. "It's mostly just a feeling," I lied, and snapped shut my Zippo. "Call it an educated guess."

His eyebrows, full and dark, climbed. "Well. An educated guess from Mike Hammer in this kind of situation can't be ignored."

"Appreciate the confidence."

He leaned forward, painfully earnest. "Look, you take *care* of that girl, Mike. She's a great talent and a nice lady, but also… this club is just another joint without Victoria Valance."

Did Sonny have a yen for her, too?

I let some smoke out. "You mind if I ask how you and Packy got so tight?"

With a shrug, the club manager said, "Packy was pals with Jack Dragna. They lived on opposite coasts, but they shared Vegas interests and had mutual friends here in New York."

After Bugsy Siegel got knocked off, Dragna had become the West Coast's Capone.

Sonny continued: "I grew up in Los Angeles. Got on as one of Mr. Dragna's bodyguards right out of high school, and started doing, uh, you know... odd jobs for him."

"Odd jobs" likely meant roughing guys up and probably the occasional hit. And as nice as he seemed in the here and now, he'd won a rep as a hotheaded kid with an itchy trigger finger.

Sonny flipped a casual hand, as if he were describing the most harmless, innocuous things. "Mr. Dragna and Mickey Cohen and some other, uh, rival factions in certain enterprises got in occasional disagreements. I was active on Mr. Dragna's behalf in some of those."

Kitty White was singing a wistful "Long Ago and Far Away."

"But Dragna died of natural causes," I said, "what, a year ago? And then, what? Mickey Cohen came looking for you?"

He straightened and suddenly seemed to be reciting from a script. "Not Cohen himself, obviously. Assorted individuals who were not of a bygones-be-bygones inclination. And Packy, as the late Mr. Dragna's good friend, stepped in and gave me sanctuary."

The club we were sitting in was hardly a church. Of course, it did serve wine.

"Also," he added, "I spent some time with Packy, Mr. Paragon, over the years. On Vegas trips and L.A. sojourns, when Packy was visiting, Mr. Dragna would loan me to him as an… assistant, like. Sort of a tour guide."

Bodyguard. Muscle.

"Sonny, could your old West Coast problems have come back to haunt Packy here?"

He shook his head almost violently. "Oh, no, no, I don't think so. That's all past history and Packy was nobody the West Coast boys would want to go up against, considering how tied in he was. You know, with the various families out here."

I stabbed out my Lucky in a Paragon ashtray. "Are you sure about that, Sonny?"

He looked damn near hurt. "What do you mean, Mike?"

I didn't want to go into too much of what Don Alberto Bonetti and I had discussed at Vitale's—this was about me *getting* information, not giving it.

Treading carefully with Sonny, I asked, "Did Packy ever mention anything to you about anyone who might be working against his interests—specifically, somebody in any of the six mob families? Maybe more than one somebody?"

"No. Nothing. Why?"

"Mostly just a hunch," I admitted.

I gestured around the club. On stage Kitty White had paused to go over sheet music with the accompanist. The young women were still cleaning tabletops. The bartender was clinking bottles as he straightened and checked their levels.

"On opening night," I said, "Packy was upbeat, smiling and laughing and holding court like a conquering king. But I sensed something."

He frowned. "Like what, Mike?"

I shrugged, gestured with an open hand. "A certain uneasiness. His glad-handing good mood was at least partially a front, I think. And not long after that...?"

Sonny nodded. "He was dead. Killed. But, Mike, he got that bullet when somebody emptied his safe. He wasn't the target, the *safe* was—right? Or anyway, that hundred G's was."

"The one hundred G's... or maybe a ledger worth a whole hell of a lot more?"

Sonny's eyes tightened and he shook his head slowly. "What ledger?"

I leaned back in the booth, folded my arms. "You don't know anything about a ledger Packy kept, with a record of activities over decades, implicating every one of the six families and countless crooks and cops and politicos?"

He made an incredulous face. "No. Could Packy be dumb enough to do such a thing?"

"Dumb enough. Smart enough. Depends on how you look at it. He had control of gambling in the most profitable territory on the East Coast for years. Again—decades. And when he finally got out, he'd amassed a fortune and still had an insurance policy designed to protect him while he erected this palace to himself and his young wife."

Sonny cocked his head. "Mike... Mr. Hammer? I don't know anything about any of that. But I don't think he had much of an insurance policy if he got murdered anyway and somebody else wound up with this ledger you say he had. Look—I loved the man. He was a second father to me. I'd give anything to find out who shot him. Like to kill him with my bare hands."

"Thanks, but I'll take care of that."

One eyebrow rose. "Well, if you need any backup, you know where to come."

"I will keep that in mind, Sonny."

His face hardened. "You just let me know how I can help you find whoever did it."

I locked eyes with him. "You could start with any ideas you might have about who did this, if Packy *was* the target, not incidental. I don't care if it's anything but a gut feeling—you let me know."

His expression grew thoughtful. "Well, there was no love lost between Packy and Mel Hazard, I can tell you that. Maybe you already know that. I mean, some of it had to do with *you*, Mike."

"Me?"

He nodded once, firmly. "Packy held Hazard responsible for what happened to your secretary on that Civac robbery—Velma?"

"Velda."

"Packy was convinced Hazard was behind this string of armed robberies in the papers lately, and since Packy was *killed* in an armed robbery, it makes all the sense in the world to start with that frog-faced bastard."

"You know Hazard, Sonny?"

"No. That's the problem, that's the drawback holding me back in this thing. It's why you're better positioned to do something about Packy's killing than I am. I'm too new in town. Too wet behind the ears in this part of the world. Anyway, I only saw Hazard once. And that was plenty."

"When was this?"

He glanced at the seating below us. "A day before we opened. Hazard came in when we were just putting the finishing touches on this place, and the fat little bastard started shouting and screaming—he was hopping mad that Packy wouldn't sell him some property or other." He bobbed his head back at his flat-nosed bartender, who was still sorting bottles. "Pete and me grabbed the little toad and tossed his ass out. Bodily."

"Funny," I said. "I talked to Hazard about this and he didn't mention dropping around and getting the old heave-ho."

"Imagine that," Sonny said.

I slipped out of the booth and so did my host. He stuck his hand out. "Good hunting, Mike."

I shook it and said, "Keep your eyes open, my friend, including any you might have in the back of your head. Mel Hazard's got his own gaggle of gunmen. It's always dicey dealing with slimeballs like that frog prince."

The White songbird was doing a melancholy "That's All" as I took my leave. When I stepped out under the canopy, the sky issued a growly warning, and I again snugged my hat down and turned my trench coat collar up, hoping I could make it to the corner for a cab before the overcast sky could burst.

But the guy who slipped up behind me gave me no warning at all before shoving the nose of a pistol in my spine.

I glanced back at Mel Hazard's rockabilly bully boy, Billy, who said, "This time *you're* gonna eat it, Hammer."

Then a black Fairlane roared from nowhere and squealed up to a stop like it was picking up a dignitary and a rear door opened and my last thought, before that kid clouted me on the side of the head with the barrel of his rod and I dropped into black nothingness, was that I should have heeded the advice I gave Sonny Gray.

CHAPTER TEN

My eyes opened to blackness.

To a darkness that might have been death, only when you're dead your head isn't splitting with pain and your stomach isn't roiling with nausea and your ears aren't ringing like somebody stuck your head inside a kettle that got whammed and whammed and whammed with a big metal spoon.

No, I was alive. I might be blind but I was alive. My head might be whirling, but it was still functioning in some basic manner, the pain receptors working just fine. Well, not fine, because for a while I didn't know how I got here, wherever the hell *here* was. I couldn't have told you my name for a million bucks and a free pass to anywhere.

You're Mike Hammer, schmuck.

Okay. All right. So what was this? A coma? Was I buried alive? In the trunk of a car? What? *Where?*

Something like thunder roared above me. No. Not something like thunder—*thunder!* And that was rain, a lot it, unleashed from a sky I couldn't see, hitting a roof, a roof above me somewhere, *like a thousand Nip machine guns were firing down at me from high in trees, trees I could see in my whirling brain, palms trees with fronds like sharp green pointed blades.*

Then the image dissolved like a handful of salt flung in water and the machine-gunning became rain, a steady beat on a roof, while the thunder intermittently returned, rattling things in the room—*I was in a room!* Possibly a chamber, an enclosed space but not a small one.

You're lucky, I told myself. *A blow to the head like that can kill you.*

That's what happened—I'd had a blow to the head! Somebody had whapped me alongside the skull with a gun barrel, an automatic, no, not *somebody* but that kid, that blond almost Elvis punk with the slightly bucked teeth.

And this darkness was just darkness, not a coma, and sure as hell not death. I was alive, if you called this living, and I was somewhere indoors, not out in a storm rattling the roof but not the windows... why no windows? And that thunder, that rain, it was echoing. Where in the goddamn hell was I? A church?

My brain was working, not on all cylinders, but working at least, and I sent it signals indicating I wanted to get to my feet but I couldn't. I was constricted. Constrained. *Bound.* I was seated. A chair. A wooden chair. I was tied into it!

"*Bastards!*"

Someone yelled that.

Me! That was me yelling. So I wasn't gagged.

"He's awake," somebody out there said.

Out where?

"Give him a second," somebody else said. "Let him come around."

They sounded like kids. Or anyway young.

My breath came hard as I struggled and felt the legs of the chair rise a few inches and rock and then settle again as laughter came from my unseen audience. A few claps. Claps that rang like lazy gunshots.

From the way the arched backrest felt I could tell I was in a bentwood chair like you might find in a bistro. I was bound by what must be rope. Twice around the chest, with my ankles looped around the front chair legs. As best I could tell anyway. My hands were behind me, bound together at the wrists and secured to the open backrest. I shifted my tail and could tell the seat was cane. This was a well-made chair but it was probably old, because it made noise against my protesting movements, as if it was just as unhappy having me in it as I was to be tied into it.

But I wasn't going anywhere.

I willed my breath to slow, my body to relax itself; struggling like a fish out of water wouldn't improve my situation at all, and that laughter out there in the dark made me not want to give my captors the satisfaction of seeing me flounder. And the initial fogginess in my mind seemed to be lifting.

A bright light hit me.

The effect was like the old Third Degree in some hidden corner of a cop shop, but that wasn't it, not a lamp stuck in my face at all—it was a shaft of light angling from high out in the darkness that washed my features in a brightness blurring my vision into smudgy uselessness. I blinked, turned my head away, blinked some more, and the blurriness eased and I could see that the whole area where I sat was in a puddle of light.

I was in the spotlight.

Literally. A narrow beam emanated from a grid beyond and above me. And this was a stage, my chair resting on the wooden floor of it, with enough ambient lighting created to reveal the first few rows of what I could now confirm as a theater.

And I knew where I was.

I knew right where I was. This was the old Fleur-de-lis Theater in Greenwich Village, on Christopher Street, an art house where Velda used to drag me. I had slept through some of the most celebrated foreign films in the history of cinema out there in those seats. We'd had a deal, Velda and me. I would go along for the ride as long as she gave me a gentle elbow to wake me up when one of the European gals got naked.

Not a big house—seated five hundred maybe, a three-story cream-faced affair built in the '20s that had been shuttered for a year. I'd heard somebody had bought it to make an off-Broadway playhouse out of it.

I seemed to be performing a one-man show here right now, live and in person. Live for the moment, anyway. Roped into a chair in my t-shirt and trousers, a half-baked Brando.

I grinned at my audience. Two guys in the front row, right in the middle, leaving two seats between them. Both were young, barely past college age, though I doubted these were graduates of anything but reform school.

The one at left had a flattop with so much butch wax I could almost smell it from here. His face was round with bright button eyes, a pug nose and a thick-lipped mouth that hung open like he was hoping to trap flies. He wore a two-tone sport shirt—light green with a wide band of pink—and his trousers were darker green and baggy, with a big revolver stuck in the waistband.

The one at right was skinny and he had a dark brown crew cut and a horsey face and enough muscles on a scarecrow build to show off in a blue-and-white striped t-shirt with its little sleeves rolled up and a pack of Chesterfields stuffed in one. He had a gun in his waistband, too, a .22 Browning.

I had to crane my neck to see these pimply delinquents because I was off to one side of the stage. Didn't they know who was starring in this damn production? Least they could do was place me centerstage when holding me captive.

The rain continued but it had reduced to a steady tempo and the thunder was losing its interest. My vision wasn't so blurry now. My headache had receded into a tolerable nagging presence. The ringing in my ears was gone and faint approaching music of my own creation was starting up, the crazy flutes, the banging timpanis, the symphony of death I had directed so often....

They were kids all right, these two. And somewhere my friend Billy from Mel Hazard's Glass House was lurking, another youngster dying to never grow old. My breathing was regular now. My mission clear.

These students needed a lesson. Maybe a final one.

The flattop nodded to the crew cut and each rose and the first went left and the other went right and headed for the little stairs up onto the stage on either side. The crew cut got there first, because I was positioned stage right. He was putting his brass knuckles on. Flattop came over from the left, his footsteps echoing, taking his time, reaching in his pocket for something.

A roll of quarters.

He placed the roll of coins in his hand and squeezed a fist around it. His eyes were a gray-blue that would have looked great on a pretty girl and not a round-faced horror with a fly-catcher yap. He strolled over and slammed a fist into my belly but I'd clenched and it damn near bounced off. The crew cut rapped me in the side of the face and the brass knuckles bit and tore and my teeth rattled.

It was an annoyance.

Didn't they know I was busy?

This was not the first time Michael Hammer had been taken for a ride. Not the first time his hands had been tied behind his back. Not the first time he'd had to make use of the safety-razor blade kept in the open seam between the double layer of cloth in back under his belt.

My belt.

Them working me over made it tricky getting to that razor blade, however. Neither had a lot of power but they were young and had energy. And my wrists were tied together, which was awkward, and if a blow hit at the wrong time, if I didn't anticipate right, they might make me drop the razor blade before I even got it all the way out, or had it positioned in the fingers of my right hand well enough to start working on the ropes binding those wrists.

And the knots were strong and the hemp rope was thick and required a steady sawing motion, which could be hard to maintain when some punk was slamming a bony fist gripping a roll of quarters into your left temple. The worst of it was when the crew cut got ambitious and slammed the brass knuckles into my mouth. My teeth held but my lips went mushy, and the coppery taste of blood made me choke.

"*Cool it!*"

The voice came from the wings.

I glanced over there as Billy, who was in a James Dean jacket and a t-shirt and blue denims, strode out onto the stage, footsteps echoing with the rain a percussive accompaniment. He was clicking his switchblade open, closing it, clicking it open, closing it.

He took his time getting over to me, and his two buddies stepped aside to let him in between so the rightful leader could stand right in front of me, opening the knife, closing it, opening, closing.

"That's just a taste," Billy said, nodding once each to his two associates. "But you can avoid getting the full course, Hammer. All you have to do is tell me where it is."

"Look between a girl's legs," I said. "Hasn't your daddy told you the facts of life yet?"

He didn't find that amusing and gave me a backhand with more power than either of his boys could manage with the help of quarters and knucks. And the razor blade damn near slipped from my grasp!

No question about it—Billy was the most dangerous one here. Well. Second most dangerous...

He again opened the knife, and the spotlight beam winked off it; then he closed it, *open, wink, close, open, wink, close....*

Rain drummed in a slow, steady, almost lulling beat.

"Where is it, Hammer?"

"Be more specific."

"The book. The ledger."

"You tell me. I'm looking for it myself."

"I don't think so."

Another backhand, then the routine with the knife repeated, quicker now, *click, open, close, click, open, close, click, open, close.*

"When I get out of this chair," I told him, "I'm going to open you up with that thing. Your guts'll come tumbling out on this stage like blood sausage they haven't cut in links yet."

The flattop looked over at the crew cut, who looked back. If my life depended on it, I couldn't tell you who looked more pale.

Billy tried to look contemptuous but couldn't quite pull it off. He gave himself away twice: he backed up a step, and he stopped doing his open/close knife routine.

But then he said something terrible.

"Get her," he ordered the flattop. Then to the crew cut he said, "Get the spot."

They both nodded, with the round-faced mouth-breather heading to the wings at stage left and the tall skinny greaser going down the stairs at stage right into the house and disappearing into the darkness.

Seconds went by torturously and then another spotlight from that grid illuminated an area at my left, still with most of centerstage dark between the two pools of light.

And into that second pool of light, the flattop dragged someone tied into another bentwood chair. The human cargo was Victoria Valance and the rear chair legs as they dragged it across the stage screamed, almost as if she were on vocals. But she didn't look conscious, so it wasn't her.

And when she was positioned in the spotlight, facing front like me, her head hung.

She was stark naked!

That beautiful body was defiled by bruises and welts and cigarette burns and her face was a puffy welter of contusions and smears of already caked blood. The hemp ropes cut her flesh, unrelenting in their tightness, the globes of her breasts and the long lovely legs spared none of the violent indignities.

My yell boomed through the theater, blotting out the rain and thunder. "*Vickie!*"

The flattop patted her on the shoulder and she stirred a little. His open mouth in the round face made an amused O and a chortle fell out like food from the mouth of a baby who didn't know how to chew yet; then he walked over to where I sat, attended by Billy and the skinny lighting man, who had returned dutifully to the stage.

My second yell—"*Vick—eee!*"—broke in the middle, like a kid whose voice was changing. Like Henry Aldrich calling for Mother. Which made these three kids laugh.

Billy pawed the air dismissively. "Ah, she'll be fine. She'll heal up like a champ... if we don't have to put her lights out, that is. You wouldn't like that, would you, Hammer? They filled me in about you. They say you got a real taste for dames. Long, leggy ones with them Jane Russell kazongas."

"Let her go," I said. "Give her back her clothes and let her go. Do that, and I'll let you live. All three of you. I'm feeling generous today."

He leaned in so close our noses almost touched. I could barely hear him *over the pounding drums and screeching horns and howling flutes screaming their kill-crazy symphony in my brain.*

But this is what he said: "Mr. Hazard wants to know where the ledger is."

I ignored that, swung my face toward her. "Vickie, I will get you out of this."

She could barely raise her head, but she did. She looked at me through half-lidded eyes and her voice was a pitiful thing. "Mike… Mike… it hurts…"

"Tommy," Billy said.

The flattop—whose name apparently was Tommy—nodded and returned to the wings, stage left. He came back with an old-fashioned brass blow torch and he was grinning like a kid with his first popsicle. He worked the little wheel and the blue-orange flame leapt to life with a whisper of harsh death.

Tommy, eyes bright, approached Vickie, who recoiled and yelled, "Mike! *Please!*"

The blow torch sang its throaty song.

"That," Billy said, "is what she'll get. It's called irony. They filled me in on that, too. She's a torch singer and that's a torch—get it?"

"Someone will," I said. "Tell that slimeball to turn that thing off."

"Sure, Hammer. We're not monsters…. Tommy! That's enough… for now."

Tommy turned the wheel and the flame went away. He carted the thing back to the wings and returned empty-handed, rubbing his hands together like he'd just finished a big satisfying meal. Vickie's breathing grew more regular, but her eyes remained full of terror.

"You tell Hazard," I said, "I'll give him the ledger when I know the woman is safe. Not till then. If you're going to kill us both, go ahead. Do it right now. Cut out this schoolboy tearing the wings off flies routine."

Billy seemed surprised. "You'll do it? Hand it over?"

"I will. I don't want the damn thing." Didn't have the damn thing, but that wasn't what Billy or Hazard wanted to hear. "Mel can have it. No charge. Just give us our lives. I can see what I'm up against. I'm no fool, kid."

"Okay. Okay." He told his boys, "Get her out of here."

They nodded and hustled over, got behind her and dragged her out, one on either side grabbing the backrest, the screeching fading as they disappeared. Vickie's wide-eyed expression mingled hope and fear.

Billy gave me a sneering little smile. "But, uh… just one thing, Hammer."

"Yeah?"

He leaned in. The buck teeth really took the edge off his good looks. "Something personal. Between us. That's another thing they filled me in on. You hold grudges. You take things real, real personal."

"I do."

"So you'll dig this. Not 'dig' as in *like* it, but… you'll get it."

"Will I?"

His buddies were returning from the wings and he said to them, "Now," and they positioned themselves on either side of him.

Billy dug in his pocket and I thought he was going to come back with the switchblade and go into that shtick again. But no— he just got something out of his pocket, like maybe he'd dug out a coin for a parking meter outside.

He held the object between the thumb and middle finger of his right hand—a .45 cartridge.

"You're gonna eat this, Hammer. I mean, it's yours. I'm giving it back. And do I have to tell where it's been? How I… retrieved it?"

"Spare me."

"Open wide…"

I opened my mouth. Took in the cartridge, and if the taste was foul, I didn't notice, with all the caked coppery blood in there. I spit it in his face, put some real velocity into it, and it bounced off his nose. His eyes closed and a hand went to where the bullet hit, like he'd been stung by a bee.

His boys closed in on me and my hands came out from behind me, freed by my razor blade, and with precision timing any theatrical director would have lauded, I yanked the guns from their waistbands, the .38 revolver from Tommy's and the .22 auto from his pal's, and crossed my hands like a posing pirate and triggered bullets from the guns of each into the other. Tommy's mouth was already open wide but now so was his crew cut buddy's and then they both did backward stumbles and tumbled into the orchestra pit and landed with thuds, leaving slimy trails on the stage floor provided by the insides of their heads.

It made me laugh.

Billy was clawing for his switchblade as I threw myself backward onto the stage, hard, and the spindly chair broke into kindling and the loose ropes fell away like so much yarn and I leapt up at him and a right preceded a left in pummeling his face and in just those two blows his features became a bloody smear. He dropped the switchblade reflexively and I scooped it up and it opened with a click and sank into his belly with barely a sound at all.

I pushed him down onto his back and he was staring up and trying to say something but he couldn't even summon a scream, or maybe he did and I couldn't hear it over the crazy music in my brain as I cut through his t-shirt and set his guts free. I got up and he curled into a fetal position and was looking down at the red slimy things as they crawled out of him as if escaping when he died.

I ran to the wings.

No Vickie, but the stage door opened onto the alley, where they could have shoved her into a waiting car. The rain had turned the alley glossy but the thunder was a half-hearted distant thing now, the downpour replaced with the kind of steady rain sleepy afternoons are made for.

My shirt, tie, suitcoat, trench coat and hat were in an untidy pile in the wings, and I reclaimed them. In a dressing room backstage I found a working sink and cleaned the gore and blood off of me. I would rub any fingerprints off weapons before I went.

But right now, I could only look at myself in the mirror and say, "They've snatched another one out from under you, Hammer. Goddamnit! You've lost *another* one...."

CHAPTER ELEVEN

When I hopped a cab on Christopher Street, the rain was still coming down steady. I gave Velda's address, not mine, wanting to see how Hazard's boys had got in to grab Vickie. The overcast afternoon's fake night was the real thing now, the wet street and sidewalks reflecting the garish lights of the city like shiny black mirrors.

The cabbie didn't comment on my physical condition, the puffiness of eyes and lips, much less my rumpled wardrobe. So I'd taken a beating. He'd picked me up in Greenwich Village. Probably I'd been mugged. Maybe I insulted the wrong party. This was New York. What else was new?

At Velda's, no evidence of a break-in awaited. Not even the scratchy signs of somebody working with lock picks. I went down and checked with the landlady and Mrs. Murphy hadn't seen anything unusual. That could mean Vickie had let her captors in, suggesting someone was along who she knew and trusted before they snagged her.

Back upstairs, my first move was to call Pat.

"Am I out of favors?" I asked.

"Since about two years ago." Good will was not dripping off the line. "What do you have in mind?"

My Zippo fired up the Lucky waiting in my poor puffy lips. "You trust anybody in Vice?"

"I know a guy or two. Why?"

"I want you to order up a raid on the Glass House. On 52nd Street?"

"I know it and I know where it is and I know who runs it. That human toad Mel Hazard."

"That's a nasty thing to say about toads. Mel baby runs a backroom casino, wide open, so he's protected."

"This is a news flash how?"

I let smoke drift out like a ghost looking for a house to haunt. "You just need to be careful who knows about the raid. I don't want Hazard warned. If he's tipped, this does me no good."

"How does it do you good if he isn't?"

Carefully, I said, "I think he snatched Victoria Valance. He may be holding her somewhere at the Glass House."

A long pause. "You seem to be making a habit out of misplacing the women in your life, Mike. If it's a kidnapping, I need to call the FBI. That's a federal crime. Maybe you read about the Lindbergh baby in the newspapers when you were a lad."

If I shared the real circumstances with him, I'd be cooked. So I just said, "Vickie isn't even a missing person yet. Hasn't been twenty-four hours. Too early to call the PD in officially, let alone the feds."

"So what is this, then—a hunch?"

"It's a request from one old friend to another. I'll stay away, but I want you to go along. Tell whoever your honest pal in Vice is that you think Hazard is a suspect in the Paragon slaying and you want him rousted."

"Haul him in, you mean."

"No!"

"No? What the hell, Mike…."

I sighed smoke. "Raid him. Chase the customers out. The locals, whether they're posh or street, won't think twice about it. The tourists will have a story to tell when they get back to Peoria. Round up all the employees and get 'em out of there. If your friend in Vice finds Victoria and frees her, *then* have him arrest Mel's froggy ass. If she's not there, leave Mr. Hazard behind with a warning."

His grunt was kind of a laugh. "So you can come in after the public servants have departed, right? Why, so you can beat Hazard to a pulp? Or rig one of your famous self-defense pleas?"

"Pat, I need you to do this. I think Vickie is in real danger. Neither one of us wants another Velda situation."

"…Goddamn you, Mike."

"Is that a yes?"

"It's a yes." A sigh. "It'll take a couple hours to put this together."

"Works for me."

"Well, that's all that counts, right?"

And he hung up.

Nonetheless, I smiled at the receiver in my hand and said, "Thanks, buddy," and cradled it.

I started with a hot shower. A few places on my face could use Band-aids, which made me look like nothing more than the victim of a careless shave, if you factored out the puffy eyes and lips. I gobbled some aspirin and found Velda's ice pack and filled it with cubes from the freezer and wrapped the thing in a washcloth. Then I sat in Velda's reading chair and leaned back with the coolness on my face.

A half hour of that seemed to help. I still looked like a boxer who lost the big match, but might not scare any small children now, the more resilient ones anyway. I'd brought some spare clothes over when I started babysitting Vickie and it felt good getting into fresh things. The sport coat had been tailored for the .45, so I went to the dresser drawer in the bedroom to retrieve the weapon.

The shoulder sling was there but not the gun.

I didn't know what to make of that. The only scenario that made sense was a knock at the door prompting Vickie to bring along my .45 when she answered it, only to be overcome before she could use it.

Which meant somebody out there had my rod and I didn't like that at all. It was like finding out my right hand with all its fingers had been mislaid.

In the bottom drawer of that dresser in a small wooden box I found one of Velda's handguns, a Browning FN Model 1910, and a box of .32 cartridges. It would have to do for now. I loaded the weapon—its magazine took seven rounds—and filled a spare magazine; but the piece was way too small for the shoulder sling, which I left behind, tucking the .32 and spare clip in my right-hand sport jacket pocket.

I skipped a cab this time and instead paid the ransom on the maroon Ford from the garage and headed over to 52nd Street— mostly in case it turned out I'd need a trunk to stow a corpse in for disposal. Better safe than sorry.

When I positioned myself in a booth in the twenty-four-hour diner across the way, a couple of black-and-whites, their rooftop lights smearing the night red, were out front of the Glass House, bookending a paddy wagon receiving a put-upon parade of employees. I recognized the bartender, Joe, among those being collected by the boys in blue. The rain was just a drizzle now and two plainclothes cops in raincoats and brim-down hats were supervising. One I didn't know.

The other was Pat.

The load-in of Glass House dealers, croupiers, cashiers, waitresses, strippers, musicians, and bouncers was complete in another ten minutes or so. The plainclothes cop I didn't recognize gave Pat a little salute and wandered off. I left the booth, went out front and stuck two fingers in my yap and whistled.

Pat heard and in another minute we were back in my booth at a window covered in the tears of the petering out rainstorm.

"No sign of Victoria Valance," he said. He was looking at me like Daddy whose teenage son had borrowed the car without asking. "We gave it a thorough look, back room included, Hazard's office too."

"How did Mel take it?"

"About like any club owner paying protection who got rousted unaware. But I don't think he made anything particularly suspicious out of it."

"Including that you hauled in everybody but him?"

"He was told to come to Centre Street tomorrow afternoon for questioning. But not about what. He said he'd be there with bells on."

"And his attorney."

Pat slid out of the booth. "I'll let you get to it. I don't know how long Mel is likely to hang around with his place closed up on him for the night."

I got out as well, leaving a few dollars for a coffee and hamburger I'd consumed while waiting. "Thanks, pal."

"You're not going to kill anybody tonight, are you, Mike?"

"If I do, you'll be the first to know." I shrugged. "One of the first."

He shook his head, sighed again, and went out into a night too cold and rainy for any respectable summer to brag about.

As I'd requested, the Glass House door had been left unlocked, though when I stepped into that outer bar area with the booths and the little stage faced by chairs the lights were off, only the beer signs on here and there, their mostly red letters throwing a faint demonic cast. I slipped my hand in my suitcoat pocket and came back with Velda's .32 Browning, then eased through the curtains between the stage and the booths that led to the casino.

That was a generous description—*casino*—as it was just a long narrow room with the personality of a mess hall, just a blank space with a painted cement floor and gambling tables positioned under florescent lights fixtures, also shut off. The only light in here right now came from slot machines along the left and right walls, lined up like gangsters at the St. Valentine's Day massacre, and more beer signs at a secondary, smaller bar way down on the other end. Red letters glowed EXIT above a hallway that included SETTERS and POINTERS doors (always an indication of a class joint) and PRIVATE—EMPLOYEES ONLY.

An edge of light ran along the latter door.

I returned the .32 to my sport coat pocket and went in, not bothering to knock.

Mel Hazard had put considerably more money into his private office than the bar/"cabaret" in front and the casino in back. The oak-paneled chamber was home to modern wood-and-metal furniture, lime-green cushioned chairs, hunter-green wall-to-wall carpet, and seafoam-shaded lamps. Along one wall, a suspiciously comfortable-looking, overstuffed and not at all modern-looking brown-leather couch lurked beneath a big framed color photo of a Vegas showgirl. Somehow, I just knew unspeakable things had occurred there.

Me invading his private bog put an unpleasantly surprised expression on that jowly pan, his eyes bugging out even more than usual. No green wardrobe tonight, though. He perched behind his wood-topped metal desk, his suit a conservative dark brown, shirt tan, tie taupe, with only an emerald stickpin to maintain the One Froggy Night theme he'd apparently decided he might as well embrace.

"What did you do, Hammer?" came his amused raspy welcome. "Walk into a door?"

He was hanging up his phone, which was dark green of course. I'd interrupted a call, probably to his bent cop on the Vice Squad. The only other thing he seemed to be working on was a bottle of Jack Daniels, a half tumbler of which was nearby.

I took the orange-cushioned chair opposite him. Sat casually. Made my puffy lips form an even worse smile than usual.

I said, "Disappointed in you, Mel. Sending around those refugees from an Alan Freed concert to play tough with me."

Somehow those bulgy eyes managed to narrow and the big head on no neck swiveled. "What the hell are you talking about?"

I jerked a thumb toward the front. "Billy boy. The one I fed the bullet to. This time I fed him his switchblade. Skipped the gullet stage and went right for the stomach."

The squat shape shifted in its chair. "He doesn't work for me anymore, Hammer."

"He doesn't work for anybody anymore, Mel. Neither do his buddies. They're like those brats who hang around with Peter Pan. Little boys who'll never grow up."

He swallowed thickly, raised his hands shoulder-level, palms out, like I was already holding a gun on him. "I don't know any buddies of Billy's, and I fired the little shit after he embarrassed himself with you out front the other day. If he gave you any trouble..." Hazard shrugged. "...he must've been trying to get back at you. You know, for cutting him down to size and losing him his job."

"Getting back at me was not what he was after. You *know* what he was after, Mel."

The liver-spotted puss pretended to be bored. "I don't know, Hammer. No idea."

"Come on, Mel. Don't kid a kidder. They were after that ledger. The one you think I have."

His smile was as insincere as it was wide. "Mike, Mike, Mike. Why would I hire you to find something I think you already have?"

He had a point, but it only irritated me. "I'm asking the questions, Mel."

He slammed a fist on his desk and the phone jumped. So did the Jack Daniels bottle. "Well, you're asking the wrong ones! Whoever killed *Packy* got the ledger. And we both know that wasn't you. And if it was *me,* why would I send Billy around to shake the thing out of you?"

I was tired of dancing with this swamp dweller.

I slammed a fist on the desk and the phone jumped again, the bottle too, but this time so did Hazard. "*Where* is *she, Mel?*"

His tongue flicked out and wet his lips and went back in. "Where is who?"

I leaned across the desk and with my left hand yanked him close by his taupe tie and with my right gave him a backhand. Then I gave him another.

"Where *is* she, Mel?"

He was shivering now, fear running down from his slicked-back thinning black hair in tiny glittering beads. Blood trickled out a corner of his mouth and I was almost surprised it wasn't green. Then I reached across and shook him by the lapels.

"Do you want to get on my bad side, Mel?"

"Where is… who…? *Who…?*"

"Don't play owl with me, you slimy bullfrog! *Victoria Valance!* You took her!"

"But I didn't!"

"No, your little snot-nosed creeps did. They snatched her and now the only way you see tomorrow is to give her back tonight!"

I gave him a grapefruit-in-the-puss Cagney shove and he flopped back in his chair, which bounced him back and forth a few times without any further help from me.

He was shaking. He was crying. And begging.

"I don't have her, Hammer! I didn't take her! Don't know a goddamn thing about it! You *gotta* believe me.... You just... just settle down and I'll tell you everything I know. *Everything!*"

Shit.

I believed him. I could barely hear him over the crazy music blaring in my skull, but I did believe him. And whatever he knew that I didn't, I needed.

"Don't you want to know who's masterminding these robberies?" he sputtered.

I was breathing hard. But I sat down. I slipped my hand in the sport jacket pocket and around the grip of Velda's gun.

"Tell me," I said.

"For one thing, it's not me. Think about it. It's somebody new, nobody in any of the families, a real outsider making a name for himself, carving out a place."

"What name is he carving, Mel?"

"I'll get to it. Don't get excited, Mike... don't lose your cool."

"I never lose my cool," I said.

"Right. Yeah. You just need to know I am not your, what, *kingpin* in this thing. I *am* involved.... Sit back down! Settle! I will tell you what you want to know if you just agree to leave me out of it. You don't tell the cops, and you just make this guy go away."

"And you take over?"

"No! With how things have got out of hand, if it gets back to the families I was part of this, I am out of the club business. Maybe out of the breathing business."

"What was your role in this robbery spree?"

A fat hand waved the question away before he answered it. "A conduit for the kind of people this ambitious newcomer needed in our part of the world. A kind of… talent scout. I just… helped make things happen."

My smile hurt my face. My hands wanted his throat. "Things like… getting Velda killed?"

He got to his feet and gestured to himself. "No! God, no. I was no part of any of that. And this is where you've had it *wrong* from the start, Mike. That Civac kidnap was *not* the work of one of our crews. Whoever it was wanted to make it *look* like a heist, because the papers had been full of these jewel robberies. But word is it was really a kidnapping all along. You've been going down a blind alley, Mike."

Could he be right?

"Who's your boss, Mel?"

"You'll protect me?"

"Guaranteed."

The shot went right over me where I sat and into Mel Hazard's forehead where he stood; his eyes made big circles, his mouth a much bigger one, but the important circle was small—with scorched edging and a teardrop of blood dripping out of its circumference.

So much for guaranteeing my work.

Mel flopped forward across the desk, making the phone and whiskey bottle jump one last time.

A big tan good-looking guy in a raincoat hanging open over an Aloha shirt stood in the doorway. He had a gun in his fist, a familiar gun—my .45!

In one second so many thoughts can come together—like Packy Paragon knowing surrogate son Sonny Gray from L.A. was the robbery-crew kingpin, but also that Velda's kidnapping was unrelated. Leading to Packy tipping me off to the Greenway heist to shut me down while giving me closure. Then Sonny killing Packy and stealing the ledger. And Sonny at the Paragon bar today alerting his Dead End Kids he'd stall me till they could pick me up for my theatrical debut at the Fleur-de-lis. Assorted thoughts that in an instant became one realization.

Had Sonny really been worth a damn he would have used that second to squeeze the trigger on my .45, and not give me time to grab the Jack Daniels bottle by its neck and hurl it at him. It landed hard enough across his forehead to shatter the glass and he fell backward with his pretty boy tanned features covered in dripping booze and blood, the alcohol meeting plentiful cuts on his face and making him scream in stinging pain.

But even as he lost his balance, falling backward, he got off a wild shot that hit the desk the late Mel Hazard was sprawled over, the dead frog making one last pitiful hop. I was already barreling at Sonny and he had the presence of mind at least to scramble to his feet and go scurrying back out into the narrow corridor.

I was on his heels, the .32 out of my pocket and gripped tight, but now we were both in a big room where the lighting was all but dark, with only slot machines and beer signs to delineate the shapes of gaming tables—roulette, craps, blackjack—and he ducked down an aisle where, by the time I came around the corner, he was out of sight.

Staying low, I prowled, stopping at crossing aisles to listen for movement. I heard nothing but a refrigeration unit humming behind the bar and the faint ticks of various clocks. Along the walls with those illuminated slots, or down at the far end where the bar and its beer signs were, spotting my prey would've been no sweat at all. Here—in the midst of the sizeable dark room with these tables of varied size and shape, draped in black—what little light there was threw shadows, the hunting dismal.

My left hand brought out the Zippo and I thumbed it to flame.

Held it up like I was signaling, not searching.

And there he was!

Three tables down this very aisle. He'd got cute, climbing up on top of one and lying flat, waiting for me to come by so he could jump me. The flame caught his attention, though, and he looked back with the startled eyes of a stalked deer and rolled off the table down into the aisle.

I could have shot him with the .22 and *goddamn* did I want to. But I had questions that still needed answering, questions Mel Hazard couldn't have answered even if he hadn't been dead, starting with: where was Victoria Valance being held?

And if Vickie was dead, Sonny would die begging for a mercy I had no intention of granting.

By now my night vision had kicked in, which—combined with the nearby bar light—enabled pursuit, and I was at a dead run when I took him down in a tackle, hard, knocking the air out of him in a noisy gush. But in the process, I lost my .22—I heard the gun bounce away. Still, I had him, I was on top of him— only he had muscle and size and wriggled and writhed and turned under me and then we were wrestling, and grappling for my .45 in his hand. I swung his gun-in-hand up and the rod's nose was under his chin when I turned his wrist under the gun-in-hand and reflexively his finger pressed the trigger and the bullet came out the top of his head and killed a Miller High Life sign over the bar.

Killed Sonny Gray, too, the ragged hole in his skull spraying bone, brains and blood onto the cement floor. I was close enough to the remaining beer signs to see that clearly—not that I needed any convincing. His face was a welter of glass cuts, with some shards still stuck here and there in the flesh, and blood drizzled down his face like ghastly cherry topping.

I got to my feet, breathing hard. Relieved to be alive, frustrated he was dead. Who was going to answer my damn questions?

That was when somebody punched me in the back.

I dropped to my knees, as if in prayer, knowing I'd been shot. Only a few seconds were left to me before I passed out, but I would have sworn I smelled Chanel No. 5.

Was that a dying sense memory of Velda before I slipped into eternal black?

CHAPTER TWELVE

The windows in the barely lighted room were shaking, rattling, keeping the storm at bay but having to work at it. The angle of the rain made the plump drops pelt the panes, exploding as they hit into small globules of moisture that dissolved into jagged streaks running down the glass in a race to nowhere, illuminated by flashes of lightning that accompanied thunder roaring from the sky like the howl of a mammoth unrestrained jungle beast.

Despite a sluggish thickness in my skull, I knew almost at once that I was in a hospital room, a bed, with an IV bottle my only company and the illumination at a bare minimum—just enough for a patient to navigate to the bathroom and for nurses and any medic unlucky enough to be on night duty to attend their patient. The pain was dull, knocked back by whatever cocktail the hanging bottle was serving up. But mostly I felt like I was caught in a slow-motion sequence in a black-and-white film, a special effect in search of a story.

I had been in the hospital before and knew how to work the little call button. I did this and, exhausted from the effort, lay back and waited.

"You're awake," a female voice said.

A pleasant-looking redheaded nurse with as many freckles as Howdy Doody was leaning in, smiling over me.

"Yeah," I said. "I have a question."

"Certainly, Mr. Hammer."

"Will you marry me? You're the best-looking woman I've seen lately."

Her smile was tolerantly amused. "Well, at least in two weeks."

"Oh?"

She was wheeling away. "That's how long you've been out, Mr. Hammer. I'll get Dr. Meadows. He's on duty now and happens to be the attending physician when they checked you in. He'll be delighted to find you among the living again."

I glanced at the wet-streaked window. "Has it been raining for two weeks?"

She paused at the door. "Gracious, no. Just since about four o'clock this afternoon. A dilly of a downpour, though."

"Where am I, by the way?"

"Bellevue."

"The nutcase wing?"

"Certainly not! This is just a regular hospital floor."

"That's a relief."

Then she smiled, shook her head, said, "You're going to be a handful from now on, I can tell," and went out. Nice little shape on her. I decided to let the marriage offer stand.

The doctor was small and black-haired with a mustache and kind dark eyes, all in white of course but for his red-and-black tie. His name tag confirmed him as DR. MEADOWS. His smile seemed genuine.

"Welcome back, Mr. Hammer. You are a lucky man."

"Why, my ticket to the Irish sweepstakes come through?"

He shook his head, the smile settling in one cheek. "No. But the bullet went in and out. Didn't get near your spine and we patched the rest of you up the night you joined us."

"Why was I out so long?"

He adjusted the stethoscope around his neck. "You lost a lot of blood. You weren't found for a while. Sorry to interrupt your beauty rest, but I'm going to have a look at you now."

"Be my guest."

After he'd completed his examination, I asked him, "If I go back to sleep, doc, will I wake up again?"

His smile turned into a grin. "Good odds on that, Mr. Hammer. Much better than the Irish sweepstakes."

I woke up the next morning in time for an oatmeal breakfast and orange juice and to get my temperature taken orally by a good-looking blonde nurse whose sour expression didn't rate her a proposal. After a while, a little orderly who looked a little like Leo Gorcey came in on bedpan duty and I had a confidential chat with him; he was cooperative where a couple of requests I made were concerned. Then I had my first nap of the day.

When I woke again, at about ten a.m., Pat was sitting in a chair by the window, which looked like shimmery pebbled glass, thanks to the storm easing to a drizzle. The day out there remained dark, however, the lighting in my room low-key enough to create a perfect mood for a cop to glower at you. Pat's raincoat rode the back of the chair and his hat was in his lap, as were his hands. His legs were crossed.

"You must have a hell of a time," he said, "buying life insurance."

I shrugged, which took real effort. "Stopped trying a long time ago."

He scooted the chair closer and it screeched at the imposition. "Did you see who did it, Mike?"

"No."

His sigh started around his shoes. "Are we going straight to the lies or are you leveling for a change?"

I raised a palm as if swearing in at court. "No secrets, Pat. I'm not saying I won't play a card or two close to the vest, if it's called for. But no lies."

"Well, we may have a lead on who shot you." His voice had a touch of archness in it.

But I bit, anyway: "Oh? Who?"

"Bullet that took a nickel tour of your insides is a .32. Ballistics ties it to a Browning FN Model 1910 registered to a Miss Velda Sterling."

I frowned. "I was carrying that gun, Pat. But I dropped it at the scene. Somebody must've scooped it up and helped themselves to a crack at me. You found my .45 in Sonny Gray's mitt, right?"

Pat nodded. "Gun that killed him. Some of your fingerprints were on it too, by the way."

"No shit—it's my .45. His prints mostly—on the butt, right?"

My friend nodded slowly. The gray-blue eyes were unblinkingly suspicious. "You wouldn't want to tell me what happened when you went calling on Mel Hazard, I suppose? I mean, Hazard was also killed with a slug from your .45, but of course that's a trifling detail."

He was starting to piss me off. "I said I'd level with you, Pat, and I will."

So I gave him the works, starting with my getting grabbed at the Paragon and how Victoria Valance had been snatched and tortured, too, then dragged off God knew where. How I went to the apartment and made that call, "To you, Pat, remember?" Then how I discovered my .45 was missing, and had to take along Velda's .32 instead. And about dropping in on Mel Hazard and the gist of our conversation, which was interrupted by Sonny Gray with my rod in his fist, followed by the cat-and-mouse game in the darkened casino.

Everything.

By the time I wrapped it up, his expression had softened but his eyes were alert, even taking time to blink now and then.

"Your turn," I said.

He thought about that, drew in some breath, let it out, and was about to speak when the Bowery Boy orderly bounded in, saw somebody was with me, got wide-eyed and started to scurry back out.

"Kid!" I said. "It's fine. He's a friend."

The orderly swallowed, then smiled nervously at my guest and came over to my bedside, conveying the brown paper bag of goodies I'd requested.

"Hey Pat, I don't have any dough in my hospital gown. Give this kid a sawbuck, would you? Second thought, if you got it, make that a double sawbuck."

The captain of Homicide made a face, but he was already reaching for his wallet. The orderly went over, nodded and smiled nervously again, and took the twenty-dollar bill with a nod of thanks.

From the paper bag I withdrew a pint of Seagram's Seven, a Lucky Strikes carton, and a book of matches. All of this I stowed in the drawer of my bedside stand—after I filled my water glass with whiskey, that is, and had a few satisfying sips.

The orderly said, "Smoking's fine, of course, but be careful with the booze. Somebody'll conference skate it."

The kid even talked like Leo Gorcey.

Then he was gone and Pat said, "So much for you being off the sauce."

"When somebody shoots you in the back, you look at the world different. I'd offer you a snort but you're on duty and I got a limited supply. Where were we? Oh. It was your turn."

Pat sat back and folded his arms, cocked his head. "All I knew about Victoria Valance was that you said you thought she'd been kidnapped. I caught up with her at the Riverside apartment the morning after you were found shot at the Glass House. Her story tallies with yours— that she'd been kidnapped by those three overgrown delinquents… who you killed at that theater, by the way, and self-defense or not you are going to face charges for walking away from—"

"Let's not get picky, Pat."

He growled to himself, then: "Anyway, somebody—the Valance dame doesn't know who—dumped her outside the Paragon. She wasn't badly hurt but she suffered some bruising and was pretty shaken up apparently, because her personal physician was called and he got her back to her apartment and in bed, where she stayed for several days. My understanding is she tried to come and see you, but your visitors have been restricted to family and you don't have any living relations that I know of."

"They made an exception for you, I see."

He shook his head. "Not till you came around out of your coma, they didn't."

"I wouldn't have been much of a conversationalist before then, anyway."

"You aren't now. Anyway, I talked to the woman. She's worried about you, but Sonny Gray dying put that club of hers in turmoil. Press landed all over it, and she's stepping up to do something about the bad publicity. Or maybe take advantage of it."

"Stepping up how?"

He flipped a hand. "She's opening at the Paragon in a couple of days. Wants to show the world none of this has gotten her down, I guess."

"Maybe I'll take in opening night."

"Not hardly." He smirked at me. "I talked to your doctor. He says it'll be a couple of weeks anyway before you're out of here. And you won't be fully recovered for maybe a year."

I grinned at him. "Don't kid yourself, Pat. I know more about gunshot wounds than anybody on the damn Bellevue staff."

"About *causing* them. Not treating them. You better take this time to finally get your damn head on straight. Relax. Heal up." He got to his feet, slipped on his raincoat. Snugged on his hat. "I'll let you get to it."

He was at the door, a hand on the knob, when I called quietly out to him. "Pat..."

"Yeah?"

"Anything on the Velda front?"

He sighed. Shook his head glumly. "I think you need to accept it, Mike. I think we both do. She's gone."

I refilled my water glass with Seagram's. "Get another water glass out of the john, buddy. Join me in a toast to her."

He took a few steps back into the room, but that was all. His expression was grave. "No, Mike. You need to lay off that stuff."

"What Mel Hazard told me is true, ol' chum. I screwed the pooch on this one. Froggie the Gremlin was right—this is a blind goddamn alley I been running down. Looks like the Civac robbery was staged by somebody taking advantage of that rash of jewelry heists as a front for something else. The press bought it, you cops bought it, hell... *I* bought it."

A frown clenched his forehead. "It was about kidnapping Velda all along?"

"Her and maybe Civac. They snipped the old dame's fingers and dropped her in the drink because they didn't need her, and it made their story play. Jewels and murder, good headline material, and something for you cops to chew on... but it must have been about something else."

I threw the whiskey down and refilled the glass.

At the door again, with it open and ready for his exit, Pat said, "You keep that up, Mike, and you'll wind up in the gutter."

I shrugged. Drank.

"You'll know where to find me," I said.

CHAPTER THIRTEEN

The grand reopening of the Paragon found Victoria Valance top-billed with Kitty White reduced to an opening act. Two torch singers on one program may have been redundant, but it didn't hurt the turnout—an array of Manhattan celebrities were on hand plus assorted Hollywood visitors. These famous faces were sprinkled like expensive seasoning around the cozy club with its red booths and white-linen-clothed tables, its fieldstone fireplace and open beams and modest stage with piano, standing microphone and fiery-curtain backdrop. In the entryway, the standee of the star faced outward now, Victoria's sultry sad expression and low-cut gown bidding you a reluctant welcome.

"We were lucky to get this booth," Velda said.

"I know people. I know what strings to pull."

"Know how to frighten them, you mean."

"Come on, Kitten. You know I'm a pussycat."

A waiter brought me the highball I'd ordered. It went down cold. It went down easy. It nuzzled the bottom of my belly, wonderfully warm, lingered a while, then made its stealthy way through me, spreading its glow.

"I thought you were quitting, Mike."

"Gimme a break, baby. A hardworking guy needs a little pick-me-up at the end of—"

"Shhhhh, Mike… the show is starting."

Kitty White opened with that Nat King Cole number and Velda hugged my arm and whispered, "Oh, she's good, Mike. She's really good."

The black songbird in a glittery white gown, borrowing Victoria's accompanist, ran through all the songs I'd heard her rehearse here not long ago. I had only stayed in that hospital room until the weekend came. They'd shifted me to pain pills, so I didn't even have to yank the IV out of the back of my hand before I found my clothes and discharged myself. People yelled at me, but I'd been yelled at before.

When the singer from L.A. left the stage, the lights in the smoky chamber stayed down and a palpable tension was in the air, with only the occasional clink of a cocktail glass to break the pregnant silence. The papers had told the story of a woman widowed by gunfire and then kidnapped by young hooligans—Vickie had decided to show the world what being a real trouper was all about.

A voice came over the sound system: "Ladies and gentlemen…"

Packy Paragon's voice!

"…Rendezvous Records Recording artist…"

Oh. A tape. Chilling, nonetheless.

"…*Victoria Valance!*"

When, finally, she glided out in a black gown with her chin high and her bare shoulders back, brushed by that golden waterfall, her magnificent breasts thrust forward like a dare, the songbird didn't even acknowledge the audience and their thunderous applause with a nod. She just stood there proudly, eyes hooded, and the piano intro led her into her signature song, her big hit, "My Old Flame."

"She's wonderful, Mike," Velda whispered.

The program was nearly the same as opening night—"The Man I Love," "Lover Man," "Don't Smoke in Bed," and when Vickie went into "Since I Fell For You," Velda whispered, "*Did* she fall for you, Mike? You certainly fell for her...."

I looked at Velda but of course she wasn't there. Had I imagined her presence? Was I high on morphine? Was she dead and doing a *Topper* routine on her old boss? Or did I just want her to be there? Whether I did or not, she was. Right there inside my brain. Right there inside my goddamn heart....

The headliner got called back for an encore. She rarely gave them—it was part of the melancholy persona she adopted for the stage. But tonight she capitulated, and delivered a haunting "One For My Baby (And One More For the Road)."

A drinking song. My kind of music.

The crowd begged for more. Marlene Dietrich started the standing ovation and Rocky Graziano got it going on the other side of the room. But it did no good. The sultry torch singer had given them all she was willing to.

Something about this night—though it was unspoken—made it a memorial service for Packy Paragon, one of those decent-seeming hoodlums who show-business types often loved. Perhaps it was because they were forced in their line of work to put up with so many unpleasant hoods, or maybe it was that even the classiest of them was a carnie at heart. After all, show business was made up of nothing but carnival people—Cary

Grant was a circus acrobat and so was Burt Lancaster. And nothing wrong with that.

But a respect and even love for Packy had dropped a post-show pall on the club and no revelry followed Victoria Valance's performance, no giddy laughter, merely a slow shuffling out the door of mourners in dinner jackets and gowns, a murmur of reminiscences following them, leaving the club empty well before midnight.

A waitress in red came to the booth where I sat with a last-call highball, having become the only customer left in the Paragon.

"Sir, we're closing up," the waitress said, apologetic. She was a pixie-cut, tawny-haired kid who looked like a college student. She probably was.

"Okay, honey," I said, but soon another waitress tried to block me, in her pleasant way, when I headed toward the backstage door.

"The exits are up front, sir," she said.

"Mrs. Paragon is expecting me," I said.

I wasn't challenged, maybe because I'd said "Mrs. Paragon" rather than "Miss Valance," or maybe I'm just intimidating to little girls. But soon I was slipping through the door with an unspecified glittery gold star on it.

The spacious dressing room I entered lived up to the description of it tossed my way weeks ago by Sonny Gray—a couch, several chairs, a light-bulb-rimmed make-up table, and a private bathroom, its door ajar, the shower making its percussive music, steam filling the little bathroom and fogging its mirror.

At the dressing table, the surrounding lights unlit, I idly examined the make-up lined up there—the cosmetics that made a woman like Victoria Valance seem so effortlessly beautiful...

foundations, rouges, lip colors, eyebrow and lip pencils, and even something to make her *feel* beautiful, Chanel No. 5 Eau De Cologne. I picked up the bottle and looked close at the label. The upper right corner had peeled back just a touch.

I glanced in some drawers and found nothing of interest except, in one, some theatrical make-up—spirit gum, jarred wax, stage blood. Then I wandered over to a 12" by 12" framed color photo, the almost bosom-baring shot used on Vickie's bestselling LP album cover, but without the lettering.

My God, she was a lovely woman.

The downpour in the shower stopped. I went over and sat on the couch opposite the make-up table and the framed picture on the wall beside it, the bathroom just to the left. I could hear her step from the shower, even make out the rustle of cloth against skin as she stood drying off. Then she came out toweling her hair, her somewhat damp body making the pink dressing gown cling—an echo of that comic moment when she interrupted Velda's landlady, Mrs. Murphy, and me.

"Hi, baby," I said.

Vickie looked up, frozen, two hands holding the loose towel to her head, and then smiled in surprise. "So I *did* spot you out there—I thought I was dreaming."

She came over and I stood and held her close for a few seconds, then she took a step back and those wide-set green eyes got even bigger, as if she still didn't quite believe them. "What are you doing out of the hospital? You were supposed to be in such serious condition they wouldn't let me in to visit you! I didn't even bother calling. Now, here you are, larger than life!"

"And twice as ugly."

She went quickly to her mirrored table, hit a switch and the bulbs glowed. Sitting on a plump round stool, toweling off her hair, looking at me in the glass, she said, "You don't mind me saying so, you don't look completely yourself. So skinny… pale. Are you sure you should even be out walking around?"

"Never felt better," I said, settling back on the couch. "And you never *sang* better. Wow. You are one crazy performer, kid."

"Thanks." Her smile was almost pixie-ish in the mirror. "Had 'em in the palm of my hands, didn't I?"

"Sure did. Never mind me being out of the hospital. What are you doing back on stage so soon?"

"Oh, the publicity has been at once terrible and terrific. They made me out to be some pitiful victim of those punks on the one hand, and an inconsolable widow on the other. Your pals Hy Gardner and Earl Wilson started asking, what is to become of the popular Paragon club? So I decided I'd show 'em."

"As in, 'the show must go on.'"

She grinned at me, abandoning the towel and allowing the golden hair, browned with moisture, to hang in tendrils as she started putting on her make-up, foundation first.

Looking at herself, she said, "Well, some people will think less of me and others will think more. But either way they'll be talking about Victoria Valance *and* the Paragon, and that's just how Packy would have wanted it."

"I, for one, am impressed."

"Thank you, Mike."

"Take that Central Park performance, for example."

"Central Park... what?" Now she frowned at me in the mirror, mirror... as she worked to make herself the fairest one of all.

"Your performance in the Park," I said. "Worthy of a Tony. Starting with maneuvering me to the Tavern on the Green—then, after a swell intimate dinner, you guide me to the very spot where your accomplices are waiting. At least one was tied to one of the armed robbery crews—the one I shot with his own gun. Was I always intended to interrupt the kidnapping or were you planning to slip loose to help convince me you were innocent of Packy's murder?"

She was using her eyebrow pencil now. "Oh, Mike. You can't be serious. You can't think that of me...."

"That's two faked kidnappings, baby, if you're keeping score. By the way, I saw the stage blood and such in your drawer—that was some fine stagecraft. You had Billy and his boys position you far enough away that I couldn't tell the cigarette burns and bruises and blood were make-believe. And you made sure they dragged you off before I could 'save' you."

She was applying mascara now with a little wand. "Are you listening to yourself? To how absurd this all sounds?"

"Then why don't you open that robe so I can see how your wounds are healing? My review of that little one-act play in Greenwich Village is that you and Sonny were in this together from the start. Between sets at the club on the murder night, Sonny picked you up and the two of you acted fast—a tight timetable, but you could, and did, make it. In the apartment you led Sonny to the study where Packy was unwittingly waiting for a bullet. You went to the safe, didn't you, doll? That's why Packy was looking in that direction when he died! With a killer pointing a gun at him, he turned away to look at you."

Her mouth was wide as she applied a deep red lipstick. "Why would I want my husband dead, the man who built a damn temple to me with the Paragon? Why in hell would I 'steal' anything from a safe in my own apartment?"

"I'm not sure whether you knew the combination or not. Maybe he kept it from you, and you got it out of him when his surrogate son held him at gunpoint. Doesn't matter. You wanted to get your hands on that ledger. I'm not positive why, beyond it being valuable as hell... but I think I know."

She was dabbing on rouge, a finishing touch. "Then tell me, why don't you, Mike? Tell me right now."

I took the .45 out from under my left arm in the suitcoat, slowly. No hurry at all.

I said, "My guess is that Packy really did want to pack it in. Essentially retire as far as the mob stuff went, and concentrate on the woman he loved. Her career. Her art. And you're an artist, all right—but versatile, and so very ambitious. You came up the hard way, bouncing from one syndicate slimeball to the next, climbing one rung of a nasty damn ladder after another. Lately you've done Vegas dates, and I think that's where you connected with Sonny. He made a good second-in-command—just smart enough to be useful, just dumb enough to control. *He* wasn't the kingpin behind the armed robbery crews, was he? *You* are. Queen Victoria. Packy guarded that ledger like his life depended on it, and of course it did. And now you have the most popular book in town. What are you going to do with it?"

She swung around on the stool and faced me, her make-up complete. But the sweet, loving mask was gone. What was revealed was still beautiful. Perfection. Surprisingly, the absence of pretense had not turned her ugly at all. Just strong and confident.

"I *have* the ledger," she said, matter of fact. "Your pal Pat Chambers is in it, by the way—or anyway how he got to be a captain at so very young and tender an age. You can have it, Mike, for the asking. You say I'm a queen? Well, you can rule at my side. Sonny was just another rung on the ladder. You make a worthy partner. You are the strong man I've been seeking."

"Not Packy?"

Her hands were on her gowned knees, her nipples poking at the pink fabric. "Packy! Not hardly! Maybe once upon a time... but he'd grown weak. He'd gone straight, or very nearly so— wanting to use the ledger only as leverage, not to gain power, not to build and earn and grow."

I gestured with my free hand. "This club. Your recording career. TV spots. Headlining in Vegas. Your dead husband's money. What *more* do you want, Vickie?"

Her eyes showed white all around and the redness of her mouth burned. "*I want it all!* I want to use that ledger to build my career all right, and have the sublime pleasure and triumph of a successful public persona... but *also* behind-the-scenes control of every pie the six families have their fingers in, and more! A woman has never *in history* wielded that kind of power in organized crime! Those robbery crews were just a start. And you can be part of it, Mike. You can be the strong man at my side. You may not believe me, but I do love you. You have proven yourself to me and I will tell you from the bottom of my grasping heart that I do *love* you!"

"Shooting me in the back is a funny way of showing it."

Her hand waved that off, erasing the notion. "No. It wasn't me. I don't know who did that... not Mel, he was dead, not Sonny, he was gone, but... one of these... the peripheral figures."

"No, honey. *You.*"

She flew to her feet. *"You don't know that!"*

"I do know. I caught the scent of Velda's Chanel from the bottle you stole from her apartment, you little thief—I gave it to her for her birthday and got a discount 'cause the label was frayed. I'm just glad when you stole my .45, you gave it to Sonny. You wound up having to shoot me with Velda's .32. Otherwise, I'd probably be as dead as everybody else who's come in contact with you."

"Don't be so sanctimonious. *You're* the real killer here!"

She wasn't wrong. But I had promised myself I would never drop the hammer on another woman. Still... you know what they say—promises are made to be broken.

Victoria Valance raised her hands, held them palms out. She was nervous now. She knew the guy with the scythe was knocking at her door. Probably that's why this was the moment she chose to slowly open the robe and let it slip caressingly down her gorgeous body to puddle at her feet.

This time her stark nakedness was unspoiled by stage blood and wax appliances. Her breasts rode full and high, her waist tapering, hips flaring, golden triangle pointing the way to paradise above those endless, smooth yet muscular legs. This was female beauty as pure as she was not.

And she said, "A peace offering."

"How do you spell it?"

The red mouth twisted into a smile. "Any way you like. I will give you the ledger. Right now. And you can tear out your policeman friend's pages. Destroy them. But if you kill me, Mike, or turn me over to your Captain Chambers, that ledger will come back to haunt you. You don't know where it is! And I *do*."

"I'm not falling for some sucker play, baby, where you lure me off to—"

"No! No, it's right here. Don't… don't do anything rash, Mike."

She turned slowly and that view was stunning, too, as she moved nakedly to the framed photo portrait of herself. She swung it open and revealed a wall safe. There had been a wall safe at the Greenway place, and another at the Riverside apartment. And now this. The final one.

This took a combination she knew, and as the round door swung open, I could see the thick ledger book resting at the bottom of the safe, but when she reached in, she sent her delicate fingers in deeper, over the book, and she came back fast, with a little handgun tight in her fist and glittering madness in her eyes and the clenched teeth of a rabid dog about to bite….

I was getting soft. A killer like this deserved the slow death of a bullet in the belly. And hadn't she shot me in the back, and left me to die? But I let her off easy.

When the .45 slug burst her lovely head into puzzle pieces, she probably only heard a fraction of the roar and experienced just a flash of terrible pain.

And I was glad.

When you love a woman, you don't like to see her suffer.

EPILOGUE

The message from their Moscow correspondent came into the New York Herald-Tribune *foreign desk and, decoded, was as follows:*

Beautiful black-haired female American agent recalled to active duty reputedly in hiding behind Iron Curtain. Said to have uncovered information that could impact Soviet espionage system.

Please advise.

The foreign desk editor told his underling, "Inform our correspondent we need more than a squib like this to take it any farther."

And the message was spiked as the busy newsroom pursued more important matters, such as a union dispute at the docks, a Hollywood star picked up for drunk driving, and the death of a recording artist, shot in self-defense by a private investigator investigating her husband's murder.

THE 75TH ANNIVERSARY
OF MIKE HAMMER

CO-AUTHOR'S NOTE

The resolution of the loose end hanging like a sword of Damocles over *Kill Me If You Can* results from it serving as a bridge between *Kiss Me, Deadly* (1952) and Mickey Spillane's subsequent Mike Hammer novel, *The Girl Hunters* (1962). The latter, which marked Mike Hammer's comeback, solves the riddle of Velda's absence and the mystery surrounding it.

The Girl Hunters is part of Volume Three of *The Mike Hammer Collection*, which includes *The Snake* (the next story chronologically) and *The Twisted Thing* (from Penguin Publishing Group). The novel is easily available in various other editions, and the 1964 film version, which Mickey starred in as Mike Hammer and co-scripted, is available on Blu-ray, DVD and various streaming services.

Complex 90 (Spillane/Collins, Titan Books, 2013) concludes the cycle of tales begun by *Kill Me If You Can* bearing on Velda's disappearance.

* * *

When *I, the Jury* emerged from the respectable publishing house of E.P. Dutton in 1947—a novel that would soon earn fame for being anything *but* respectable—it arrived in the literary world with a resounding thud.

And not even very resounding.

To the first round of critics, *I, the Jury* was just another hardboiled detective novel, its content perhaps more violent and overtly sexual than the rest of the field, but not worth working up a post-war lather over. Sales were respectable, too, but not enough to convince the powers-that-be at Dutton to accept a second Mike Hammer novel (*For Whom the Gods Would Destroy*) by the young author, who scurried back into writing comic books for Marvel and selling ties in Gimbels' basement.

Then in 1948 Signet published *I, the Jury* in paperback with a provocative cover depicting its famous last scene—Mike Hammer training a gun on a beautiful blonde who appeared to be undressing—and the rest (as they say) is history.

Almost overnight, Mike Hammer became the most famous fictional private eye of all, and one of the most famous fictional detectives, period. Simultaneously, Mickey Spillane became the most popular—and controversial—writer of the coming decade, his name synonymous with sex and violence, his background as a comic book writer a bloodless bludgeon used to batter the young writer by deeply offended critics. One such critic, at a garden party, once told Mickey how awful it was that seven Spillane novels were among the top ten bestsellers of all time. Mickey replied: "Aw, shut up or I'll write three more."

Indeed at that point (the early 1960s) Mickey had only written seven novels, six of them Mike Hammer mysteries. The bulk were published between 1950 and '52, and the titles remain famous to this day: *I, the Jury*; *My Gun is Quick*; *Vengeance is Mine!*; *One Lonely Night*; *The Big Kill*; and *Kiss Me, Deadly*. The lone non-Mike Hammer, *The Long Wait*, might well describe the near decade-long pause between Spillane novels. (*For Whom the Gods Would Destroy*, despite Dutton and Signet begging the writer to resubmit it, would not be published till 1966, when Spillane sent it in as *The Twisted Thing*, rather than miss a deadline for *The Big Bang*, the novel he was working on.)

Spillane stopping the flow of his Mike Hammer and other novels at the peak of his popularity would be akin to Stephen King taking a decade off after *The Stand*. The stoppage bewildered readers and frustrated publishers (Signet turned to the UK for what they thought would be a temporary replacement: James Bond, the British Mike Hammer). It's a question with multiple answers.

Spillane famously announced his conversion to the Jehovah's Witnesses and indicated he would no longer be writing the kind of blood-sex-and-thunder material that had made him rich and famous. The latter two things, however, provided another facet of the answer: he did not need the money, and was taking the opportunity of his new-found fame to have some fun.

He pursued various macho interests—stockcar driving, deep sea diving, undercover police work, movie stardom, even touring with Clyde Beatty's circus as a trampoline artist (and getting shot out of a cannon, something one does not see a celebrity do every day of the week). He would write up these activities in various men's adventure magazines—*Cavalier, Saga, True,* and *Male,* as well as the latter-day pulp *Manhunt*—for the blue-collar males who understandably identified with one of their own.

He also wrote fiction for those same magazines—novellas, mostly—perhaps in part by way of payback for publishers and editors who'd bought his comic-book scripts before and after he served in the Army Air Corps during World War Two. He identified with his fellow ex-GIs, and his fictional heroes—Mike Hammer very much included—were part of their ranks.

That Spillane wrote material for low-end magazines—when he could have been getting top dollar in major markets or certainly by writing more books—is something of a mystery in itself. The importance of loyalty to friends is definitely part of it—that aspect of Hammer's character is as key as his love for good women and his hatred for bad guys. But it also allowed Spillane to hone his craft further while flying under the radar. The men's adventure magazine stories were just as sexy and violent as anything he'd written in his notorious seven novels, which undermines the notion that his religious conversion kept him from writing what he'd become famous for.

If Mickey was not always a savvy businessman, he was ever the shrewd marketer, and he withheld the Hammer character from any of those stories published between 1953 and 1961. He knew when Mike Hammer returned, it needed to be a big deal.

During that long wait, there were Mike Hammer movies, a comic strip, a radio show and two seasons of the Darren McGavin television series, *Mickey Spillane's Mike Hammer* (1958–59). The novels continued to rack up millions of copies in sales, while Mickey consciously held back his "bread and butter boy" (as he called Hammer) from the book market for just the right moment.

After all, readers weren't even sure Hammer was still alive! In *Kiss Me, Deadly*, he'd been left gut-shot in a burning building, wondering if he had enough left in him to make it to the door. So when *The Girl Hunters* finally appeared in 1962, revealing Mike Hammer had been on a seven-year bender, blaming himself for the apparent death of his beloved secretary/partner Velda, the reading public returned in droves to the notorious PI.

Just two years later Mickey himself—never happy with Hollywood's take on Hammer—was on the big screen in his own adaptation of *The Girl Hunters*, where the opening titles boldly stated MICKEY SPILLANE IS MIKE HAMMER. (Mickey had starred as a Hammer-like version of himself in John Wayne's production *Ring of Fear* in 1954.) Great publicity was generated, and critics loved him as Hammer—and why not? Did Conan Doyle ever play Holmes, or Agatha Christie portray Miss Marple? And could they have done so as effectively?

But the timing was poor. Some of the funding had fallen through and plans to shoot the film in color were unrealized (although black-and-white was probably more *noir*-ishly suitable in the long run). Spillane ran into the competition he had unwittingly encouraged by his long lay-off: Ian Fleming was now selling millions of copies for Mickey's publisher, Signet, and James Bond was hitting the big screen in *Dr. No* in blazing color. Ironically, the British-shot film of *The Girl Hunters* wound up a year later in a double feature hitting the drive-in circuit riding the coattails of *Goldfinger*, whose "golden girl" Shirley Eaton had co-starred with Mickey.

Nonetheless, *The Girl Hunters* film was successful enough to lead to Mickey's eighteen-year run in amusing, well-crafted commercials for Miller Lite in which he wore a porkpie hat and trench coat and spoofed himself and Hammer, sharing the stage with the "Doll" —Lee Meredith of *The Producers* fame.

Once again, Spillane found himself involved in a profitable enterprise as "a beer salesman," with constant filming and touring compromising his writing time. After a decade or more away from the Witnesses—during which he wrote some of his most sexually explicit and typically violent novels (the non-Hammer *The Erection Set*, 1972, and *The Last Cop Out*, 1973)—he returned to the fold. Throughout the rest of his life, a push-pull between his church and his career meant that numerous Hammer novels were begun and set aside.

I know this because Mickey—in the last week of his life—asked me to take charge of his unfinished material and complete that material as I saw fit. We had become friends in the early '80s and had collaborated on numerous projects, including half a dozen anthologies, a *Mike Danger* comic book, and my biographical documentary, *Mike Hammer's Mickey Spillane* (1999).

Mickey had told his wife Jane there would be "a treasure hunt around here" after his passing, and that she was to give all of the material to me ("Max will know what to do"). Jane warned him: "You know, Mickey, Max is not a Jehovah's Witness. He's not going to hesitate about what he puts in there." And Mickey had given his blessing.

Since Mickey's death in 2006, I have completed thirteen Mike Hammer novels, including the very first Hammer, *Killing Town*, and sequels to *I, the Jury* (*Lady, Go Die!*) and *Kiss Me, Deadly* (*Kill Me, Darling*).

Mickey completed and published thirteen Mike Hammer novels during his lifetime. With this novel, *Kill Me If You Can*, the number of Mike Hammer novels has been doubled. This is significant because Hammer is one of the few famous fictional detectives whose published body of work spans so few novels. Mickey published no Hammer short stories or novellas, either, though that was a form he preferred to novels.

Rex Stout wrote thirty-three Nero Wolfe novels (and forty-one novellas and short stories). Erle Stanley Gardner's Perry Mason appears in eighty-two novels and four short stories. Agatha Christie's Hercule Poirot is seen in thirty-three novels and fifty-some short stories.

My mandate has been not to create new Mike Hammer novels, but to complete the ones Mickey either began or envisioned. Most of the novels that share our byline have substantial Spillane content—drafts of eighty to a hundred double-spaced typewritten pages for eight of them, shorter drafts but with notes and endings in two more, and another two developed from synopses Mickey produced. (I also developed, from less substantial Spillane fragments, the Hammer short stories collected in *A Long Time Dead: A Mike Hammer Casebook*.)

Kill Me If You Can I set aside knowing we would want something special for the 75th anniversary of Mike Hammer's first appearance. This story dates to around 1954 and was the first Hammer story Mickey wrote after *Kiss Me, Deadly*. He created three versions—two teleplays, one designed for a sixty-minute time slot and another for a half-hour time slot; and a radio version. None were produced.

A brief word about *Kill Me, Darling* (2015), which I developed from a substantial Spillane false start on *The Girl Hunters*. In *Kill Me, Darling*, Velda disappears and turns up in Florida. In *The Girl Hunters*, Velda disappears behind the Iron Curtain for those now-famous seven years. In completing both novels, I have developed a timeline and continuity that accommodates both. (No mention of Velda is made in any of Mickey's three versions of *Kill Me If You Can*, which he titled variously *The Night I Died* and *Tonight I Died*. That aspect of the novel is part of my contribution.)

Like many of the great mystery writers—Stout, Gardner and Christie among them—Mickey in his famous series played fast and loose with continuity. I have attempted to shore that up, as unlike the other greats mentioned he wrote Hammer in a manner that indicated passage of time—with Mike Hammer aging, if not the way the rest of us do, but indeed aged. When I complete a Hammer novel from Mickey's material, I do my best to keep in mind where Mike Hammer is in the loose continuity of the novels, and where Mickey's head was at when he wrote the material.

This sometimes frustrates readers, who wish I would only concentrate on the young, psychotic Mike Hammer. I enjoy charting the character's growth, and the twists and turns of that troubled psyche. But for those readers, I am offering up *Kill Me If You Can*, an early 1950s version of the character in his key decade.

As a part of the celebration of the anniversary of Mike Hammer's first appearance, five short stories developed by me from unpublished Spillane material are included here as a sort of bonus feature. Two of these are rare Mike Hammer stories, both of which have particular significance to the canon. Each is introduced, revealing its origin and specific aspects of what we might call the Hammer-verse.

Max Allan Collins
August 2021

THE BIG RUN

This story is based on a television play written for Suspense, *a well-known program of its day. "The Big Run" was scheduled to be presented in March of 1954, but apparently was not produced. Had it been, the presentation would have been a live one, as was common in the early days of TV. The cast included Spillane's friend Jack Stang, who had starred with Mickey in* Ring of Fear *that same year, and the screen's first Mike Hammer, Biff Elliot, as well as comedian Jonathan Winters portraying the plainclothes cop transporting a convicted killer.*

I saw them on the platform of the railroad station—two uniformed cops, a tall and a short. I watched from the recession of the doorway as a guy came around the corner and into the illuminated area of the cold, misty night only to get grabbed and patted down and made to display his driver's license. Then they let him step onto the waiting train.

Another guy came along, in work-clothes and cap, and he got the same procedure, even though he protested. "Hey! I'm with the railroad here! Platform man in the station."

"Okay, feller," one of the cops said. "Go on ahead."

The platform man frowned at them and straightened himself, and went off to take his position.

The tall cop said to the short one, "This town used to be nice and quiet."

The other cop said, "It ain't so noisy at the moment."

"With all the law they got running around here, how noisy can it get?"

"Toss that cigarette—here comes the captain."

From within the station came a broad-shouldered guy in plainclothes. He took a look around the platform. He didn't see me in my shadowed doorway.

"Anything?" the captain asked.

"No, sir. Everybody's checked out clean so far."

The captain glanced around again. "Well, he's here, all right."

The tall cop asked, "They find the car?"

The captain nodded. "In an alley. Not far from the bank. He must've got spooked or he'd have hit it. Half-empty box of .38 shells in the glove compartment. So he's probably loaded."

The other cop asked, "We still supposed to shoot on sight?"

"That's right. He only has one known kill in this country, but he racked up plenty overseas."

Of course, they gave me medals for those.

The captain was saying, "There are only two other guys in the whole damn country who're wanted more than him."

The short cop, suddenly cocky, said, "He won't make it out of town."

The captain gave his man a contemptuous look. "Really? He's smart, this one. Smarter than us, so far."

The tall cop said, "You don't really think that, d'you, Captain?"

His laugh lacked humor. "He's spent the last year slippin' out of one tight spot after another. What I don't get is why he hasn't taken all his money and run. Really run south of the border... *way* south."

The short cop said, "Then maybe he isn't so smart."

"All I know is..." The rest of his words had a musing quality. "...he'd have made a hell of a cop."

The captain headed into the station.

I pulled the trench coat collars up and my fedora down, then I waited till the two cops were looking elsewhere and stepped out onto the platform, heading toward that waiting train, its lighted windows throwing distorted yellow squares onto the platform.

I had damn near walked right by them, to where I could step up onto the train, when the tall one called out: "Hey you! Buddy!"

I went over to them, in no hurry. They didn't look stupid. But they didn't look smart. I got out my wallet and flipped it open and showed them the badge.

"New York," I said. "Things popping yet?"

"Oh," the short one said. "City cop.... No, not a thing."

I checked my watch. Yawned. "Well... you guys hold down the fort. I go off duty when the train pulls out."

"Tell me something," the tall cop asked. "Do you big city boys get expense accounts and everything?"

I gave him half a smirk. "Yeah—three whole bucks a day for meals."

"Well, you'll be eating better soon. This'll be over 'fore you know it. He won't get away. Bus station's covered, our little airport, too."

"Roadblocks," the short cop said, grinning. "They never learn."

"No," I said. "They never do, do they? They never get away. They run… and run. Till one day the game stops being fun and they don't feel like running anymore. Because they're alone. All alone. Dirty and wanted by nobody but the law and no damn good to anyone at all. Imagine it—being no good to anybody. Just something to hunt down."

The short cop laughed. "Are all you city dicks philosophers?"

I grinned at him. "We're big thinkers, to a man. You boys stay awake. You never know what a guy like this will pull next."

I walked toward the train and, as I went, had a look in the station windows. Good to know how many more in blue and/or plainclothes might be waiting.

Then suddenly it happens.

The thing that could never happen.

She's right there, just a few feet and a window away, and cold chills are crawling across your back. She's with a big heavyset dick who is talking to the stationmaster behind his cage. You knew her at once, though a dozen years had passed, since before you went off to do Uncle Sugar's bidding—the girl you left behind who was gone when you got back. There she stands, beyond all logic and reason, and you feel sick with the knowledge that the reunion happened too late. She was still blonde and beautiful, with those big sky-blue eyes, but now she's mink and money and everything you could never be. Never in the world could she let you back into her life… all you can do is look.

And want.

Then she saw me. And knew me. Her surprised recognition turned into something sad, and she looked away.

Then just as suddenly you are *wanted—because as the big guy escorts Gloria out of the station and onto the platform, you see the glitter of handcuffs that shackle her to him, and then all the self-pity gets wiped away and the hunt is on... only this time* you *become the hunter....*

I stepped inside the station and went to the window.

"Friend," I said to the man in his cage. He was in his fifties with a walrus mustache and wire-rim glasses.

"Yeah?"

"Who's the blonde?"

"Who are you?"

I showed him the badge.

The stationmaster said, "You're a cop and you didn't spot her? What are you *here* for, anyway?"

"You didn't look close enough to that badge, friend. I'm from the city. After that wanted murderer—John Murphy. The one they call 'Irish.'"

"Oh, you're down here on that manhunt, too, eh?" He glanced toward the door. "Well, that's Gloria Dell herself. Killed her rich husband, she did. Now she's getting life. Tonight's her last train ride."

"Must have been mostly *women* on that jury."

"You ain't wrong, mister."

As I started to board the train, the tall cop was right there with a hand on my arm. "Hey, how far off duty are you going, anyway?"

"Real far, friend. I got a train detail going back. If our boy pulls a cute one and hops on here, *somebody* has to be aboard to nail his ass."

The cop grinned at me. "Then you can lean back and take it easy, chum. That guy Irish won't make it out of town."

I gave him a grin back. "You guys don't miss much, do you?"

On board, I approached the conductor and flashed the badge again. "Where's the officer with the prisoner?"

He was a slender guy about sixty in the typical dark blue uniform with brass buttons and a cap. "In the club car." He pointed. "Right through there. Nobody back there right now but him and his prisoner."

"Thanks." I looked around. It was like I'd walked into 1920-something. "How old is this thing, anyway?"

"Ha! Been around longer than me."

Then the train started up and so did I, heading back to that club car, where I dumped my trench coat and hat on the first seat. She was seated in a tandem club seat next to her companion, a big dick about forty, reading a paper. She was staring straight ahead. Behind them, nearby, was a small bar with nobody on duty. A topcoat that the big round-faced dick didn't really need was slung over her right wrist and his left one.

The handcuffs would be under there.

Her eyes met mine. No surprise now. Perhaps regret. Sadness, at what we'd missed. But I gave her a little smile and she returned it, just barely, those lovely blue eyes lighting up. *I'm yours*, she seemed to say. *If you can take me.*

"Gloria!" I said, all happy surprise.

The dick lowered his paper and glowered over it.

"John," she said warmly. Hot syrup on a griddlecake.

"Imagine seeing you here," I said, pulling over a single seat and dropping into it. "What's it been? Ten years? I almost didn't know you."

"I *have* changed," she admitted.

"Look, bud," the dick growled, "find another place to park it."

I put on a look that was mostly confusion with a dab of irritation.

"What do you mean? Look, mister, she and I go way back...."

Gloria gave the dick a quick pleading look and said, "Oh... John, this is my Uncle Andy. Uncle Andy, John and I... a long, long time ago, Johnny and I were in love."

The dick made a face. "Look..."

She whispered to him. What she said I couldn't hear, but her lips spoke to me. "He doesn't know. Please."

The dick looked at her, then he looked at me, and a sigh started down around his shoes. "Sure, John. Stick around. Catch up a little."

I leaned toward her a little. "You've grown even more beautiful, honey."

"That's because I was just a kid," she said, smiling just enough, "and you've been away so long."

"I've dreamed about you, sugar. So many times. I'd be in the mud but your face was in the clouds... or on the ceiling, when I was lying in a field hospital."

She glanced at the dick and he seemed uneasy, almost embarrassed.

I said, "Where are you off to, honey?"

"I'm, just... you know. Going away. Visiting family."

"You can't run off, not now. Not when I finally bump into you after so long. Could we a least... talk a little? In private, maybe."

She glanced at the dick. But he was looking at me, reading me.

"Korea?" he asked.

"No. The dust-up before that. Pacific." Then I said to her, "Let's go get a drink. Hey, Uncle Andy—Gloria and me, we got so much to talk about.... What do you say, Uncle Andy?" I stood and gestured for her to get up, too. "Come on, Gloria."

She looked at him. "Couldn't we? I mean, I'm going to be away for... *so* long...."

The dick thought about it. Then he forced a smile and aimed it at me. "Listen, John—why don't you go pour yourself a couple, and then you two kids can catch up."

"Thanks, Uncle Andy," I said, and went to the bar. I fixed us some bourbon and ginger ale.

The dick didn't know I heard their hushed conversation.

"You play me for a sucker, babe," he said, and then came the click that I knew was the handcuff key working, "and I'll shoot you *and* your pal. Nothing funny better happen."

"What could happen?"

"Go easy on the slob. Don't tell him you grew up to be a killer. Let him have his drink and his old flame and his face in the clouds he saw from the mud and the field hospital. Because if he wants to see you again, there'll be a heavy screen between you two."

"You have a funny way of showing a girl a little pity."

"Maybe I just want to see you sweat."

"Thank you, anyway."

Then she was beside me. She held out her hands and I drew her close. We never touched the drinks, just leaned against the bar.

"You lost track of me," she said very softly, "but I keep track of you. They call you 'Irish.' They're looking for you like they were looking for me."

"And now," I said, just as softly, "we're two of a kind."

"Not really," she said, as she took my hand and led me to another tandem seat, away from and behind her cop companion. We settled in, and she said, "I'll tell you what I told them all, and nobody believed.

I'll tell you I'm supposed to be a killer only it never happened that way. But they said it did, and took the rest of my life away. You were part of that life once, and now, for just a moment, we're young again. And in love. But before we can pick up where we left off… it's over."

"You're wrong."

"Am I?"

"It's only just starting. See, I didn't do what they say I did, either. The world's wrong about both of us, baby. And we're paying through the nose for it."

"What can we do, Johnny?"

I grinned at her. "Me, I like a challenge. I like going up against the smart boys. Nobody believes us, but we believe each other. They took us down, one at a time, but now we're a couple. Fred and Ginger, Bonnie and Clyde. We make a go of it, together. We might die in the process, but it'll be fun while it lasts."

Those blue eyes were wider now—excited, filled with love, and belief in me. Somebody had put the two of us together on this old-fashioned train moving through a cold, damp night—call it kismet or God or maybe just sheer coincidence. But the two of us had found each other in the darkness, and the sparks we made gave us a chance.

The conductor came in and rushed up to me and said, "Look here, officer. This just came in."

I took the telegram and read: "WANTED MURDERER JOHN 'IRISH' MURPHY ABOARD SOUTHEAST SPECIAL. DANGEROUS, PROBABLY ARMED. HOLD FOR ARREST. POLICE BOARDING EMERGENCY STOP. REPEAT DANGEROUS AND PROBABLY ARMED."

I asked the conductor, "Think you'd recognize him? Have you seen his picture, in the papers maybe?"

"No."

I put a hand on his shoulder. "Well, I have, Pop. If he's here, I'll find him. And get him."

The conductor gulped. "What shall I do?"

"Not a thing. Don't alarm the guy."

The conductor nodded and, looking spooked, went off.

I slipped an arm around Gloria's waist. "They know I'm here, kitten."

"What do you have in mind?"

"Working on that," I said.

Then I saw that the dick had stopped the conductor and was talking to him, and they both looked back at us, the conductor in fear, the dick in rage.

The cloak was ripped from our deception and there stood the law, indignant, outraged. The big man approached me, coat unbuttoned, hand over the .38 on his hip.

"You made a sucker out of me, Irish," he said. The trembling in his voice had nothing to do with justice and everything to do with anger. "Brother, did I get took. I let the babe soft-soap me and make a mark out of me."

I said, "Is that so, Uncle Andy?"

"You're dead, boy."

"Don't make the big try, friend. I'm a little younger. A little faster... and I got more to live for—now, anyway." The conductor, to the rear of the dick, was going for the emergency cord. "Don't pull that thing, Pop!"

The dick asked, "You heeled, Irish?"

"Make a guess. But make it good—nobody wants to die for your kind of paycheck."

Gloria's smile was beautiful and awful. "You're sweating, Uncle Andy. What's the matter?"

"You two are crazy," the dick said. "You won't live the night out."

I said, "Care to bet?"

"You'll have to go through me first, Irish."

"You married?"

That threw the big man. "…Yeah."

"Kids?"

The dick swallowed and nodded.

"Want to risk all that?" I asked. "Make the try if you want, but remember—I have the edge."

Another swallow, another nod.

With two careful fingers, the dick removed the .38 from the hip holster, slowly. He bent and tossed it gently away—he knew not to throw it down hard and risk it going off.

I leaned down to pick it up and he was on me. It was a sucker play and I fell for it. But neither one of us got the rod—Gloria got there first and used it to hold the conductor at bay, the old boy goggling at the two men thrashing on the carpet. The dick was heavy and he was on top of me, but then my knee found just the right place and he rolled off, groaning. Then I was on him, when I threw a punch that might not have put Marciano out, but sent this overweight copper to dreamland.

I got the handcuff key out of his pocket, undid the loose cuff on his wrist and tossed the cuffs to Gloria, who caught them one-handed; she was smiling like a beauty queen in a parade as she snapped the cuffs on the conductor and found him a seat.

Everything was going swell till the assistant conductor came in, a guy in his thirties with a halfback build. He was blurting, "They're flagging down the train! They're—"

Before he knew what was going on, I belted him and he hit the deck. Gloria held the gun on him.

"Get up and tell the boy at the throttle to keep going," she said. "We don't stop, understand?"

I was grinning. "That's my girl."

She shook the gun at the young trainman, who was on the floor in a half-lying, half-sitting position, his cap knocked off, his hair mussed, his expression dazed.

"Do it quick!" she demanded.

He winced up at her. "You're crazy, lady. There are cops out there! You know what they want?"

With a toss of her blonde hair, she said, "Yes. Yes, I think do. I think they'd tell you they want to see justice done. Don't *you* want that?"

The trainman, scared now, looked from Gloria to me; then he nodded nervously.

"Would it be just," I asked, "for that man on the floor to die? He's a cop himself. Or your friend the conductor?"

One eyebrow was raised as she said to the young guy, "Justice can be served in any number of ways. Go tell the engineer. We'll wait."

He got up slowly, his cheeks flushed red. "Not on your life. Not on anybody's life. I *know* who you are—both of you. So you can stuff it. Go tell him yourself—but first you gotta go through me."

The dick was coming around. He looked up from the floor and said, "Go tell the engineer, son—they'll kill you."

"I looked down a gun before," the trainman said. There was as much pride as anger in it. He looked right at me. "But you got to get through me first. Lady, hand him the gun. He'll need it."

I held up a hand to stop her. Handing the .38 over would be just the distraction he'd need to throw himself at me.

I said, "You and I were in the same war, friend. And it wasn't Korea—right?"

He gave me a slow nod. "That's right. But now we have our *own* war, don't we?"

I nodded. "Hang onto the gun, sugar," I told Gloria, "and keep a close eye on Uncle Andy…."

"Johnny," she said, "I don't get it…."

I nodded toward the trainman. "He fought for the right to challenge something like this. What branch, bud?"

"Marine. Second division."

"Army," I said. "Infantry."

He came forward with his fists ready, and when he threw his first punch, I ducked it and swung a right at his chin. But he was no easy mark like Uncle Andy—he ducked that and stepped in to give me one that doubled me over. Much as that hurt, even with my wind knocked out, it left me in a position to tackle him and I took him down hard. He was on his back when I slammed a combination of rights and lefts into his chin, his face, that bloodied his mouth and his nose and though he wasn't out all the way, he was finished. And knew it.

Gloria's attention on our struggle was enough to give the dick a moment he could use to snatch the gun out of her hand. He held it on me and his expression was flat—too tired and beat up to summon any more rage.

He said, "Okay, you two… it's over."

She was at my side now.

I said to her, "It never really had a chance to start, did it?"

She kissed me—nothing fancy, just a quick sweet goodbye before all of this caught up with us.

The dick reached for the emergency cord, but before he made contact, a foot reached out and spilled him, landing him hard.

The ex-marine gave me a grin and a wink. With a glance at the dick, who was down and dazed again, he said, "Get out, buddy. Get out fast!"

Then Gloria and I were between cars and the wind was whipping us and the wheels were grinding. She was in my arms as if we were in a ballroom somewhere, and she asked, "What now?"

"Now we run."

"Run where?"

"Somewhere to hole up till we're very old news. Then maybe we come back and quietly prove ourselves innocent. Or maybe we just enjoy a new life somewhere. Live the right way and enjoy that life. But first we run."

"It'll be a hell of a run," she said.

"Maybe we make it, maybe we don't. But at least we try it together."

Another kiss and we watched for the right moment.

To jump.

And start the run.

And I could swear I saw two faces in the window of that club car—that trainman giving me a thumbs-up and a glum Uncle Andy, looking like he thought he'd be better off jumping, too.

A KILLER IS LOOSE!

This story has been adapted from an unproduced radio script, circa 1953. It demonstrates Spillane's early fascination with Post Traumatic Stress Disorder long before the term had been coined.

Alone.

Alone. I'm alone. For how long? For how long before one of them wants to be a hero and comes up here after me?

Look at them, look at them—you can see them out the window.

A mob.

No, not an angry mob, a very patient mob. Waiting. Waiting to kill a killer. And that killer is me.

They don't know I'm up here. All they know is that someplace in this building that has no exit, no escape, is a killer—a cold, terrifying killer who has no escape. So they wait patiently and they're right. They're right. He'll never get away.

They don't know who I am—all they want to see is one dead body, that's all. They don't know who the killer is—but whoever dies in this building is the man they want, the man they've cornered....

Soon, one of them will come up. One cop who wants to be a hero and maybe he'll get me. But maybe not, too. There are still three shots left in the gun. Maybe even two will come up and each time one comes, someone will die.

Maybe the hero, and maybe me.

So I stand here at the window with the darkness wrapped around me like a shroud and look at the mob in blue, knowing that someplace is a gun that will spit a bullet into me... as soon as one of those blue uniforms decides to be a hero.

I should have known.

No exit. No escape. No nothing. Only a hole in the ground—a grave someplace. Yeah, I should have known. I should have felt it coming on two years ago in the mud and slime of a Korean rice field. I should have felt it coming on in the antiseptic halls of the hospital. I should have felt it coming on then.

But no, I waited until Grace was there.

Grace out of my past. Grace of eight years ago. Grace. The only girl who cared enough to come to me—Grace. I'd like to see you once more, but I won't be able to. I'll only be able to think of you in what little time is left. I can still remember that morning, when you walked into the hospital....

They'd moved me to a small ward with bars on the windows. I had a little area of my own for my bed and a nightstand. My hospital gown had been exchanged for dungarees, a blue work shirt and the kind of shoes that don't need laces. This wasn't prison. But it was close.

I was sitting in a chair by the window, and the doc, a guy about forty, skinny as hell with gray eyes that didn't blink enough, sat next to me. I stared out the window. He stared at me.

He said, "We need to go back to these periods of unconsciousness...."

"Go back then."

"You have no memory at all of what—"

I shot him a glare. "What are you bothering me for? You know what it's like as well as I do."

"Mr. Devlin... Terry... we're here to help you."

"Sure, sure. Then help me by getting my ass out of here. If not, just beat it. Leave me the hell alone."

He stayed cool. "About these... rages that precede the loss of consciousness—"

"Look, doc—I don't know why it happens. I just get mad. I burn up. I think I'm going to bust wide open, and then I lose it. Ask the guy in the next bed, he'll tell you. They used to call it shell shock. Then they got polite and named it battle fatigue. The guy one bed over, he's real bright—to him I'm a gutless S.O.B. ready for a permanent padded cell."

The doctor said nothing, smug bastard.

"Say it, doc—go ahead. I'm almost in that padded pad right now—bars on the windows, the doors stay locked. We eat everything with spoons."

A male orderly of about twenty-five stepped in just in time to hear me tell the doc, "Get the hell outa here! Go on, get away from me before I take you apart, you *and* your stinking hospital."

The orderly said, "You need any help, doctor?"

"No. No, I guess not." He turned to me with a thin smile that was like a cut in his face. "Okay, Terry, if that's the way you want it. But we *will* talk later."

The orderly said, "Uh, pardon me, doctor, but there's a young lady here to see Mr. Devlin."

The doc frowned over at his helper. "Young lady?"

"I'm afraid she has a court order with her."

The unflappable doc was suddenly good and flapped—his anger trumped by his amazement.

"Fools," he muttered. Then he blurted, "What's the matter with them? What has to happen to make them understand?"

Then he realized he'd said too much, but I read the rest in his gray eyes: *Open the doors of the cage too soon and somebody will have to die before the fools understand.*

The doc was saying, "Where is she?"

"Out in the hall."

"Bring her in." He turned back to me. "You heard that, Terry? You heard what he said?"

"Sure, I heard it. Stop bellyaching, doc. You can't keep me here forever. Who's the babe?"

His voice was soft but with an edge: "Whoever she is, she's a fool."

"Seems like everybody who disagrees with you is a fool."

She was blonde and about thirty, and her orange and yellow dress had an abstract pattern but there was nothing abstract about that body. The guys in this ward may have been nuts, but they weren't *that* nuts: wolf whistles cut the air, and guys were yelling out, "Get a load of *that*!", "Oh, *man*!", "*Somebody's* lucky!"

"Doctor Thayer?" she asked. Her voice was a low, familiar purr, though I hadn't heard it in years.

He rose and went to her, saying, "That's right."

"I'm Grace Walsh. Did your orderly—"

"He told me. May I see that court order?"

"Certainly."

She handed it to him and he rustled through the several sheets. Then he said, "May I speak to you outside a moment, Miss Walsh?"

She hadn't looked at me yet. "Gladly, doctor."

They went out, but the door remained ajar. Nobody was there to stop me from going over and eavesdropping.

"I'm afraid, Miss Walsh, you're treating this situation as if this were a jail."

"Isn't it?"

"This is a hospital."

"I know—where men are statistics. Where human frailties are analyzed and then talked about in college classrooms. Where all is white and clean and cold. Sometimes a little human understanding, doctor—or better, love—can do things all of science finds impossible."

The doc sighed. "Terry Devlin should not leave this facility. Not yet."

"Is he sick?"

"No... not exactly."

"Is he sane? ...Well, *is* he?"

"I'm afraid you don't quite understand, Miss Walsh."

"I'm afraid I do understand, doctor. You can't quite put your finger on what sanity is and what it isn't. There is no way you can really judge. So you prefer to keep him here until you find out. By that time, there'll *be* no doubt—he will be sane or insane, however you choose to label him. No, doctor, Terry served his time in the army. As you said, this is not a jail, and I came to take him home. You see, I love the guy. Is that so hard to understand?"

"You're a young fool if—"

"Can I see him now?"

"...Yes. I'll have his things packed." Another sigh. "He can go home whenever you're ready. Have him sign out with the supervisor."

I could hear the doc clip-clop off down the hall, and I returned to my chair at the window.

She entered and got no wolf whistles this time, though the men's eyes all went to her. She came over and stood by the empty chair next to me, and smiled down. "Hello, Terry."

"Hello, Grace."

"We can go now."

I laughed, once. "You—of all the girls... the only one who gives a damn is you. Of all the nasty deals I've handed out, you got the worst, and yet you still come back. You should hate me."

She sat and her smile was like sun coming through clouds. "We ended badly, but I know what you've been through. And I know I want to love you again, Terry. I'll... I'll take what's left of you if I have to. If all I ever get is... only a little bit of you, then that's enough." She stood and moved away, saying, "I'll be waiting outside for you, Terry."

So we went out. Into the daylight of early summer, into the days and nights that had almost become forgotten memories, into a world of color and smell where white was only a word and antiseptic an alien odor.

A world where you could fold a woman into your arms and know that she had forgotten what you had done to her a long time ago....

Her little house off the park hadn't changed since I'd been there last, and I was glad of that. I never wanted anything to change again. I wanted everything to stay just the way it was. From the parlor, a tinkling of jazz piano said someone had beat us here.

"Who's that?" I asked.

She laughed lightly. "That's Joey. My little brother, all grown up. Joey, honey! Come here..."

Tall, well filled-out, but with the same boyish face, Joey Walsh ambled in. He'd been a piano prodigy as a kid, and apparently was still at it. He was in a white short-sleeve shirt and black slacks and black-and-white loafers.

"Hiya, Terry," he said. His voice had changed but his tenor still had some squeak. "It's sure good to see you."

"Brother, did you stretch out," I said, and we shook hands. "Last time I saw you, you were operating a tricycle."

Grace took her brother's elbow and looked at him with pride. "He's the man of the house now, Terry. Isn't he big? But big as he is, I can still hug him."

And she did.

"Or," she said mock-threateningly, "whack him one if he gets out of line."

"Gimme your jacket, Terry," he said, rolling his eyes at his sis. "We have lots to talk about."

"Joey," Grace said reprovingly. "Later..."

I said, "That's okay, Grace. We'll talk. First, though, I want to hear about you."

We sat on the couch, Joey saying, "Aw, nothing ever happens to me. I wasn't old enough for the last war and flubbed a physical for this one, so I keep at the piano playing to waste time."

From the kitchen, Grace called, "Don't let him kid you! He's good. He's up for a try-out with the Copa orchestra. An agent thinks he can get Joey in."

"Wow," I said. "That's the big time. How about playing something for me while your sis gets supper ready?"

"Sure. Any requests?"

"I was always a sucker for Gershwin."

"No problem."

He did "Summertime" and a piece of "Rhapsody in Blue," and then he played something that he said was original, a moody, jazzy piece that had nice melodies but a darkness, too....

And it's the first night you're home, but while you're sitting there listening to the music, you feel the horrible spasm of maddening thought that tries to beat your consciousness into the black uncertainty that breaks down the order of sanity... but you think of Grace and that strange new feeling you have for her, and it goes away.

For a little while.

Only at night it comes again and you wake up trying to stifle a scream. And you do, for the sake of the beautiful woman sleeping in the room next door—you keep it back.

And then one morning, maybe a week later, when you come in for breakfast, you find that lovely woman giving you a sideways nervous glance.

"Terry," she said, setting the table. "Hello."

"Morning." I sat. "What's the matter?"

She paused. "Terry, honey... last night. You were *home*, all night?"

"Well, sure. Where d'you think I was? Didn't I go off to bed while you and Joey were going over his music?"

"I... I know. I'm sorry. Guess I'm just jumpy this morning."

She was serving me up some scrambled eggs when Joey came into the kitchen, eyes wild. "Hey, sis! Hey, did you see..." Then he noticed me and swallowed and said, "Hi, Terry."

"What do you say, kid? Where you been, so early?"

"The store. How's... how's everything, Terry?"

"Great. Why?" I looked from him to her. "What's eating you two?"

Grace laughed as she sat down with her own plate of food. "I guess we're both nervous trying to keep a secret. You see... that Copa audition has come through."

"I said he'd make good, didn't I?" I sipped orange juice. "When's it coming off, Joey?"

"A month from tomorrow. A pretty big break for me."

"Don't get yourself worked up in a bundle of nerves, kid. You'll do fine. Let me see the paper, while you grab a bite."

"The paper?" Joey glanced at Grace. "Uh, I gave it to Ben next door—he was after the box scores. I'll go get it back from him, after I eat."

"Forget it. I'll get one myself." I pushed my cleaned plate away and stood. "You two go ahead and chow down. I'll see you both in a little while." I patted my belly. "Better walk this off."

Grace leaned forward. "Terry..."

"Yeah?"

"...nothing."

I laughed. "You two are nuttier than a Baby Ruth today. Kid, you let yourself build up a month's worth of stage fright, and you'll blow it. Cool it, now, okay?"

He smiled. "Okay."

But they both still seemed tighter than a snare drum. What the hell was up?

I'd barely stepped out of the front door into a summer breeze when a familiar figure fell in alongside me. No hospital whites, a distinguished business suit, but the same gray eyes.

"Well, Dr. Thayer," I said. "Checking up on your old patient?"

"That's right, Terry. How're you getting along?"

"Look…"

"Let's keep it pleasant, Terry. I'm not here to give you a bad time, I'm just interested. Whatever you do could have a great effect on the future of other patients."

"So I'm a test case, huh? Well, I don't mind. Come on, we can walk and talk at the same time."

That was when I noticed another familiar face: the doc's orderly, still in white, seated in a blue Chevy at the curb, on the passenger side. He leaned his buzz-cut head out and said, "Want me to come along, doctor?"

"Sure," Thayer said. "No sense you staying in the car, nice day like this."

I gave the doc a look. "You figure you need a bodyguard?"

"He's come in handy before."

We began to walk with the orderly trailing us.

The doctor asked, "How've you been feeling lately?"

"Guess."

"All right, I will. Your days are better. Your hopes brighter. You've got something to look at, and forward to, now. But at night…?"

"Yeah."

"At night, the fears come back. You feel the emptiness… and the thing inside you starts to work again. You lie in bed all tightened up with the sweat pouring off you."

"Then I get it under control," I said, "and go to sleep."

"Go to sleep? Or do you black out, Terry? Is it *really* sleep?"

I stopped and faced him. "Why don't you shut the hell up?"

"I'm only guessing, Terry."

"Guess again, then."

We walked some more. A kid on the corner was peddling his papers and asked, "Paper, mister?"

"Yeah." I gave him a dime and had a look at the front page and went cold all over. The tabloid headline screamed: A KILLER IS LOOSE!

"Look at that picture close, Terry," Thayer said, at my shoulder. "He's dead. Brutally murdered. Young college kid taking a walk in the park last night. Nothing taken from him. No known enemies. Just a sudden attack and a brutal murder. As if… as if a maniac had jumped him."

I muttered, "You're the maniac…."

"Me?"

"Hell, doc, I was in bed. I went to sleep. Grace and Joey—"

"I know. I spoke to them already…. Terry, I think—"

I took him and shook him by his fancy lapels. "I got a prescription for you, doc—get your ass out of here. Get out of here before you get hurt."

The orderly was moving forward, saying, "Doctor?"

I let him go, and the doc said, "No, it's all right. Terry… I'll be seeing you again."

"Yeah. Nice to have something to look forward to."

And that night I couldn't sleep at all, or the next night. Then finally I was so tired, I stretched out in my clothes to relax and read a little, but I couldn't stay awake and that was the night it happened again.

Frantic knocks at the guest room door awoke me, accompanied by Grace's muffled cries of: "Terry! Terry! You there? ...*Terry!*"

Then Joey's voice: "I'll try it, sis—*Terry!*"

"Yeah!" I said, sitting up, mind and mouth still thick with sleep. "Yeah, what's the matter? Wait a minute." I got into my shoes and went over and opened the door.

Grace, in a silk robe, was trying to stay calm but I could see alarm in her eyes. "You're... dressed."

"*Still* dressed. Fell asleep in my clothes. I was dead tired."

"You *have* been here, haven't you? Right here?"

"Of course. I was sleeping. What time is it anyway?"

"Three in the morning," she said.

Joey, in his pajamas, his gaze piercing in that baby face, asked, "You haven't gone out?"

I looked from Grace to Joey and back again. "What happened?"

Grace's voice was soft with fear. "A woman's been killed, Terry. In the park. I'm surprised the commotion outside didn't wake you, too.... Where are you *going?*"

I said, "I want to see for myself."

Joey said, "Wait'll I get dressed. I'll go with you! I'll—"

"Don't bother, kid. I'd sooner go alone."

Then you go out and the darkness outside is almost the same darkness that crowds in on you when you feel that strange emptiness in your mind. Even the sounds are there, but they turn out to be the voices of a milling, curious mob. A mad mob whose anger is tinged with a deadly, righteous indignation.

Then there's one face in a uniform standing over a blanketed form on the ground and you hear his voice, too.

The cop stuck his flashlight in my face and asked, "Who are you, mister?"

"Get that damn light out of my eyes."

"I asked you something."

"Terry Devlin. I live on Westchester, right beside the park."

"Well, you can go on back. There's nothing here to see."

I nodded toward the spectators. "Yeah, sure."

But as I turned to go, he called out, "Wait a minute! Haven't I seen you around before?"

"Probably. Like I said, I live right over there."

"I don't mean on the street."

"Maybe you saw my picture in the papers."

"Why would I do that?"

I made a face. "I was a war hero. At least that's what they said."

"Really? Well, the war's over. You can go home now."

So I turned away and started back through the mob, even became part of it for a few minutes, long enough to hear what they were thinking.

A middle-aged guy was saying, "Sure, the police give the same old story—he'll be apprehended. They got clues, they say. So what happens in the meantime? I got to cross this park every night after work. Maybe I should get myself an armed guard!"

"Quit yapping," his pal said. "The cops—"

"Hell with the cops. We're supposed to sit around and worry about our families, too, I suppose? Maybe that killer will take it into his batty head to go looking in houses for somebody to bump off, if the park is empty. I'm not sweating my family out every night. From now on, I go out with a gun, and I'm not the only one. We'll get the neighbors together. We'll patrol the place until we get him, no matter how long it takes."

I got out of there fast. I wanted to scream at him, to tell him, no! It shouldn't be done like that. The killer is a sick man. *He's sick!* You can't just murder a sick man, even if he is a killer!

But I got out because you don't let them know those feelings. It might make them start thinking…

And all the way home you feel the surging of your mind trying to break out of its prison, but the lock is still too strong while you're awake and you keep it in place.

And for two days you sleep all day, staying awake at night, so you can control that other person inside you….

Joey was in the parlor playing his jazz compositions. I liked the kid's stuff, but that bluesy undercurrent brought out dark thoughts in me. Next to me on the couch in the front room, Grace put a hand on my arm.

"Why don't you go to bed, Terry?"

"I can't, honey. I like to stay awake and just look at you."

Her smile was lovely and loving. "Remember a long time ago? How we used to stay up all night, watching the moon play tricks on the water?"

"I wish there'd never been any years in between."

"There never will again. I love you, Terry."

"Grace… come here." I kissed her, and her mouth was a giving thing, soft and warm and wet. "I love you, baby. I wish we were back there again. I wouldn't hurt you this time."

She drew away a little. "No… we're older now. It's better this way. It's easier to forgive… forget. It's easier to love, completely now." She shook her head and the blonde locks bounced. "No, I wouldn't go back. You're all mine now, Terry. I wouldn't go back because… well, back there I lost you. And I don't ever want to lose you again."

"Baby, you're the only one who ever really wanted me."

"That's why I never stopped loving you."

We kissed again, and she whispered, "You could sleep with me tonight. I could watch over you.…"

"What about your brother?"

"None of his business. He'll be out of here before you know it, if that Copa job takes off."

"It will. Why don't we wait till then?"

She looked a little hurt, but then said, "Sure. A few days or even weeks won't be anything."

I wasn't ready to take a chance on hurting her again. If I was doing these things, did she really want to have shared a bed with a killer? Could I trust myself not to make her the next victim?

The doorbell rang and Grace said, "I'll go," and got it.

I couldn't see the door from where I sat, but I heard her voice go from a warm, "Yes?" to an icy, "Oh… well."

Dr. Thayer said, "May I come in?"

Joey's piano playing had stopped when the bell rang and he called, "Who is it, sis?"

Thayer called back, "A friend!"

I joined Grace at the doorway and met the doc's gray eyes. "What do you want?"

"I thought I'd come back to see how things were going," he said to me. Then to Grace: "Do you mind?"

Resigned, she said, "No, doctor, not at all. Come in please."

Hatless, he was again in a crisp business suit. "It was quite a trial getting here—I had to cross the park and cut between the citizens and the police, who've got a cordon around the place. I was stopped four times."

"Yes," Grace said, "there's been more… trouble."

"Worse than trouble, Miss Walsh. Murders."

Joey came in from the parlor and frowned at the doc. "Say, aren't you—"

"That's right, Joey," Grace said. "This is Terry's doctor. Will you sit down, Dr. Thayer?"

"I can't stay long. I would like to speak to you alone, however."

Grace turned to us. "Terry… Joey… do you mind?"

"No," Joey said with a shrug. "No, it's okay. We'll hop out to the kitchen and make a drink."

The kid nodded to me and I followed him. He went to the cupboard where Grace kept the hard stuff and I sat at the kitchen table.

Joey asked, "What's this all about, Terry?"

"You know these medics, they're always sticking their noses in."

"Ah, sis can handle him." Now he was looking in the fridge. "See any ginger ale around?"

"We're all out."

"Hold the fort—I'll go pick some up next door."

He went out the back way and I took the opportunity to get up and move closer to the archway between rooms, where I could hear them talking out there.

About me.

Thayer was saying, "You sure about this?"

"I'm telling you, doctor," Grace said, "there has been no sign of any recurrence of his trouble. Oh, he's been moody at times, and perhaps depressed, but that's common to all of us."

"I'm not accusing him. My concern is deeper than that. I told you before that he wasn't ready yet. Now there's this trouble."

"Doctor..."

"Inside each of us are two persons—one is generally benign, a social creature that represents everything positive we as a species are capable of. The other person within us can be a very destructive force. It causes trouble, murder, war. Usually it's under control. In some cases it can be partially controlled, and for that brief span of time it's a clever, crafty, murderous thing. You see, I've seen Terry when he's gone into those periods of black transformation... when he is lost to that other, darker self. It was that other person who allowed him to kill so violently in Korea that got him his medals. It was that crafty other person that kept him alive.... I'm hoping *we* can still keep him alive."

"We will, doctor. Terry's the only one I've ever wanted... or loved. I'll always be with him."

"I hope so. I hope so. You're his one best hope. You are the personification of our better self, if I may be forgiven for saying so. Now... if you'll excuse me..."

Joey came in through the back door with a bottle of Canada Dry and said, "Now, let's make up those drinks."

I turned toward him. "No thanks, Joey."

"What are you staring at, Terry? You're giving me the creeps...."

"I have to prove something, kid." I headed for the back door.

He gave me an alarmed look. "Terry, where are you going?"

"It's night. When the blackness comes."

"What are you *talking* about?"

"If anything should happen to me, let it happen tonight.... I'm going for a walk through the park."

"You crazy? With that mob out there? With all those cops wanting to be heroes? You out of your mind, Terry?"

"That's what I want to find out, kid."

Joey was heading toward the other room, saying, "No, you *can't* go.... Sis will—"

But that was all I heard as the door slammed behind me.

Then you're outside where the air is fresh and clean and the sharp pounding in your head doesn't seem to hurt so much. And for some reason, as you walk along the stone barricade that encloses the park, your eyes suddenly get sharper, your ears pick up every note of sound, and strangely enough the pain goes away and you're a new man, a different man.

You feel huge and strong and mad. The anger is a boiling thing and you see the shadows that are people trying to stay hidden, but they can't hide from your eyes. Then suddenly your whole mind seems to go to pieces and you hurdle the wall and cling to the trees inside the park, stumbling through the bushes aimlessly.

Then the darkness closes in completely, even before you let out that feeble call to Grace, to come help you....

It's the whistle that shatters the darkness you were in for God knows how long... a police whistle... and you hear voices...

"Another dead one. I passed here two minutes ago. He can't be too far away. Search the area. Snap it up!"

That shrill police whistle again, and men moving through bushes... and you know what happened, and you *know* who they want, not just to arrest, but to kill!

Then you run blindly, seeking escape. But they hear you, and see the fresh, torn trail you leave behind. And one of them is right there in front of you.

He can't get the whistle up in time, or the gun. My fists are a blur and I have no sense of propelling them at him, a shape in blue with a red smear for a face going down like a bag of laundry off the back of a truck.

And now I have his gun. *I have his gun!* I won't be so easy to take now....

Maybe twenty feet to the street. I run, then stop short, panting— the way back home blocked off by cops and their sawhorses. And the citizens, my good neighbors, are all over the park, prowling in packs of two and three, trigger-happy jerks with guns somebody brought home from one war or another... looking for me. But if

I can get over there to the buildings and cross the roofs...

The pounding of my running feet cannot blot out more shrill police whistles.

"There he goes! Watch it... he's got my gun!"

"Under the light...by the wall..."

They see me... they're closing in...

"Keep him away from the warehouses!"

Then when you're clear and the doorway to escape is open, a blue shape steps out of the shadows and without thinking you smash the gun across his jaw and he goes down.

You don't go in—there may be more inside.

So you just run, past the vacant lot, to the one building left, and you do it without thinking, because suddenly you're inside the darkness of the entrance, and too late you remember that this building stands alone, a wide border of empty lots around it... with no way to escape.

"He's in there!"

"He can't get away. Cover all exits. Sergeant—go around the back with a few men. Tell Warren to put in a call for the Riot Squad."

"Who is he? Anybody see who he is?"

*"Nobody got a good look. But he's the only one in that abandoned building, unless some tramp is camping out. Whoever is in that building, that's the one we want. Keep this mob under control! He can't get away from us now....
Come on, let's try the front arch."*

You feel behind you for a door. It's there, and it's open. Then you step inside and see the outlines of the steps that disappear above you into the darkness and you hear them coming closer. You run up into that darkness and let it take you....

* * *

So now I'm alone with the patient mob down there waiting for me. And at least one cop wanting to be a hero. Yeah, a hero. He'll want to be a hero, so soon he'll come up. The hero cop.

Grace, if I could see you just once more… just once more before I die. But I won't. I'll only be able to think of you in what little time is left.

I hear faint scraping and I know—*somebody got in!*

Somebody's here in this room with me now. He's being quiet, but he isn't quiet enough. I can see him now. His eyes aren't adjusted to the darkness yet, like mine. He's standing over there in a corner.

I raise the gun. "Drop it, copper."

I hear the gun clatter to the floorboards, and a sharp intake of breath. "Terry… it's me… Joey."

"Joey?"

"I came to get you out of here. Look, I played around this building when I was a kid. There's one exit here that isn't covered—the coal chute. There's a ladder in it. We can get out, Terry. I can get you out."

"You're crazy, kid, coming up here. That mob downstairs doesn't care who they find dead! All they want is a body…." Juices flow through you, survival juices that haven't flowed through your veins since you were in a tropical hell.

"Terry?"

"…You know something, kid?"

"What?"

"If I killed you… and they found you? Their killer would be dead. They wouldn't look any farther, Joey."

"Terry... cut it out, Terry!"

"Why'd you bring a gun, Joey?"

"You think it was to kill you with? Don't be a jerk. If that's what I wanted, I could let that mob or the cops get you! The gun was for anybody who tried to stop me." Even in the near darkness, the tears glisten as they roll down his cheeks. "I don't care what you did. I don't care. Terry, you're the only thing in the world that Grace wants, and I'm not letting a goddamn mob or those cops get you!"

"You think you can stop them?"

"We start by getting you out of here. Let's go, Terry. Let's get the hell out of here!"

"No. No. They'll keep looking. I don't want them to look anymore. I want them to find their killer, Joey. The cops down there want to be heroes—one or two in particular sure want to be, after I roughed them up. So I'll let one be a hero."

"What?"

"Go over by that window, kid. Stand there where they can see you to shoot at. I want them to get their killer. Then I'll go back— alone. I know how to get out now, thanks."

"Terry... no..."

"Go ahead, Joey. Move. Grace will get what she wants. She'll get me. You ought to be happy about that."

Light lances through the window; the searchlights are on. Pretty soon there won't even be a shadow in this place.

"Move over to the window, kid."

He's bawling now.

"Do it, kid."

"No, Terry... no..."

The gunshot comes sharp, like a whip crack out of the blackness.

I twist around, but only see the hero cop for a second before he ducks back down the stairwell.

My back hurts. It feels all empty inside me. They can turn the lights off now. They have their killer.

You'd think they heard me—the beams are cutting off, all but one, which catches Joey as he crawls out, stark white light painting his face. *His face!*

Kill-crazy ecstasy... a madman's face...

Hell—I wasn't the killer: *Joey was.*

Gunshots echo up the stairwell, and Joey's scream starts strong and dwindles as he falls down the stairs. The hero cop thinks he's just given me a second slug—he's wrong—but he got the right guy.

I'm almost dead now, and Joey is too, a shot-up pile of torn flesh and broken bones at the bottom of those stairs... but a killer is still loose.

A killer named Grace.

Lovely Grace, wonderful Grace, nurturing Grace... who took a guy the doctors thought was insane out of a hospital. Thoughtful Grace, who needed a fall guy to pin a murder rap on because her brother was a killer.

That hero cop didn't kill me, really—she did. For her baby brother, who made the mad music.

She set me up out of love, and love makes even normal people do crazy things. Like me. I'm going to die loving her in spite of it, so turns out the doc was right.

I am out of my mind.

KILLER'S ALLEY

A MIKE HAMMER STORY

In 1953, Mickey Spillane wrote and directed a short film starring his friend Jack Stang as a screen test of sorts. Mickey wanted to demonstrate to film producer Victor Saville that ex-marine/current cop Stang would make an effective Mike Hammer in the upcoming film, I, the Jury *(not* Kiss Me, Deadly *as has been previously reported). Saville did not agree, casting Biff Elliott instead.*

The test film—which also featured legendary comedian Jonathan Winters and future Ben Casey *TV star Betty Ackerman—is lost to time; but Spillane's friend Stang did go on to appear as a Hammer-like character in* Ring of Fear *(1954), in which Mickey played himself for producer John Wayne. Mickey came across more like Hammer than his friend, however, which led eventually to Spillane playing the iconic private eye in* The Girl Hunters *(1963) and spoofing his mystery writer persona in the long-running Miller Lite commercials.*

This short story derives from Mickey's script for that missing film. It takes place early in Hammer's career, and reflects Spillane fitting as much as possible about his unique private eye character and his noir *world into one small package.*

The street.

Killer's Alley. Putrid Place. Murderer's Row. Hell, the locals called it every foul thing you can think of. One street that wasn't a living thing and yet bred murderers and millionaires. Not a Skid Row where you wound up after a life gone wrong, but a swamp where quicksand held you in place till it dragged you down gasping, or sent you fleeing to bigger, better environs with your soul scarred and your way of seeing things skewed.

One street.

Not in Manhattan, but on Brooklyn's east side, a nasty stretch in a nasty neighborhood called Brownsville—so-called Murder Capital of New York. Crumbling tenements and crummy public housing, the place factory workers escaped to out of the Lower East Side only to find a refuge fouler than what they'd fled. "Murder, Incorporated" happened here, and leave it to Brownsville to make a business out of homicide.

For a week this four-block stretch of honky-tonks and gin mills and the kind of diner where they serve up a side of Ptomaine poisoning, no extra charge, had seen twelve innocent people die, if anybody on this foul stretch of Rockaway Avenue could be called innocent. Most had been strangled, a few had been shot. The killer was versatile.

I grew up here. My old man was his own bartender at Hammer's, not far from the mouth of the alley where I now stood and lighted up a Lucky but inhaled mostly the stench of garbage. You can't go home again, they say, but they were dead wrong. I'd been poking around the old neighborhood for a couple of days now, working for a citizen's group who found my little office at the Hackard Building in Manhattan all by themselves—maybe they were better detectives than I was.

Or maybe they smelled Brownsville on me, that same garbage smell I was soaking up now, like it or not, and it led them to me.

They were business owners. Never mind that their businesses were saloons and greasy spoons and a pawn shop. There were no churches on Killer's Alley, after all, so no rabbi or priest or Holy Roller made it onto this bedraggled team.

They smelled of Brownsville, too.

"The cops aren't doing a thing," the pawnbroker said. He was small and his eyes were big and rheumy behind thick glasses, but he was the only one not wearing a secondhand suit. Wouldn't you know it?

"The papers say it's Honeyboy Malone," I said. "Somebody helped him bust out of that upstate Laughing Academy. Left four orderlies almost as big as he is with their necks twisted and their eyes popping out."

"You got bounced off the force," said Gus, the flat-nosed, burly bartender who ran Hammer's now. My old man sold out, then died, while I was off painting the Pacific red.

I let some smoke escape my lungs. "Like the man said, they didn't fire me, I quit."

"They stuck you on a desk. Because you don't take crap from criminals."

"Nobody put that down in writing, but that's the size of it."

A skinny hash slinger whose threadbare clothes were as greasy as any apron he might use to protect them said, "What's your rate for a day's work?"

"Twenty-five," I said.

"How about ten and you get free eats at my joint, and beer at Hammer's... within reason."

The pawnbroker said, "Don't you think you owe the old neighborhood something?"

I did at that, but arson was illegal.

"Looks like you could use the business," the bartender said, taking a look around at my not-much-of-anything. "You don't even have a secretary."

"Not yet. Give me a break. I only been open a few months."

"Seems like you can *use* ten bucks and meals," the pawnbroker observed.

So I took the job and called my friend Pat Chambers, who had just made detective with the same police department that didn't like my attitude.

"I realize it's Brooklyn," I said. "But a dozen kills on one small stretch, and you cops aren't doing anything about it? The papers are making monkeys out of you."

"Not our turf," Pat said, but I could hear he was holding back.

"Come on, Pat. Spill."

His voice got hushed. "I didn't tell you this."

"Not yet, you didn't. Cough it up."

I heard his chair squeak—he had his own desk to ride. "We're doing a joint investigation with the Brooklyn boys. They figure it's Harold Malone, all right."

"Honeyboy."

"He used to be muscle for Murder, Inc., before he went completely off his gourd. He knows guys from the old days who'd hide him. He could be holed up anywhere in Brooklyn. Probably anywhere but his killing grounds in Brownsville."

Maybe the dead dozen weren't so innocent after all. Maybe some hoods were cleaning house, or using a psycho slob to scare my ragtag clients into closing up shop and getting taken over, for cheap.

Pat said, "We learned something from the upstate shrinks."

"What, that you hate your mother? Or did your old man spank you?"

He grunted a laugh. "Maybe it's that I grew up around the wrong kind of playmate. No, Honeyboy has a special kind of complex, they say."

"Oh, they diagnosed him as off his rocker, did they? The medical strides they're making these days."

Pat's voice grew tight. "Mike, Honeyboy hates that street— that stretch of Rockaway Avenue with the dives. Killer's Row, remember?"

"Killer's Alley."

"Alley. Putrid Place, Murderer's Row."

"A rose by any other. What about it?"

Pat's words came quick. "Honeyboy blames the street for what he became, the docs say. For his unnatural impulses. For the discordant music he hears in his head that makes him go kill-crazy."

I wonder if his head hired the same musicians mine did.

"So he's strangling his way up one side of the street," I said, "and blasting his way down another? Getting even with the past? *That's* the screwball idea?"

"That's the idea… the idea behind—Mike, you're not going to like this part."

My turn to laugh. "Do I like any of what's led up to it?"

Pat's voice took on an odd timbre—like he was sharing an old secret. "Honeyboy had a thing in high school for Betty Watson. You remember."

I remembered.

Elizabeth Watson had been my girl back in school. A nice kid from a nice family. Before I enlisted, right after Pearl Harbor, she and I got engaged. But when I got back, she was married. Bagged a much-married silver spoon playboy, Bruce Cummings with that Wall Street old man, and moved into a Park Avenue pad, and that was all she wrote. Then just a month ago I'd heard from her for the first time since I was back from the war. She'd busted up with Moneybags and needed a shoulder to cry on. I had two.

"You remember wrong, Pat," I said.

"I do?"

"Yeah. Honeyboy never made it to high school. He flunked out on his third try at the seventh grade. But he had a thing for Betty, all right."

The words came slow and considered now. "Here's the part you're not going to like. The Homicide boys reached out to the former Betty Watson for help. They're going to cover Killer's Alley like a righteous fog blew in."

I felt rage rising, but I didn't want to show Pat. Not yet, anyway. I just listened.

He was saying, "Betty's going to make herself seen. Walk down that street and then back up, from gin mill to gin mill. The sidewalks are damn empty after what's been going on. And each bar will have plainclothes men dressed as bums."

I kept the rage from bubbling over somehow, and just said, "You gonna be one of them, Pat?"

"Never mind that, Mike. Listen, I know you and Betty are back together now, and I figure if she wanted you to know about this, she'd have told you. And she *didn't*, did she? Or you'd have stopped her!"

He wasn't wrong.

I said, "Funny."

"What's funny?"

The words caught in my throat. "I was with her last night. I asked her to marry me, Pat."

"Hell you say! Did she bite?"

"You up for bein' best man?"

"Damnit, Mike." I could almost hear the wheels turning. "Listen, this is a big, multi-departmental operation. Don't go interfering. If the brass finds out I clued you in, I'll be pounding a beat on Staten Island."

"When is this happening, this big operation?"

"Friday night. He struck yesterday."

"Yeah, I saw the *News*. And he always puts a few days between kills. It's like his thirst gets quenched, for a time."

"For a time." Pat sighed. "Mike, it's like he wants to wipe out that whole damn street, piece by piece."

So I had poked around Brooklyn, talking to mobbed-up guys and their victims past and present, to see if I could get a whisper of where Honeyboy was, figure what hole he crawled into, waiting even now to crawl back out again, when the darkness came.

Friday night.

Cold, drizzling.

A quarter till midnight and the neons of Putrid Place were winking at me like whores with symptoms. I stood at the mouth of the alley, not daring to lean against anything in this area. That was rich, an alley in Killer's Alley, between two buildings housing rare respectable businesses (auto parts, secondhand furniture) on this stinking stretch, the kind that did their business by daylight—when a bum came stumbling by.

"Hi, Pat," I said.

"Mike," he said, startled. "What the hell…"

"It's Old Home Week. I mean, here we both are, ol' buddy. Wanna go over to Hammer's? I still got pull there. Listen, you look ratty enough, but your teeth are too good. You make a crap undercover man, pal."

He had a shapeless fedora tugged over his blond head and he looked too well fed to be housed in his tattered mismatched suitcoat and pants, his shoes scuffed and peeling. Couple days' growth of beard.

"Get out of here, Mike," he said crossly. "We're closing in on the bastard. Got everything covered. He's trapped."

"Where?"

His shrug didn't sell it. "Around here someplace. You seen Betty?"

"Yeah."

His eyes popped like *he'd* been strangled. "Tell me you didn't talk to her!"

"No. She didn't spot me, either, and I didn't need any corny Halloween hobo threads to hide in, either."

He snorted a derisive laugh. "The great Mike Hammer. Nothing bothers you. Not even a maniac with hands that grip like a vise."

"It's the right stretch for vice."

He was shaking his head. "You being here, Mike, it's wrong. It puts everything at risk. Man, you're going to get your girl killed!"

"No, Pat. You idiot cops will do that, if anybody does. Using her for bait. You make me sick."

He edged closer. "She's the one person Honeyboy won't kill, Mike. She'll draw him out. She's the only part of this foul street that loon doesn't hate."

Pat was my best friend but he rated a sneer. "How do you know he doesn't hate her most of all? That he doesn't feel like she went off and turned her back on the Brownsville rabble to marry some High and Mighty? And now *despises* her for it? Ever think maybe Betty is who he *really* came back to kill, Pat?"

He looked like the saddest hobo in town. "Mike—go home. Stay out of this. For the love of God, Mike. For the love... for the love of *Betty*."

The Lucky was down to the nub and I tossed it, where it found foul liquid in the gutter to sizzle out in. I was lighting up another when Pat shook his head and went wandering off, looking about as much like a bum as a kid in a school play.

Why hadn't I confronted Betty, and stopped her from playing her part in this dumb-ass charade? Like I told Pat, I'd seen her walking from one dive to another, cheese tempting some unseen rat, the come-on for a killer. I could have shoved her in a taxi and sent her away from this lousy slice of hell.

Why hadn't I?

Was something wrong with me? What had combat turned me into? Why did the face in the morning mirror look back at me with dead man's eyes when all I was trying to do was shave without cutting my damn throat?

But at least I felt something here, in this alley, in this bog of human misery where I'd been bred and raised. I was shaking, yet I felt alive.

Not so dead inside.

Was this where I belonged?

High heels clicked on the sidewalk.

I took a step out of the alley and she saw me and, for a moment, her eyes were wide, startled, but then a smile blossomed. And she came to me, that lovely blonde, wrapped up in a London Fog raincoat, hands in her pockets, nothing but big blue eyes and a red lovely gash of a mouth.

Then she folded herself into my arms and we moved instinctively deeper into the alley, getting some privacy.

"Mike... Mike..."

"Easy, kid."

Her eyes, alarmed, searched my face for clues. "Mike... you *know* what I'm doing? What I... *agreed* to do?"

"I know. You must be out of your mind, going along with this. *Why*, Betty?"

Those eyes were so big and so blue, swimming with tears that somehow didn't overflow. "Mike... oh, Mike... I'm here because the police asked me to be—you must know that. I thought... maybe I thought it would make you *proud* of me. If I... I..."

"Baited a homicidal maniac?"

She pulled away, just a little. "I wanted to help. To make it up to you for turning my back on you, and on who I was. But now I'm scared..."

From the street came tinny jukebox music. A distant siren provided non-harmony—an ambulance making a hospital run. Not Honeyboy captured. That siren would have been closer, louder. A scream in the night.

"I grew up on this street myself, kid," I reminded her. "I'm one of the memories Honeyboy wants to erase. Didn't you think I'd *have* to be in on this?"

"He must be scared," she said, looking around furtively. "I almost pity him. A cornered beast. You don't know what it's *like* to be scared like that, Mike!"

I grinned. "Don't I?"

She was shaking her head, all that blonde hair swinging, tumbling. "Not like this. Not like an animal... trapped here on this street someplace."

I shrugged. "There's nowhere for him to hide now. Not when his mind's filled with a crazy obsession formed by a twisted lifetime of murder and madness. That was the diagnosis the shrinks came up with. That he hates this street so hard he wanted to kill everybody on it. One stinking street that makes up your whole background that you can never escape from. Can you imagine that, kid?"

A slower head shake now. "No, Mike, I can't. It's incredible... it seems almost *impossible*..."

"Does it?"

She winced at me. "Your eyes... don't *do* that!"

"Do what, kitten?"

"Stare at me like that. It's like you're not... not even *looking* at me anymore."

"Sure I am, baby. Well... I'm watching you."

She came closer. "Mike..."

I stroked her cheek. "You're easy to love, Betty. Beautiful, gifted, enough so to marry a rich man and trade this street for Park Avenue. But Killer's Alley was still here, wasn't it? Waiting.

You couldn't escape it. Some twisted thing in your make-up reared its head and it showed on you, your husband saw that side of you. What did you do, baby? Did some female you were jealous of have a suspicious accident? Did your rich hubby have a kid brother who fell out a window and out of the will? ...Your meal ticket got wise somehow or maybe just scared for his own safety. Anyway, Mr. Park Avenue gave you the heave-ho, and that left you with just the hate...."

"Quit talking crazy," she said, yet somehow there was a look of incredible curiosity in her look. I was the doctor now, delivering my diagnosis. And some part of her wanted to hear it.

I said, "Imagine hating one street so much you break a crazy man out of an asylum and have him try to kill off the whole damn thing for you? It took a kind of genius to pull that off, kid. Twisted enough to conceive that. Genius enough to fool me."

Her chin was quivering. "Mike... please. You don't realize.... Honeyboy is still out there, killing, right now! Not ten minutes ago he shot that bartender, Gus, back of Hammer's, and—"

"Honeyboy wasn't the only maniac who came home again, Betty. He killed for you because he loved you. Like I loved you. Or thought I did."

"Mike." She was crying now. Not for us, because there was no "us," and never was.

For herself. Only for herself. Like all psychopaths.

Still, she tried to sell it: "We were going to be *married*... you said you *loved* me yesterday! And I love *you* right now..."

The alley had the slightest echo. And somewhere out there, on the street, people were laughing drunkenly.

I said, "So we were in love. So what? Should that make a difference? A dozen dead people, lover. But I'll do you a favor, Betty, and it won't be easy. You have family and people who love you, like I loved you, so I'll make sure nobody knows. They'll think Honeyboy got to you and then I got to Honeyboy...."

"No! *Honeyboy* is the maniac...."

"One of them," I admitted, taking her by the arm and dragging her deeper into the alley's darkness. "But he was dead before the last murder. I shot him right here...."

And now she saw the body sprawled between garbage cans. It wasn't so dark that she couldn't make that out.

"Mike, you can't..." She grimaced and for an instant the madwoman behind the mask revealed herself, and she dug fiercely into a raincoat pocket. Came back with a little revolver.

I took her hand and turned it on her. And one of us pulled the trigger.

THE PUNK

"The Punk" is based on an unproduced TV script written by Mickey in the 1950s. The subject matter makes it unlikely that even a bestselling writer like Spillane could have seen it produced at that time. It might have been a pilot script for an anthology series he would have hosted, that would have been produced by his friend Gene Roddenberry. It's a rare instance where the writer focused on a criminal and not a hero, plumbing the depths of Mike Hammer's sometimes nightmarish New York City world.

This rainy night would be the punk's last.

As he stands looking through the dirty moisture-streaked storefront window, studying a clock, he is not counting the hours or the minutes or even seconds. Although he is already condemned to death, he has no knowledge of his sentence.

He doesn't even know he's going to die, that somewhere in the night someone waits—unwittingly, at the moment—to take this ancient young man's life.

The skinny punk in the sopping work shirt and denims hears the approaching car, sluicing through the rain, but thinks nothing of it till he hears it slow. He turns and is washed in white as a mounted spotlight makes a momentary star out of a minor player.

He cannot see the two cops in the car, but he hears them, talking about him as if he weren't there at all.

"You make him?" one cop asks.

"Yeah. A punk. Jo Jo something. He's got a lot of workhouse time. Heroin addict."

"Want to shake him?"

"Not in this damn rain. He'd be clean anyway. Let him make his connection and we'll reach out later. Let's go."

As the cop car pulls away, Jo Jo spits back at the rain. "Lousy bastards," he mutters.

Somebody is walking, coming from the direction the cop car did—heavy footsteps splashing rain. Then an indistinct figure becomes plain as a beat cop, swinging his stick, steps under a streetlamp, pausing for an up-and-down-the-thoroughfare look.

Jo Jo retreats into the recession of a shop doorway. Waits and watches till the beat cop, swinging that stick, moves on.

Another car rounds the corner, pulling to a stop on the opposite side, down a ways. A driver sits waiting, and Jo Jo—still out of the rain, tucked in the doorway—lights up a cigarette with a kitchen match. The flare illuminates the punk's face and announces his presence.

Jo Jo takes a drag and flips the cig prematurely away, to sizzle briefly until the rain kills it. Soon a car door has slammed and footsteps approach, and Jo Jo smiles.

The guy might have been a plainclothes cop in the raincoat and snugged-down fedora. But he isn't.

Jo Jo asks, "Got it, Rock?"

"Yeah. *You* got it?"

"Sure, sure."

"Get it up, then."

Jo Jo digs out two wristwatches from a pants pocket. The connection slips out of the rain into the doorway recess, accepts the watches, looks them over without enthusiasm, his fedora emptying some rain between them.

"That all?" The guy sounds disgusted.

Jo Jo's face gets hot. "What do you mean, that all? Gold casing and Swiss works, man…."

"So?"

"So… how many are those good for?"

"Just one. You'll get one and count yourself lucky."

"You crazy? These didn't come out of some tenement!"

"So they're Swiss with gold cases. You want I should start dancing? By the time I dump this crap, I got nickels and dimes."

Jo Jo almost calls the connection a cheat, then thinks better of it, licks his lips and says, "Okay, Rock. Gimme."

The connection pockets the watches, then drops a lone capsule in Jo Jo's begging palm. There's something both nasty and superior in the connection's grin. Then he winks at the punk and walks back into the rain and gone.

Jo Jo studies the single capsule in his palm and says to no one, "Stinking cheat!"

Now he has to get out of the rain. He ducks into a nearby alley, moves past garbage cans and boxes, stops to kneel down at a basement window. The well of the window is both his hiding place, under a loose brick, and his tabletop, where the angle of rain doesn't intrude. He sets a flashlight on the brick to illuminate his work.

Spoon.

Candle.

Dope melting down.

Hypo needle drawing in the stuff.

Yanks back a sleeve, exposes his inside forearm, dotted with marks. Shoots the stuff. Withdraws the needle. Kisses his arm.

"You beautiful white horse you," he says.

His ecstatic expression looks back at him from the reflection in the basement window. But he doesn't see it. He's gone, man. Real gone.

But not so far gone he can't, from his kneeling position, wrap up his stuff and put it back in the window well. He rises with loose, easy confidence and walks out of the alley.

He emerges a new man—bigger now, tougher, owning the world. The rain is letting up, as if he told it to. He pauses, grinning as he reaches into his breast pocket and takes out two diamond rings. He thumbs the stones. Puts the rings back. Laughs and walks off.

"How do you like that, Rock, you goddamn cheat?" he asks the night.

The candy store is a shoddy thing, hard to imagine a mom allowing a child inside. Behind the counter is an equally shoddy, heavy-set proprietor, in suspenders and leaning on the counter, reading a racing form. The fat man with the wolfish, bearded face looks up when he hears the door open to let the sound of diminishing rain and a customer in.

"What do you want, Jo Jo?" Lupo asks.

Jo Jo, closing the door, grins and walks to the counter, leaning on it. "What d'you *think*, Daddy Lupo?"

Lupo appraises him with a smile that would be sad if its owner had any humanity left. "I think you're flyin'…. Well, look, I'm not cashing in any more of your loot. I caught a squeal on it last time, punk. Nice job. Your own uptown *sister* you rob? Who'll come next—*me*? I buy from you, then you steal the swag back, that it?"

The snick of Jo Jo's switchblade is the immediate answer. Then the punk leans across the counter and mock-shaves the fence with the blade.

"Thanks for the tip, Daddy Lupo. Maybe you're just who I got in mind."

The automatic comes up from behind the counter. "Back off, punk."

Jo Jo scowls but it turns into a grin. "Bang me with that and the blues'll tear this place apart. And what'll they find, Daddy Lupo? How much hot stuff you got stashed here, huh?"

Disgusted, Lupo says, "Okay, punk. Stow the blade and we go in back."

The knife gets tucked away, the rod, too. Lupo leads Jo Jo through curtains behind the counter into a box-piled storeroom.

"Let's see what you brung me, Jo Jo."

Jo Jo gets out the rings and hands them over. Lupo has a look at them with a jeweler's eyepiece. "These from your sister's?"

"What do you care?"

"Just asking."

"Where else would I score like that? What'll you go on them?"

Lupo studies the diamonds some more, then drops the loup into his palm. "Go a hundred on each…. Don't argue. Take it or blow."

"There's a couple of *grand* wrapped up in 'em!"

"Then go someplace else and get more. From me, two yards is the limit. And show me that blade again and you won't get any."

Jo Jo considers. Then he says, "Gimme the green."

"Go back out front."

"What, afraid I'll see where you hide the stuff, and help myself?"

"Out front, punk."

Jo Jo pushes back out through the curtains, wanders over to a penny gumball machine. Drops a coin in. Pops a gumball into his mouth and chews. Soon Daddy Lupo is back and hands over the cash. Fives, tens, twenties. Nice fat little roll.

Lupo's smile has some sneer in it. "What're you shooting a day, punk?"

"Two hundred a day's plenty to send me flyin'. Cruise over the rooftops and even do stunts. Man, I leave streamers in the sky."

"Sounds like you got a big night planned."

"Who knows, Daddy? Night's young, like me. I just live it up, long as guys like you are around to put gas in the flyin' machine…. See you later, Daddy. Be good, hear?"

Jo Jo is at the door when Lupo says, "Don't come back."

The punk wheels. "I'll be back when I want."

A smile flashes in Lupo's beard. "Then do me a favor and bring that shiv along."

"Why's that, Daddy?"

"Because I'm gonna shoot you up but not the way you like. With that knife on you, I can kill your skinny ass and tag it a hold-up."

"And if I leave it behind, the shiv?"

"I'll plant one on you anyway, when you're bleeding out on the floor."

Jo Jo knows his fear is showing, so he laughs it off. "You kill me, man," he says and goes out into the night.

He doesn't hear Lupo say, "That's the idea."

Jo Jo turns his collar up to the rain, which has built again. He's moving down the sidewalk, fast, pausing only to shake a fist and swear at a car that goes by with a splash that gets all over him.

"Jo Jo! Hey, Jo Jo!"

The voice comes from a dark doorway. Jo Jo ignores it, but a skinny, pitiful figure stumbles out—Pikey, a hype who makes Jo Jo seem normal.

Jo Jo doesn't break his stride. "Whaddya want, Pikey?"

"Man, I'm hurting. You got any stuff? I gotta blast one or I'm gone."

"Get lost."

Pikey falls in alongside Jo Jo, saying, "Man, I gotta have it! That monkey's scratching hard. Man, you know what it's like!"

"I shot my last cap. I'm scrounging up some fresh stuff."

"You ain't got a couple to spare?"

"Not hardly."

"How about a fin, then? Just a fin. I'm *hurtin'*, Jo Jo. Hurtin' bad."

"Tough shit!"

"Come on, Jo Jo. We're pals!"

Jo Jo stops and grabs Pikey by his sopping shirt. "Look, you drippy hophead. That lousy Rock only gimme one round for prime swag. Get off my back! You wanna blast one, get some loot the hard way, same as everybody else."

Jo Jo thrusts the bundle of bones against a building and Pikey— hurting, in early narcotic convulsions—reaches out pathetically.

"Don't go, Jo Jo! We're pals, remember?" Pikey is sobbing, then the sobs turn to retching, but Jo Jo doesn't see or care. He's heading toward a glowing neon sign in the mist, at the end of the street.

Stepping inside the dive, Jo Jo lights up a cigarette. Takes a drag, looks around. Smoke in here is thick as fog if fog made you cough. A couple of frowsy babes at the bar wave hello. Jo Jo yells hello back and heads for the jukebox. Looks at his choice of tunes, drops a quarter in the slot and soon is swaying lazily to Bill Haley.

A tall, wide-shouldered junkie pal of Jo Jo's—flesh hanging on him as a reminder of how he once got his moniker, So Big—slaps the punk on the shoulder.

"Hey there, Jo Jo boy. Where you been this crazy night?"

"Out and about, So Big. *You're* happy."

"Had a real warm fix 'bout an hour ago and found a real cool mouse to cuddle up with. Wait'll you meet her."

Jo Jo makes a face around his cig. "You and your mice. What rathole did you snag this one out of?"

"This one's different, Jo Jo. She's class, real class." So Big leans in, puts a hand on Jo Jo's shoulder. Winks. "So far everybody's been nudging me for a intro. Only I ain't sharing. But for *you*, buddy boy, I will make an exception. Come on."

So Big walks Jo Jo back to a booth. For once, So Big is right— the dame is class all the way, good-looking, nicely dressed, real wrong for this place, yet something about her is... offbeat. She's got a streak, Jo Jo can tell, the kind of streak that can lead a girl from the right side of town to check out a wrong joint like this.

Blonde, blue eyes, cheekbones like Bacall, long-sleeve dress that hugs her shapely slender frame—Jo Jo would be in love, if he didn't already have a thing for the stuff.

"Meet Francine," So Big says, as Jo Jo slides in next to her and So Big crawls in across. "Francine, meet Jo Jo Tea. From the old days uptown, we're pals."

Jo Jo says, "Hi, Francine."

She smiles at him but says nothing.

"Ain't she something?" So Big says. Then he calls to a waitress: "Hey, Red! Bring us three ryes on the rocks! Big ones! And get us another bowl of potato chips!"

Jo Jo can't stop looking at her. He licks his lips and she only smiles. Sultry, dangerous. She's heroin in a long-sleeve dress.

"Isn't she something?" So Big asks him.

"Yeah. Real something."

She says, "I'm sitting right here, boys." Voice as sultry as her looks. She gets in her purse, comes back with her cigarettes.

"Some mouse," So Big says. "Up till now all I get is pigs, dogs and dragons."

Jo Jo asks, "What's a dragon?"

"A pig with make-up."

Lighting her cig, Francine says, "What is this, the animal kingdom?"

The drinks arrive.

The waitress, a cute redheaded kid on a fast track to old age, says, "That'll be a buck twenty."

Jo Jo digs out his roll, peels off a five. "Here you go, honey. Keep it, okay?"

She looks at it like it's milk for a baby that doesn't have a daddy. "Thanks, mister. That's real okay."

She drifts off and So Big has big eyes for Jo Jo's roll of green.

"Man, catch the bundle on the boy," he says. "You're traveling *loaded* tonight, more ways than one!"

Jo Jo pockets his roll. "Fun money, son. It's playtime. Where that came from, there's plenty more."

Francine's eyes are all over him now. She nods toward the dance floor. "So let's play a little. Mind if I dance with your friend, So Big?"

"Naw, go ahead! Fly some. Toss me that bundle, boy, and I'll bust it up some!"

Jo Jo shrugs, digs out the roll, tosses it to So Big.

"Buy your friends a drink or two," Jo Jo says. "It's only play money. When we run out we'll get some more."

The dance floor has maybe a dozen couples clinging to a slow Sinatra number. There's room enough for Jo Jo and Francine and she lets him hold her close, but not so close that they can't look at each other.

"You a big man here, Jo Jo?" she asks him.

"Pretty big."

"How big do you go?"

"Way up. So far sometimes I can even reach out and touch a classy girl like you." He frowns at her in a friendly way. "Francine, why a slob like So Big?"

"I thought he was your friend."

"He is my friend. He's also a slob."

She shrugs. "I'm slumming."

"Someplace *you're* big."

"Someplace."

"How did you get here?"

"By car. Jaguar. From real far away."

"But I could reach you there, kid. I can reach anybody anywhere or anyplace."

"How do *you* travel, man?"

"Not by Jaguar."

"How?"

"By horse. It's faster."

"Back to the animal kingdom?"

"Different kind of horse, kid."

"Think I know the kind."

"You do?"

"I ride it myself."

Jo Jo pauses and they stand still while he draws back her left sleeve and her forearm tells the puncture-mark tale. He tugs the sleeve back down.

"You ride hard and fast, honey."

"No other way. It's a short race. Fast. But short."

They hold each other close a while, dance to the Voice.

Jo Jo whispers, "Where do you get the dough for your thrills, Francine?"

"Some here, some there. You know."

"Around the house? Daddy's money, Mommy's baubles?"

"Pretty tapped out there."

He squeezes her to him. "Don't even think about it."

"About what?"

"Workin' the street. A clown like So Big isn't gonna help you make what you need."

"From him I already got what I need."

"Yeah?"

"Yeah. In one night. All at once. I met *you*."

That plays for a moment, but then Jo Jo laughs. "You mean you met that *bundle* of mine. Honey it'll probably be half gone before we get back there…. Catch that slob over there, playing king."

He gestures to their booth, where So Big is holding court with B-girls and boozers, everybody laughing—and drinking—it up.

Francine looks at him, hard. "You came from money, too, didn't you? Till Mommy and Daddy cut you off for not being a good boy."

"Something like that. Think I shoulda hung around, and played the game?"

"Naw… money anybody can get." She was smiling at him now, the kind of smile that registers below a guy's belt. "But you, man… you got more to offer than money. This lady jockey is lookin' for a fresh steed. You know?"

"Back with animals, are we?"

"Yeah. Horses."

He nods. "White ones."

She nods. "Pretty ones. Fast ones."

"Prettier and faster than So Big can give?"

"He's nothing, man. He popped a little one an hour ago that he shook some kid down for. We rode together, but it was an awfully short trip."

She's not talking sex.

"What's he got on you?" Jo Jo asks. "How does a pig like So Big come up with a doll like you, even for one night?"

She shrugs in his arms. "We went to grade school together. When he saw me down here, he tried to shake me down—then he took a closer look and knew what I was after. Even if I had dough, what good would it do? My connection got picked up last week and there's nobody I can reach. Heat's on uptown. Got pretty bad for a while."

"Think about maybe kicking it?"

"You kidding? What *else* do I have? My family gave me the boot a month ago when they found out I was using. The old man told me the only money I had coming to me was for funeral expenses. Kick? Me? That's a laugh."

She stops and so does he, mid-floor.

"Listen," she says, "I'm gonna need to fix pretty damn soon. You with me?"

"Babe like you, anything. You know? *Anything.*" He takes her hand and starts leading her off the dance floor. "We'll get what's left of that roll back from So Big and take off."

But at the booth, they find So Big slumped over, his face cut up and bleeding, a dark bruise on his forehead.

Jo Jo grabs a guy going by. "*Hey!* What's this?"

The guy, bigger than Jo Jo, shakes him off. "Hands to yourself, bud!"

"*You* were drinking with him! What went down?"

Guy shrugs. "Ask your pal."

The redheaded waitress who Jo Jo tipped earlier is going by. He stops her. "What gives?"

She speaks low. "Listen, Jo Jo, all I know is you better get him outa here before Buck comes over. He sees this mess, then out you go, sailing."

He shoves her away. "You dumb little bitch…."

But she's gone.

He bends toward the booth and puts a hand on So Big's limp shoulder, shakes him. "*So Big!* Come out of it, man!"

Francine asks, "Is he all right?"

"Somebody creamed him, that's all…. Shit, the *roll!*" He paws through the unconscious So Big's pockets.

Nothing.

"Somebody lifted it," Jo Jo says, bitter. "Some louse beat him to hell and lifted it!"

What's left of a beer is on the table and Jo Jo grabs the glass and sloshes its contents in So Big's face.

"Wake up, you slob! *Wake up!*" He grabs So Big by his jacket and shakes him violently. "Come out of it, you *hear* me!"

So Big makes a face, groans and his eyes come open. He's hurting. Jo Jo shakes him again, So Big's head banging on the back of the booth.

"What the hell happened?" Jo Jo says right in his face. "Where's my *dough?* Talk to me! Talk to me! *Talk to me!*"

"I… dunno. Got hit. Somebody hit me…."

The bartender, a big burly guy in an apron, pushes through and whacks Jo Jo's shoulder. Hard.

"All right," the bartender says, nasty. This is Buck. "Get his ass outa here! Don't give me no hard time or I'll break your neck for you. Get that bum up and out."

Jo Jo, keeping his cool, says, "Look, man, he was holding my dough. Somebody sapped him and grabbed the bundle!"

"Should I call a cop for you?" It's a question but also a joke.

"No. Hell no."

"Good. Then get out the hell out of here!"

The bartender shoves Jo Jo in the general direction of the door. Jo Jo takes a fighting stance, pulls back a fist and then has himself a real good look at the bartender.

"Go right ahead, punk," the big man says, grinning. "Throw it… and I'll break it off and give it back."

Jo Jo lowers his hand, his fist becoming fingers.

The bartender says, "*Out*, punk. Take the garbage with you."

Jo Jo hauls So Big out of the booth. "Get a hold of him!" he says to Francine, who helps him, and they drunk-walk So Big out.

The rain is back. Not coming down hard, but steady. They stagger with their charge to under an awning. By the time they get there, they are as wet as the night.

Francine says, "What're we gonna do, man?"

"We'll take care of him. I'm going to find out who did this and—"

"Never mind that! I'm talking about *me*! I need a damn fix."

"Well, who doesn't? Just shut up and we'll pop one soon enough. I got to get hold of that loot."

So Big is coming around. Slowly, but around.

"Jo Jo," he says. "I'm in a… in a bad way."

Jo Jo's upper lip peels back. "*You're* in a bad way? You jerk, you stinking pig! Who got my bundle?"

"I… I didn't see…"

Jo Jo slams him against the wall, crazy mad. "I oughta make you *bleed*, man! All over the street! That was two big green yards, man. Two long fat green yards! Playing big shot… you…"

Francine, maybe a little scared now, says, "You said it was fun money, Jo Jo. Play money. Man, you can get more. Nothing can stop *you*."

Jo Jo backs off. He struts. "Yeah. You're right. You're goddamn right."

She clutches his arm. "Just make it quick, man. Pretty soon I'll be hurting *hard*."

"We'll load up, baby, don't worry. This lard head will start to pay his freight, too." Jo Jo grabs So Big by the jacket again. "So Big—you got the pitch now?"

"I'm in! Anything you say. We'll get you back your dough. No shit. And you'll get *me* fixed, too, right?"

"All right. Just shut up."

Under the awning, Francine and So Big are looking at him, waiting for his orders. Both are in a bad way. Jo Jo's not doing so good, either. But he pulls himself together.

"There's nothing going around here," he says. "We'll go down to where they come out of joints with some loot still in their pockets. They're leery of dark alleys, so we'll make it a three-way play. Lard head here is the sick husband and you're his worried wife. If we get the right sucker, I'll take him down. You got it?"

"Man," Francine says, "I'm with you. All the way."

"How much loot you got on you?"

"Six bucks."

Jo Jo holds out his hand. "Gimme. We go by cab."

Then Jo Jo whistles one down and they all pile in.

This is a street with gaudier joints on it. The cab pulls up and lets them off, Jo Jo paying the driver.

So Big is holding onto his face. It's no act. Francine looks to be in pain herself, gripping her stomach.

"Here, Jo Jo?" she asks. "We do it here?"

"Down a few stores. See that saloon neon? Honey, keep that pretty mug of yours where they can see it and they won't figure it for a boost."

But she doesn't look so pretty at the moment. "My guts are squirming, man. Better be quick."

"Cool it. We go now. Just don't hurry it till you see me wipe my mouth like this...." He shows her the gesture. "Okay. Go ahead."

Jo Jo heads through the drizzle toward the entrance of the gin mill. He doesn't go in, instead watches guys and couples exiting the saloon, scrutinizing them as they leave. They make impromptu remarks, enter cabs or walk off.

Then emerges an older, well-dressed patron, white hair, white mustache, dark tailored suit, who steps toward the curb, looking up and down the street for the next cab.

Jo Jo wipes his mouth, by way of signal, as he watches the guy.

The mark notices the pretty woman bending over the man who is on his knees. She is crying, the man is moaning. The mark goes toward them on the sidewalk.

"*Hey there!* What's the matter?"

The mark stops by the pair. Francine looks up at him. "He fell! My husband fell, slipped on this wet pavement. He can't even *speak* to me!"

The mark crouches. "No wonder—look at his head…. I'm afraid this man needs a doctor. He's pretty badly hurt."

As the mark stands, Jo Jo slips up behind him and hooks his right arm around the man's neck. Jo Jo lifts the mark high and the victim makes squeaking sounds. The mark paws at Jo Jo's arms, choking, while Francine and So Big scramble up and begin going through his pockets. Francine comes back with a wallet, waves it at Jo Jo and smiles.

Jo Jo says to So Big, "*Hit* him already!"

So Big belts the mark a hard one in the belly. Jo Jo releases the mark, who falls to the sidewalk in a pile.

"Now give him one in the head," Jo Jo says, smoothing his shirt.

So Big kicks the man in the head.

"Let's *go*, Jo Jo!" So Big says.

"Easy, man. Nobody saw us, but any time now, somebody else'll split out of that joint. So just walk. Nice and easy."

They stroll, leaving the unconscious mark behind.

Jo Jo asks, "You still got that pad back at Annie's place?"

"Yeah."

"We'll go there. You just keep Annie off our damn backs."

"I'm paid up. She won't bother us none. She does, I'll kick her teeth in."

"Just keep your feet on the ground, lard head."

Soon they are in a dingy room with the most minimal furnishings—iron bed, crummy dresser, beat-up table and chairs.

Strictly flophouse. Jo Jo slouches in a chair, Francine sits on the edge of the bed, So Big perches on a windowsill.

"How much, Jo Jo?" So Big is saying, as Jo Jo goes through the wallet.

"Thirty-six-hundred bucks."

"We hit a gold mine!"

"ID says he's an insurance collector."

"We got it *made*, Jo Jo!"

Jo Jo grins as he thumbs through the green. "You ain't wrong. We got it made good—for a month, anyway. Nothing we can't do now!"

But Francine is looking miserable and she's clutching her belly. "Then get with it, man! I don't blast one, I'm gone. It's crawling all over me. You better get to somebody fast! You got a connection?"

"One call and it's made," Jo Jo says, getting to his feet. "We make a buy they won't forget."

"Jo Jo," So Big says, "you… you *will* be back, right? You wouldn't…?"

"I wouldn't." Jo Jo's grin at Francine is a suggestive thing that tells her what this is going to cost her. "I'll be back. Don't you kids worry about that."

Down on the street, Jo Jo gets into a phone booth, pulls the door closed and drops a coin in the slot. Starts to dial.

On the other end, somebody picks up but doesn't speak.

Jo Jo says, "Rock…?"

"What do *you* want, punk?"

"Come on, man, I'm—"

"No swapping merch for product. You fence whatever you come up with first, and *then* come see me."

"Listen, you cheap bastard! I got thirty-six-hundred bucks,

cash, to make a buy. Hear me? Don't give me any of your crap. You got enough for a buy like that? If not, I go somewhere else."

Silence.

"Rock, you there?"

"…I'm here, man. I'm thinking."

"Well, stop thinking. Don't try no fancy double cuts on me. You try sugaring it down and you know what you can do with it."

"Okay, Jo Jo. I won't cut it any. Same place?"

"Same place. How long?"

"Give me twenty."

"Okay, but shake it."

The buy goes smooth, no b.s. at all, and only half an hour has gone by since Jo Jo left the flophouse room. But as he comes down the ratty hall, he can hear So Big's barely muffled voice: *"Shut up! Shut up! You're makin' me sick!"*

When he slips inside, he finds Francine on the bed, crying and retching. So Big is pacing, ready to go to pieces. But seeing Jo Jo, they freeze and the hope in their eyes blots out the despair.

"Yeah?" So Big asks.

"Yeah. Smooth."

"Gimme, gimme—where *is* it?"

Jo Jo raises a palm. "Easy, man. Don't go rushing things. You'll be okay."

Francine rolls over and looks up at Jo Jo.

He grins at her. "Time to toss that monkey off, baby, and climb back on the horse."

Somehow she's pretty again in a ragged way. "Let's go… go… go. You cook it man. I got it awful bad."

Jo Jo says, "Take it easy, baby…. Who's got the setup?"

"In my purse," she says.

Soon the ritual is under way—spoon, wooden matches, a cap a piece.

"They're hot ones, kids," Jo Jo advises. "Watch it. These'll fly you *real* high."

Melt the stuff down. Pass the hypo around. Ladies first. Francine takes a deep ecstatic breath, and passes the hypo to So Big. Then it's Jo Jo's turn.

So Big flops in a chair and Jo Jo sits by his girl on the bed and they smile in anticipation of the warm glow only it's not warm, it's hot, and within a minute all three are twitching on the floor, convulsing, frothing, puking.

Then silence.

Somewhere in the city a man who calls himself Rock has made a thirty-six-hundred-dollar score. And when three bodies are found, the wallet of a man in critical condition at Bellevue will be found on Jo Jo Tea's body, along with thirty capsules of junk cut with rat poison.

The death of a punk called Jo Jo is nothing new and no surprise, except perhaps to himself. Yet hadn't he pursued a course of death, following it closely, seeking it eagerly, if unknowingly? It was expected that he would die and he did not disappoint.

This was tonight. Who will it be tomorrow, or the night after?

TONIGHT, MY LOVE

A MIKE HAMMER STORY

This short story derives from a radio-style playlet by Spillane that was part of a Mike Hammer jazz LP produced in 1954 by the writer himself— Mickey Spillane's Mike Hammer Story, *with Mickey appearing (for the first time) as his famous detective. For any devoted Spillane/Hammer fan, the final line here will have great resonance.*

I'm going to tell you a story about trouble.

I'm going to do it fast, because there's never enough time to spell out trouble. It's a story about New York, two men, and one woman. It starts on a street corner off the Main Stem where the lights are gaudy come-ons and when you listen, you can hear the sucker music calling over the traffic.

I was on a shadow job, the kind of routine matter that keeps Mike Hammer Investigations going. But what happened that rainy night was something else again. The music right now, a pulsing jazz, was coming from the kind of club where the membership is free, if you can afford a beer and don't mind risking your life. The rain was pattering on the awning and I was keeping myself and my latest Lucky dry, thinking about whether I wanted a cab or a drink.

That was when she showed up from somewhere wearing the kind of red dress that would have looked painted-on if any living artist was only that good. Her eyes were big and dark, and her mouth the kind of lush thing that made my mouth go slack, the cigarette hanging like a guy who changed his mind and grabbed the ledge he jumped off.

"Hello," she said.

Platinum blonde with the roots starting to show. I didn't mind. We all have nasty roots that can catch up with us.

"Hi, kid," I said.

The sleek arcs of hair swung as her head bobbed toward the window behind her. "Nice music. Wish I could afford to listen to it real close."

"There's no cover charge, is there?"

She shrugged. "Only letting any fool who feels like it paw a girl."

"Are you kidding?" She was big, as in tall and as in all the right places. "You look like you can take care of yourself."

"Usually." She laughed. "Anyway, I couldn't kid you…. You're a *cop*, aren't you?"

"Of a sort."

"Tough one?"

"More than most. Not as much as some."

She was at my side now, both of us with our backs to the club window, the jazz our personal soundtrack. I was wondering when she was going to let me know whether she was just a lonely doll or was looking for a customer.

But right now she was looking toward the rain-slick street, the fading rain dimpling the black pools. I followed her eyes.

"It only took a minute," she said, "to get to like you. So do us both a favor. Don't stand here, big guy. Move along."

I was watching the dark shape emerge from an alley and head toward us.

I tossed the Lucky to sizzle itself out in the street. "You mean because that slob coming at us is liable to brace me into a payoff for tangling with his girl?"

"Something like that."

I took a good look at her. She'd been around yet she wasn't hard, not yet. Young. Beautiful. Blonde… anyway, blonde enough.

And trapped.

"Here he comes," I said, like she didn't see him moving through the slow, sporadic traffic like a bear through a forest. A bear in a suit too good for him, but good enough to make him a guy who felt he could own a woman.

"Get the hell out of here," she whispered. Her eyes were big and brown and terrified. "*Go!*"

The big square-headed, crew-cut guy was halfway to us. I'd thought at first he might be her pimp, but no. He had mob written all over him. Not a boss, but an enforcer. Somebody who kept the boss breathing.

I asked softly, "You want out, honey?"

"I want out of here. I want to get away from this creep."

"Okay," I said. I took her by the soft upper arm, gently. "Take your first step, kid. Give us a kiss."

Her look was half surprise, half alarm.

"Are you *crazy?* Here he comes!"

I kissed her. She hadn't said no, had she?

"Crazy," I said, answering her question.

"*You!*" he yelled. "*You goddamn son of a bitch!*"

I waited till his hand was on my shoulder and turned on him swinging, connecting with his face and turning his roughly handsome look into a streaming scarlet mask, thanks to the nose I'd split open. When I hit him again, on the side of his head this time, he spit blood and teeth and he went down on the sidewalk with a splash that was only partly rain. People had seen it. But nobody was sticking around to see more.

"My God," she said, curled fingers at the lush lips. "*Look* at him."

The guy was a mess, all right. I have a pretty decent right hand.

I said, "He's probably done worse to you…. Now get out of here, kid."

"He'll *follow* me!"

I shook my head. "No. He won't follow you. You see… I'm not finished with him yet."

Her dark eyes were hooded now, but her mouth was open, as if another scream was waiting. "Your eyes… they look… funny."

"Your boyfriend's not laughing."

But her eyes were locked on mine, and she seemed caught up in a weird reverie. "They don't just *look* at you, those eyes. They… *watch*."

"Yeah, and right now they're watching a kid who has one chance to get out of this nightmare if she hurries. *Run*."

She started off, then froze a few steps away and looked back, her expression curious. "What's your name?"

"Mike. Mike Hammer."

She nodded.

Then ran.

I dragged Laughing Boy's sorry ass into the nearby alley and got to work.

Maybe a year later, I found myself in the same part of town, locating a rich kid who stole his mother's jewels for dope money. I'd talked to the kid and told him he could go home, and all would be right with his world, though I would have paddled his butt if it were up to me.

Anyway, I was back on the same street, on the other side of it, across from the jazz club. It had rained again, but was trailing off—after two o'clock in the morning, Sixth Avenue going north. Traffic was light, the gaudy lights of the clubs off, their windows dark eyes in the blank faces of brick walls.

For once it was almost quiet. And for the first time in a long while, the night belonged to me alone. And my memories drifted back, and while I was thinking of that moment so many months ago, I heard a voice call out, "Mike... *Mike!*"

The blonde with the roots.

She rushed across to me. Stood close. My hands found her shoulders and I looked down at her. Her face was bruised, her mouth bleeding.

"I told you to run," I said, almost as angry with her as with the bastard who did this to her.

She nodded, breathing hard. "I did. But not the way you think."

"*What* way, then?"

With a glance from side to side, as if this street weren't as deserted as Death Valley, she said, "I'm a cop, Mike. Undercover. Vice."

I frowned. "What the hell…?"

Very quietly, she said, "Last year I was playing moll to a very bad man, gathering evidence, but…"

"But something's gone wrong. Last year you were frightened. Now there's terror in your face."

She sucked in breath, let it out with some words: "He found out. Who I was. *What* I am. He came after me. Grabbed me. Brought me back here."

I slipped an arm around her shoulder. "Then let's get you to your boss. Your *real* boss."

She shook the glimmering fake blondeness. "No, he'll come after me. I hit him with an ashtray and he went down, and I ran, this time I *really* ran! But he'll come after me!"

"Calm down. Take it easy. I'm here now."

Her eyes were wild. "When he found out about me, he figured you'd been part of it, last year. *Another* cop. That's what he wanted to know tonight, when he worked me over. He wanted your name. I wouldn't give it to him."

I grinned. "He'd like another shot at me, huh?"

The beautiful bruised face stared up at me. "He's been looking to get just one more crack at you. And now, if we don't go right *now*, I'll have led him to you… by sheer damn chance…."

"You think that slob worries me?"

Her eyes and nostrils flared. "Mike, he's a killer. He's deadly. And he hates *hard.*"

"Yeah? Well, I'm Mike Hammer. Haven't you heard? So talk to me, kitten. While we wait for him to catch up. Talk to me…."

"*Wait* for him…?"

"We make our stand here. Talk to me."

She folded herself into my arms, spoke into my chest. "Mike, I've never forgotten you. What you did for me. I *ran*, all right. Back into my own life, a real job on the department, leaving the fake identity behind. But today I got *found* by this sadistic monster... he's murderous, Mike. Likes to see things hurt. And he's *fast*, Mike, deadly with a gun. I saw that only too well, back when I was living with him. Not far from here. And now... he wants *you*."

Across the way, a shape emerged from the alley where, a year ago, I'd left him beaten and bleeding. It was like he'd been there all this while and finally recovered.

"And now," I said, "he has me."

He started across the street. Waited for a stray car to pass. Big shoulders in an expensive suit and the kind of loud tie a jerk like him would take for style. He stood in the middle of that street, like it was high noon in Dodge City.

Stood and watched me with eyes that had known hatred and vile lust for death too long. All of the things he wanted to say, all of the names he wanted to call me, were written on his face and in the dull luster of his eyes. But those eyes turned just a little bewildered because what happened was too fast to follow for a mind that had been eaten away with thoughts of murder. There I stood, with the woman who betrayed him in my arms....

"*Go ahead!*" I called to him. "Go for it!"

My words echoed off the buildings that surrounded us like the ruins of some ancient civilization.

"The only witness is the night!" I told him. "Of course, you still have the chance to walk away."

He said nothing, breathing hard. His suitcoat was unbuttoned and his right hand was hovering chest high, right where he could get at his shoulder-holstered piece, quick.

He was letting the hate get the better of him. And when you let that happen, you've caught your last trolley, man, and it's a long way to that boneyard in Brooklyn. Over there they don't even put a name on the slab. You're only a number.

I eased the girl away, saying to her, "Look at his eyes…. He wants me to make it interesting for him."

His mitt was almost set to grab that rod and bang away, and yet… he didn't. But he wasn't hesitating out of fear, or even a desire to make a case for self-defense. What the hell—in the dead of night, no one was around to witness anything.

"Okay, friend," I said, unbuttoning my jacket with my left hand. "There's only one way to find out who's the better man— go, man… *go!*"

Her scream almost blotted out the sound of the gunshot. "*Mike!*"

He was fast, all right. He had the gun out, and it was even pointed my way. But the .45 slug I'd sent through his forehead was a period at the end of his death sentence.

He dropped like a potato sack falling off the back end of a truck, his head landing in a puddle that already was glistening with green and gray globules of what had been his brains.

"Somebody should have told him," I said with a sigh.

But this was New York.

And you let them find things out for themselves.

"Mike…"

The rain had stopped and the night was clean again. And all that was left was a beautiful woman, so very alive and with love in her eyes.

"You're safe now, kitten," I said. "What's your name, anyway?"

"Velda," she said.

ABOUT THE AUTHORS

MICKEY SPILLANE and **MAX ALLAN COLLINS** collaborated on numerous projects, including twelve anthologies, three films, and the *Mike Danger* comic book series.

Spillane was the bestselling American mystery writer of the twentieth century. He introduced Mike Hammer in *I, the Jury* (1947), which sold in the millions, as did the six tough mysteries that soon followed. His controversial PI has been the subject of a radio show, comic strip, and several television series, starring Darren McGavin in the 1950s and Stacy Keach in the '80s and '90s. Numerous gritty movies have been made from Spillane novels, notably director Robert Aldrich's seminal film noir, *Kiss Me Deadly* (1955), *The Girl Hunters* (1963), in which the writer played his own famous hero, and *I, the Jury* (1982), which set the template for a decade of violent-crime-based action blockbusters.

Collins has earned an unprecedented twenty-five Private Eye Writers of America "Shamus" nominations, winning for the novels *True Detective* (1983) and *Stolen Away* (1993) in his Nathan Heller series, and in 2013 for "So Long, Chief," a Mike Hammer short story begun by Spillane and completed by Collins. His graphic novel *Road to Perdition* is the basis of the Academy Award-winning Tom Hanks/Sam Mendes film. As a filmmaker in the Midwest, he has had half a dozen feature screenplays produced, including *The Last Lullaby* (2008), based on his innovative Quarry novels, also the basis of *Quarry*, a Cinemax TV series. As "Barbara Allan," he and his wife Barbara's collaborative novels include the "Trash 'n' Treasures" mystery series (recently *Antiques Liquidation*).

The Grand Master "Edgar" Award, the highest honor bestowed by the Mystery Writers of America, was presented to Spillane in 1995 and Collins in 2017. Both Spillane (who died in 2006) and Collins also received the Private Eye Writers life achievement award, the Eye.

MIKE HAMMER NOVELS

In response to reader requests, I have assembled this chronology to indicate where the Hammer novels I've completed from Mickey Spillane's unfinished manuscripts and other materials fit into the canon. An asterisk indicates the collaborative works (thus far). J. Kingston Pierce of the fine website *The Rap Sheet* pointed out an inconsistency in this list (as it appeared with *Murder Never Knocks*) that I've corrected.

M.A.C.

*Killing Town**
I, the Jury
*Lady, Go Die!**
The Twisted Thing (published 1966, written 1949)
My Gun is Quick
Vengeance is Mine!
One Lonely Night
The Big Kill
Kiss Me, Deadly
*Kill Me, Darling**

*Kill Me If You Can**
The Girl Hunters
The Snake
*The Will to Kill**
*The Big Bang**
*Complex 90**
*Murder Never Knocks**
The Body Lovers
Survival… Zero!
*Kiss Her Goodbye**
The Killing Man
*Masquerade for Murder**
*Murder, My Love**
Black Alley
*King of the Weeds**
*The Goliath Bone**

KILL ME, DARLING

MICKEY SPILLANE & MAX ALLAN COLLINS

Mike Hammer's secretary and partner Velda has walked out on him, and Mike is just surfacing from a four-month bender. But then an old cop turns up murdered, an old cop who once worked with Velda on the N.Y.P.D. Vice Squad. What's more, Mike's pal Captain Pat Chambers has discovered that Velda is in Florida, the moll of gangster and drug runner Nolly Quinn.

Hammer hits the road and drives to Miami, where he enlists the help of a horse-faced newspaperman and a local police detective. But can they find Velda in time? And what is the connection between the murdered vice cop in Manhattan, and Mike's ex turning gun moll in Florida?

"[O]ne of his best, liberally dosed with the razor-edged prose and violence that marked the originals."
Publishers Weekly

"For Mike Hammer's fans—yes, there are still plenty of them out there—it's a sure bet."
Booklist

"It's vintage peak-era Spillane so seamless it's hard to see where the Spillane ends and the Collins picks up."
Crime Time

TITANBOOKS.COM

For more fantastic fiction, author events,
exclusive excerpts, competitions, limited editions and more

VISIT OUR WEBSITE
titanbooks.com

LIKE US ON FACEBOOK
facebook.com/titanbooks

FOLLOW US ON TWITTER AND INSTAGRAM
@TitanBooks

EMAIL US
readerfeedback@titanemail.com